AF244765

TERRAN-NOVAN UNIVERSE BOOK 3

EYE OF THE DAMNED

SANDRA BARRET

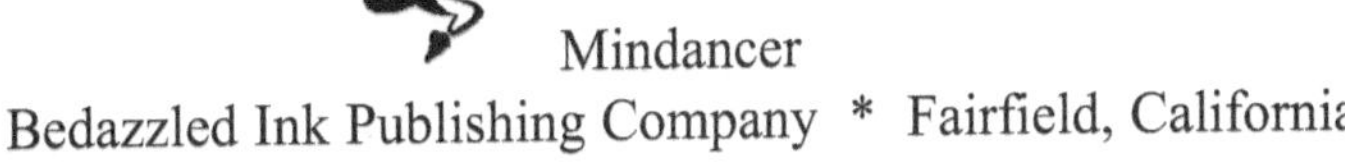

Mindancer
Bedazzled Ink Publishing Company * Fairfield, California

Cover Design
by

Mindancer Press
a division of
Bedazzled Ink Publishing Company
Fairfield, California
http://www.bedazzledink.com/

Dedicated to Leo and Ian.
You are adults now, and you inspire and amaze me.
Be proud of who you are. I sure am!

CHAPTER 1

THE SIGHT OF Varsha station expanded in the shuttle viewport from what looked like a gigantic metallic cephalopod devouring Navy ships, to a gray and black wall of plates dotted with docking rings and locking grapples. Jordan Bowers unlatched her safety harness before the shuttle engines finished their final short burst to dock. As the only passenger on the ride up from Mellick, the mineral-rich planet that stocked Varsha Station, she had no one but the shuttle pilot to glower at her for breaking regulations, and he was busy locking the rings to the shuttle dock and filling the connecting tube with human-safe atmosphere so they could disembark. Jordan floated above the hatch, waiting for the green beacon to indicate it was safe to open the hatch.

"We are docked, Captain," the pilot said. "If you would allow me to unlock the hatch?"

The beacon turned green. Jordan grabbed the latch in one hand and gave it a hard twist. The hatch swung inward. "I was flight lieutenant on the *Rubicon II* for six years, soldier. I can handle a hatch."

Fifteen years of Catholic Universalist meditation and the best she could do was grouse at a pilot for not moving fast enough for her? She blamed Dray, Dray and her damned Draybeck stubbornness.

Jordan swung through the opening and launched herself through the connecting tube to the matching open hatch on Varsha. She landed on the plasteel grating, adjusting to station gravity as she stepped through one more hatch to come face to face with yet another junior officer, this one in the deep blue of the Terran navy, the color she used to wear. Jordan straightened her black Terran Intel uniform and nodded at the officer's crisp salute.

"Welcome to the Varsha, Captain. The X.O. sends her regrets, but I've been ordered to escort you to your quarters."

"Thank you, Lieutenant, but I prefer to go directly to the dry dock where the *Rubicon* is under repairs." She knew exactly where she'd find Dray. Why waste her anger on the innocent when she could vent directly at the source?

"This way, Ma'am. The *Rubicon* is on A-pod."

Jordan followed her escort through the dock entrance, past the Bay Y-13 sign. Her come link, synced to Varsha, showed it was late second-shift, 21:00 hours station time. The station corridors the officer lead her through still buzzed with activity, a mix of Navy and shipyard personnel that tried not to get caught staring at her black uniform. Intel personnel gave regular military the creeps, but today it just added one more layer to her irritation.

"Is this your first time on Varsha, Ma'am?" her escort asked as they walked through another drab gray corridor.

Play nice, she told herself. "Yes, it is. I was stationed on the *Rubicon* up until last year, but she never needed full dry-dock repairs during my tour."

"The *Rubicon* took quite a beating, that's for sure. But Varsha's seen worse. We've got three other ships from the Chagos mission here as well. It's been busy, I can tell you."

They stepped into an elevator and he pressed A level. "Varsha has the latest vacuum robotics. On any other station, the *Rubicon*'s repairs would take a year. We'll have her back on active within seven months."

The elevator took them up, and then it was a short walk to the railcar that would speed them down the length of the pod. Her guide continued his chatter. "Varsha has eight extendible pods, each of which can handle up to three of the largest ships in the fleet. All three of the Chagos ships are on this pod, but the *Rubicon* is the largest, so she's out on the edge."

Jordan heard the dull thrumming of ship building before the railcar doors opened. The stench of dirt and grease accosted her as soon as she stepped out. Unlike the station center levels, which were set up similar to most Terran orbital stations, Varsha's A pod was visible through a protective shield. The pod was a vast open shell that hosted the three Chagos ships of different tonnage. A maze of oxygenated catwalks surrounded each ship, with the pod otherwise open to the vacuum of space. The vast distance between ships was an odd perspective, especially given the tiny dots that must be the robotic mechanics buzzing around each ship.

She locked her eyes onto the gray exterior of her former home. "That's some serious damage." The hole in the aft hull must have cost the most in human collateral, but the craters where the attack drones should have been was likely the hit that cost Dray the most.

And that's where she saw the familiar close-cropped blond hair and disheveled blue uniform on a woman staring out a catwalk porthole at the ship.

"That will be all, young man. I can find my way from here." Jordan barely acknowledged the officer's final salute as she marched across the enclosed pod base and up two ladders to reach her target. A shipyard worker sidestepped to get out of her way, but she wasn't sure if it was from the uniform or the expression on her face. Two-and-a-half weeks of interstellar transit and an extra six hour wait for a shuttle up from planetside made for a very cranky Intel captain, very cranky.

Dray turned an instant before Jordan arrived. The scar tissue and swelling around her left eye knocked some of the wind out of Jordan's anger. She'd read the medical reports, but Varsha was on a strict audio-only communications stream. This was the first time she'd seen what that Chagos mission had cost her wife. Two blue eyes stared back at her, but only one was still biological.

Dray wrapped her in a tight hug. "I thought I was meeting you on Mellick?"

Jordan accepted the quick kiss and pushed to separate them. "So did I, Helena Draybeck-Bowers," she said over the background noise of repair work surrounding them.

Dray winced at her full name, but her smile hardly wavered. "Guess I should have met your flight, eh?"

"Mellick might be a dry rock, but at least their facilities beat this. And any sensible First Lieutenant would still be in rehab, not already back on station, making a nuisance of herself."

Dray tapped her collar, widening that same pesky grin. Jordan looked down to see the newly stitched gold leaf added to the blue uniform. "You made Lieutenant Commander after all."

"Compliments of the mission. The hospital visit also gave me the chance to upgrade my hardware." Dray tapped her temple, where a small incision was visible just inside the hair line. "Promotion and selected for the latest implant prototype. There's only five of us in the program."

Jordan pinched the bridge of her nose. "That's great. Can we go to our quarters now, before my head explodes from all this noise?" Talk of implants in public always made her edgy.

"Oh, sure." Dray took her hand and led the way back down to the railcar.

When the railcar doors shut, Jordan let out a long sigh and smiled for the first time. "I am glad you're still in one piece. Watching that mission from Intel reports was a nightmare."

"Mostly in one piece." Dray tapped her scarred eyelid. "Novan Intel was one step ahead of us the whole mission. I nearly took out their precious gene bank with a drone attack, but they got those damned Black March troops through our blockade. Then the *Rubicon* was hit on our exposed planet-side from the gene bank defense grid. That pretty much took me and my drones out of the fight."

"And should have kept you in rehab." Jordan stifled a yawn. She hadn't slept in over twenty hours and it was catching up to her. "That's what a sensible person would have done."

Dray grinned as the railcar doors opened onto station central, the head of the Varsha cephalopod where every human lived. "You didn't marry a sensible person."

Jordan shook her head. "But you did. Now find your sensible wife a decent meal and a place to sleep, please."

Dray kissed her again, for real this time. It didn't melt all of Jordan's anger, but it helped, it certainly helped.

EIGHT HOURS OF sleep did improve Jordan's temper. The next morning, local time, she accepted a hot tea and cranberry muffin from Dray as the peace offering it was meant to be and took a look around the officer quarters they were assigned on-station. It was the typical utilitarian one-room set up, but with more space than they'd ever had on the *Rubicon*. Dray had already left her mark on the place, with wrinkled clothing kicked under the double bed. The small fridge was stocked with drinks and no actual food to go with the hotplate and microwave the room came with. Jordan pulled out a chair at the tiny dinette table and scanned for any sign of coffee. After her trip, she needed something stronger than tea.

Dray perched on the edge of the unmade bed, still in her light blue Navy regulation t-shirt and boxers. At twenty-eight Terran-standard years, she looked as young and incorrigibly optimistic as the day they met at the Buenos Aires Academy. The new scars marred some of that, but even those would disappear after another visit to outpatient care, if Jordan could pull Dray away from the *Rubicon* repairs long enough.

Jordan waited for the inevitable question, the one Dray held back from asking last night. She didn't have to wait long.

"So, how did it go this time?" Dray asked.

Jordan put down her tea, wishing once again it was something stronger, and shook her head. "It didn't take." She tried to ignore the stab of guilt when Dray's enthusiasm deflated a notch or two. "We did talk about this. It's very rare that Novan-Terran couples can conceive, even with the F-K procedure. The genetic material has drifted too much between our subspecies."

"You're only half Novan, and it worked for your parents, even without the F-K procedure. Have you talked to your mother?"

Jordan took a bite of her muffin before answering. "Yes, but you won't like it. She passed on both our medical and genetic records to a Gilgaran fertility clinic. Her first suggestion was that you try to have the baby instead of me. Her medical friend said you have all the markers of a real breeder."

"Me?" Dray laughed. "I guess that's an option, but what was her second suggestion?"

"That I travel to Gilgaran space and see if this clinic can help us out."

Dray perked up again. "That doesn't sound too bad."

"It doesn't sound too bad to you because you don't have to go through it all again." Jordan pushed the rest of her breakfast away. "I know you want us to have our own biological baby, but maybe all this trouble is telling us something. If by some miracle we succeed, there's still the issue that the baby could inherit detectable Novan genetics from me. I don't want our child to go through what I had to go through, hiding who she is from the Terran Purists."

Dray stood behind her and massaged the growing knot in Jordan's shoulders. "Our first bridge to cross is having the baby. We can cross the baby's genetics bridge after that. Kelvin has some options."

"I know. Your brother is my Commanding Officer at Intel. He mentioned those options to me." She let out a long sigh, releasing some of the tension she'd held overnight. "If I go through this again, I want us both to agree it's the last time."

Dray stopped the massage. Her hands lay unmoving on Jordan's shoulder. Jordan expected Dray wouldn't agree to that without a fight, but she couldn't handle the guilt and disappointment any more.

"Dray?" When she didn't answer, Jordan shifted in her chair to better see Dray's expression. Dray's electronic pupil transitioned from small to large and back again, in rapid succession. "Dray!"

Dray's arms dropped limply to her sides when Jordan moved. Otherwise, she stood still, as if in a trance. Jordan slapped her hand against the room's comm link. "Med Alert! Implant malfunction!"

UNLIKE THE VARSHA Station emergency hospital, the Navy Biotechnology Research Division headquarters on Mellick was fully equipped to handle Dray's condition and was where Dray was moved to the next night. Jordan moved their belongings to the visiting officers quarters, a drab two-story barracks that must have been one of the first built when the Navy set up facilities on Mellick. The research headquarters on the other hand, all but sparkled with newness. A glass dome covered the front foyer as Jordan approached, the lighting outlined the dome against the dark night sky. Displays showcased the latest advances in military enhancements, at least the unclassified ones anyway. Dray's prototype modifications wouldn't become public knowledge for at least two years, the average time it took for new tech to be recognized, stolen, and repurposed for the general Terran population, the ones with enough money to afford biannual upgrades.

Jordan walked past the displays and presented her credentials to the night Navy MP on duty. Since she wasn't officially Navy anymore, she'd had to get a visitor pass from Dray's implant specialist. She palmed the MP's chip ID scanner, which uploaded her name, rank, and unique ID. The chip embedded in her palm was the only piece of tech she had, too simple to detect her genetic differences. After passing through security, she took a waiting elevator up two floors to the rehab clinic, where an orderly directed her to Dray's room.

Jordan paused before entering, her mind flashing back to Dray's frightening collapse the day before. She took a deep breath. The specialist told her the crisis was over and Dray would recover fully, that's what mattered. Jordan straightened her uniform and opened the door.

Dray sat on the edge of the bed in her fatigues, bent over to pull on her boots. She looked up as Jordan entered. "Hey! Guess I gave you a fright, eh?"

"You could say that." Jordan shut the door and settled into a stiff-backed side chair. Dray's room had a bed, a window that would look out onto the neighboring barracks in daylight, a vid screen, and the chair Jordan occupied, not the most elaborate of facilities.

Jordan looked Dray over from head to toe, taking in the light blue fatigues with the *Rubicon II* insignia, her new rank, and Draybeck stitched across the front. She looked good, no obvious side effects from the implant malfunction. Even Dray's artificial eye seemed to blend in better, now. "How are you feeling?"

Dray sat up. "Good as new. They took me off sedation this morning after they re-enabled the implant. The doctor said this implant links in deeper, neurologically, and I have some minor genetic drift he hadn't seen before, but that's what caused the glitch in the interface."

"That was some glitch," Jordan said. "You were practically catatonic. What makes them think it won't happen again?"

"Good question. They put me on inactive status for the next month, just in case, and I'm stuck here for the duration. He's sending my stats to a geneticist for deeper analysis, but meanwhile, he's resynched the interface and wants to proceed with implant adaptation training."

Jordan shifted in her seat to hide a shiver. Geneticists weren't her favorite group of people, but it was Dray's Terran gene set getting analyzed, not hers. She looked around the sparse room. "This isn't the most comfortable facility to spend a month in, and neither is the barracks next door, but I guess we'll survive. Kelvin will sign off on my leave request to match your time here, I'm sure. If the implant acts up again, though, I want you to have it removed, please."

Dray gave her a sheepish look.

"Helena Draybeck," Jordan said. "We're starting a family, remember? You have responsibilities that mean you can't continue being a human lab rat for the Navy's biotech researchers, no matter how much you want to be on the bleeding edge."

Dray held up her hands. "Okay, okay. But let's give them a chance to figure out why it acted up in the first place. If they can adapt it to whatever my freaky genes require, and it works, I can keep it, right?"

Jordan sighed. "Yes, you can keep it. You and your implant toys."

"You should see what this one does. I was about to go test out a few things. Do you want to come watch?"

No, she didn't, but Jordan kept that to herself. Maybe she inherited some of her Novan father's prejudice, but the constant race to adapt and enhance based on biotech didn't sit well with her, overall. Dray excelled at that race, though, so Jordan had learned to live with it.

"Yes, in a minute," Jordan said. "Kelvin and Cara will be glad to hear you're back on your feet. Meanwhile, I've contacted that clinic we talked about."

Dray's eyes lit up. "And?"

"And, it sounds promising, and they could take me right away, but it means I'd spend most of my leave traveling there and back." And not able to keep an eye on Dray to ensure she gave herself time to recover. "They also offered to run a gene-test on the fetus at five months. We may have some hard decisions based on those results." Meaning, they would have to relocate out of Terran space if the baby didn't pass Terran purity standards, but Jordan wasn't saying that out loud in a facility she knew nothing about.

Dray stood up and pulled Jordan out of her chair to wrap her in a hug. "We'll cross that wormhole when we get to it."

Dray led the way to one of the testing rooms, what she called an implant gym. The room itself didn't look much different than the simulation rooms Jordan had used when she was still in the Navy. Banks of gray computer consoles lined one wall, with two holographic stations taking up the center portion of the room, and odd array of other equipment she didn't recognize hugging the far wall. Everything was in sleep mode, with solitary standby lights blinking on each console. Even the overhead lights were still off.

Dray stepped into the room first. "Are you ready for this?" Without waiting, her eyes drifted with a far-away look that Jordan recognized as Dray's way of accessing her implant. A heartbeat later, the overhead lights came on, along with every console in the room. The two holographic stations started their boot-up cycle.

Jordan's eyes widened. "What was that?"

"That," Dray said, pulling out a console chair, "was compliments of one BioTech lab rat." She tapped her implant as she sat with a triumphant grin. "Not bad, eh? The implant has full network connectivity, with command overrides. I can access everything in this building, and then some."

The implications were obvious and a little frightening, if that tech got into the wrong hands. Dray interrupted her train of thought before she could fully obsess over it.

"I know that look, Jordan, and you can relax. One of the reasons I'm booked to stay here for a month is so that they can keep me under control. They'll recode me today to limit my access based on my rank. No chance I'll become a power-crazed overlord." She grinned. "At least not right away."

Jordan pulled up another chair and collapsed in it. "That's good to hear. Any other party tricks I should know about?"

Dray faced the console and pulled up the holograph programming. Jordan wasn't sure she needed to do it the old fashioned way, given the capabilities of that implant, but she was glad for it anyway. A little humbleness was in order about now.

"I won't know the limits of the implant for a while, but I did want to play with the new eye. I get an extended wide spectrum range along with telescopic zoom. At least some good came out of that last mission fiasco."

Jordan read the reports on Chagos. They'd managed some heavy damage to the mining facility but their real goal, the gene bank, remained intact. A company of Novan Black March troops successfully defended it from both Terran ground troops and Dray's attempts at overhead drone bombardment. She left that out of the conversation, recognizing that Dray didn't want to hear any of the Intel details. Instead, she leaned back in her chair and relaxed while Dray warmed up to her favorite topic—her latest tech enhancements. At least it took her mind off planning the trip to yet another fertility clinic.

JORDAN'S TRIP INTO Gilgaran space proved to be an uneventful two weeks of travel. She left the day after Dray started her implant training. The shuttle from Mellick to the inter-system junction on Isere took just under two days. From there, a quick pass through Terran customs and she was on a passenger ship bound for the Gilgaran home world, a six day, multihop trip that left her stiff from too much sitting and a gravity level set just beyond the comfort zone even for her enhanced Novan bioskeletal structure. The handful of Terrans on her flight were in even worse shape when they docked at the station orbiting Gilgar. Having grown up on Gilgar as the daughter of the then-ambassador, Jordan knew those Terrans were in for a hard time. Gilgarans averaged a third taller and twice as heavy as Terrans, coming from a gravity-heavy homeworld. Most Terrans avoided Gilgar entirely, staying up on the transfer station to conduct their in-system business, but even that station operated at 1.3 times standard Terran gravity.

Jordan stretched the kinks out of her back and joined the flow of people off the ship and onto the station. She carried one travel bag that held the black Intel uniform she'd changed out of back at Isere the moment she left Terran space. It also held two spare sets of civilian clothes that matched what she was wearing now, a light blue tunic over grey slacks, and a well-insulated coat with matching gloves, though she didn't anticipate having to leave the station. Gilgaran winters were bitterly cold for Novans and Terrans.

The gray skinned station customs officer, short for a Gilgaran, scanned in her visa and handed her a breathing mask. "Welcome to The Republic of Gilgar. Please wear this mask at all times when outside the controlled atmosphere of your hotel."

Jordan strapped on the mask, inhaling the familiar sterile air as she stepped through the passageway to the station proper. Gilgar, as one of the few truly neutral cultures, gave welcome to every species and colonial transplant in nearby space, and then some. Jordan passed Gilgarans, Terrans, and Tarquins. The first Novan she passed gave her a confused smile, recognizing her from the pheromone shift they both experienced in each other's presence. He didn't need a mask to breath the station air. She didn't either, but old habits died hard, even light-years from anyone who would care whether she was half-Novan or not.

Jordan barely turned the corner from her docking bay before she was confronted.

"Jordan Bowers, ser?"

Jordan turned to the pink skinned Chameleon talking to her in Novan. "In Terran, please."

He nodded. "Yes, Ma'am. I am nurse J'lak Tremar, from the Massi Clinic. My apologies for the intrusion, but based on your limited timeframe, we would like to collect genetic samples as soon as possible."

Jordan looked around at the busy corridor. Chameleons had no sense of privacy. She sighed and rolled up the sleeve of her tunic. "Did you get the samples that I sent by fast courier?" Dray's genetics and her own previously harvested eggs.

"Yes, Ma'am." He tapped her forearm with a blood extractor, pulling a sample in seconds and sealing it. "That was why we want to rush out analysis of your genetics, to ensure a compatible recombination."

She rolled her sleeve back down. "Is there a problem?" She better not have traveled two long weeks for nothing. This was supposed to be the premier fertility clinic in the region. If she actually believed in her Catholic Universalist deity, she'd think there was a hidden message there not to procreate.

The Chameleon smiled at her. "You're results will be available by 13:00. Please reserve your questions for your assigned genetic counselor."

She didn't bother trying to read a Chameleon's nonverbal clues. "I will be at the clinic in two hours then."

He bowed and shuffled off into the crowd. Jordan made her way to her hotel for a hot meal and shower. She arrived at the clinic fifteen minutes before her appointment, sitting in the bland, light tan waiting room with a gregarious Gilgaran woman who kept up a steady stream of conversation until the nurse, J'lak, called for Jordan. He'd already shifted his skin tone to a pale orange, with contrasting green tinged hair.

"Thank you for your patience," he said as he approached a small conference room. "Please be seated. Your counselor will be with you shortly."

The room had two padded chairs, a small sofa, and paintings of the broad-leaved orange and green Gilgaran fauna. The central table was low, but had the satin finish of a touch-sensitive screen. It all spoke of a quiet comfort that put Jordan on edge. An exam room would have said "Everything's fine and we're ready to proceed."

This room said dead-end. She'd sat in enough of them over the past year and a half to recognize that.

The door slid open and a tall, broad-shouldered woman entered. She had the darker gray complexion common to older Gilgarans. She bowed and took the seat next to Jordan. "I am Vendera, your assigned counselor. To start, we do have a procedure in mind for you. I believe we can adapt to your situation, but this procedure is still in its earliest trials."

"Excellent news." Jordan wanted to relax, but their presence in a conference room and not an exam room still nagged at the back of her mind. "But I assume there is some complication?"

Vendera smiled, lightening up an otherwise severe face. "Nothing significant. There were some genetic anomalies in the Terran samples but nothing suggesting an incompatible match. These are not markers for genetic disorders of any kind, but we are required to inform you of the results before we proceed."

Interesting. After all this time blaming herself, maybe it was Dray's slight genetic shift that had been preventing earlier attempts at having a baby. Jordan smiled, thinking how Dray would take that news, especially after the implant issues.

"I understand," she said. "If there is nothing specific in your results to suggest a problem for the baby, I would like to proceed."

"No red flags. We can do a full genetic analysis of the resulting embryos before implantation if you like, but that takes up to ten days and we'll miss your optimal implantation time for your human monthly cycle. We could implant in two days, once the zygotes are proved viable, and continue with the genetic analysis after that. It would require that you stay in-system to await the results."

"That seems a logical option." The extra ten days were worth it to see the genetics inherited by their baby. That would tell her right away if they needed to plan a move out of Terran space before the child was born.

Jordan returned to the clinic two days later to receive the implants of the two strongest zygotes. She waited an extra two days until the nurse detected successful implantation in her womb. That afternoon, Jordan used her Terran Intel links to reroute an untraceable call to Dray through Terran outposts to pass on the exciting news.

Dray's face showed up on the vid screen, disheveled blond hair and eyes barely open. Her left eye had fast-healed in the two weeks

Jordan had been gone, leaving some darker shading around the nonbio eye that would fade with time.

"You know it's late shift here?" Dray said through a yawn. "Late, late shift?"

Jordan laughed. "I love you too, sleepy head. Would you rather I called you back in the morning to congratulate you?"

"Huh?" Dray scratched her head, making an even greater mess of her hair. Then her eyes opened wide. "It worked? Are you . . . ?"

"Pregnant? Yes. Possibly twins if they both take."

"Twins," Dray said in a whisper.

"Maybe. They always implant more than one, just to be sure. I'll need to wait around a few more days. The clinic is running a complete genetic map of the babies." Silly, but she'd already made the mental shift from implanted zygotes to babies.

"That's faster than my genetic results. I'm still waiting, and they tested me over a week ago." Dray let out another sizable yawn.

Jordan frowned. "That is slow. So they haven't determined why your implant malfunctioned yet?"

"Not yet, but I've been stable since that first event. They decided to keep me full-on for a while to fully test the implant's range." Dray tapped her temple. "This tech is amazing. I actually accessed bridge command on the *Rubicon* from here the other day. That got me a special visit from the Research Director, threatening to scope my implant back to access based on my rank."

"And are you behaving yourself, now?"

Dray sighed. "Yes. They threatened to turn me off entirely if I didn't." She yawned again.

"Okay, I'll let you get back to sleep. I'll call you in a few days with the test results."

Jordan spent the next three days shuttling down to Gilgar. Her mother no longer resided on-planet, having given up her post in favor of a political appointment within the Terran government, but Jordan still visited a few old friends. She was back on station when she got v-mail that the clinic had her test results.

She returned to the clinic for another ultrasound, then sat in a similar conference room from the first time, this one with only a small table and two chairs. The door opened and a tall, dark-skinned Novan clinician stepped in. He held out his hand in a greeting usually reserved for Terrans. "I am Doctor Massi. I hope you don't mind the presumption, but given your situation, your counselor and I thought it best if I spoke with you directly."

Jordan hid her shock as best she could. She'd expected test results to tell her either the child would pass as Terran or had inherited too much of her own Novan genetics. Neither result suggested she'd get such a high-profile visitor. She slid into the smooth public persona she'd perfected from years of travel with her Ambassador mother. "I'm honored that you would take the time, Doctor Massi. I did not anticipate a visit from the clinic's founder."

His smile would have been disarming in other circumstances. "The clinic provides me with research opportunities I would not experience in any other venue. And the chance to work on cases like yours."

She waved to the chair opposite her. "Please, do sit. And then you can explain why my case has drawn such esteemed interest." And why from the ranking Novan expert at that.

"Let me put you at ease," he said as he pulled the chair closer to the touch screen table. "Your babies are fine. The ultrasound proves both have implanted successfully. Nothing in the genetic results suggest you will have any complications."

"Twins." Jordan let out a slow breath. Two babies at once? Still, that wasn't why Dr. Massi himself sat across from her. What was so different about their combined gene set that warranted his attention? "Are the babies Terran or Novan?"

"Not Terran, but then the genetic combination itself made that impossible. It may be easier to show you than explain." He touched the table between them, and the screen came alive. With a few keywords entered, he pulled up a file, unnecessarily translated into Terran for her benefit. "You see, your prior unsuccessful attempts were with the F-K procedure. That procedure is predicated on the assumption that one genetic donor is Terran." He tapped the screen a couple of times and pulled up a gene-map that meant nothing to her. "The first step in that procedure is to map a fixed set of Terran markers that are most compatible with the other donor's species."

"Mixed Terran, in my case," she said, leaning over the display but making no sense of it.

"Exactly. The match should have been simplified by your partial Terran genetics. Unfortunately, there were some anomalies in your wife's gene map."

"Dray's genes?" Was this related to why her implant didn't work?

"Do you know if there are any non-Terrans in Helena's family background?"

"No. They're ancestry goes straight back to old Earth Norwegian stock."

His eyes lit up. "Most interesting. See here." He tapped the table and another gene-map overlay Dray's, with a series of markers in red and yellow. "This top map is the latest official Terran purity standard. The highlights show where your wife's genes deviate from the standard. Now genetic drift occurs all the time. That's why the Terran Purity Committee updates the standards every ten years. Yellow highlights suggest a new drift occurring and are an accepted part of an individual Terran's genetic makeup. These red highlights? These are clear violations."

Jordan studied the screen but it still didn't make sense. "What could cause something like that?"

Dr. Massi leaned back. "That's why your counselor pulled me into the case. You may not be aware, but Novan genetic modifications all carry identifiers that can trace the alteration back to its source. If I were to sequence your gene set, I could pull out exactly what makes you genetically superior to your Terran parent, what you inherited from your Novan parent. There is a universal set of genetics that separate us from Terrans on the base level. Then there are branches of alterations, based on caste and family. You are familiar with the Novan caste system?"

"Yes, military, political, religious, and clanless." He was drifting away from what she wanted to know.

"Yes, those are the high-level castes. Each caste specialized in certain genetic enhancements, and these are further specialized by clan and family, depending on wealth and access." He typed in another sequence and pulled up a more detailed view of the red highlighted area of Dray's genetic results. "This set of modifications are definitely nonTerran in origin. That's not uncommon in the past fifty years or more, at least not for Novans. But your wife's marker is definitely Novan military in source. Unfortunately, the identifier comes up as classified in my searches."

Jordan sank back in her chair. Novan genetic modifications? In Dray? It didn't make any sense. "Are you sure there was no contamination of the samples?"

He smiled again. "Quite sure. No one in this facility has these genetic modifications. We ran them against your own blood samples, and they could not have come from you either. I'm not sure where or how, but Helena Draybeck is not Terran, at least not by their latest purity tests."

Not Terran.

The urge to panic came and went with a steadying breath. She was light years away from Dray, but in front of her was one of the most gifted and well-connected geneticists in the region. *Use him,* she told herself. "You say this is a military enhancement. What else do you know about it?"

Massi leaned forward. "Military and classified is all our current records can reveal."

"Current records?"

"Yes. Given the unusual circumstances, and with your authorization, the clinic can petition for a full release of records based on the genetic IDs of the enhancements."

IDs, plural. "You have my authorization, Doctor." However the Terran government reacted, Dray would need whatever details Jordan could find on the changes and so would the babies she was carrying.

Jordan resisted the urge to shoot out of her chair. "Thank you for your consultation, Dr. Massi, and I look forward to hearing the results of the petition. If you'll excuse me, I need to return to my hotel."

Dray sat in a Terran military base, waiting for her genetic test results. Thanks to Massi, Jordan knew exactly what they'd find in those results. What she didn't know was what the military reaction would be to those results, or how long it would take them to discover the genetic differences were Novan in origin.

CHAPTER 2

REHABILITATION WARDS SUCKED, no matter how well-financed they were, and the high-caste Nassien clinic on New China was no exception. Kay pulled herself out of the indoor lap pool and sat on the edge while the water dripped from her collar-length blond hair. She still hadn't gotten used to that. Years of short-cropped hair biochemically altered to a less-conspicuous black was a hard habit to give up. The worst, though, was leaving her eyes their natural blue. Novans didn't have blue eyes. They might alter them to any other color, but not blue. Terrans had blue eyes. If her lack of Novan pheromones didn't make it obvious, her natural blue eyes did. She was Terran, an unaltered Terran clone, gene line KDTU-02128, property of the Nassien Military Research Division to be precise. Even that designation was losing significance under the ever-vigilant eye of one Ayaan Nassien-Nomani, Novan Black March Lieutenant Colonel. Or was it full Colonel now? Kay couldn't remember. The gratuitous promotions had come fast and furious during the last days of the Chagos mission, even for her.

If she looked at her room chart, it stated the ridiculous rank of Sergeant, as if a grunt like her was ever meant to get that high in the military food chain. Jax would have had a good long laugh on that one. If he wasn't dead. If she hadn't shot him to save his traitorous ass from something even worse.

She grabbed a gray and white towel and rubbed her damp hair with a vengeance. Too much change, too fast, and shit-all she could do about it. Guess her life hadn't changed that much after all. Grunts took orders, whether they were in active duty, or in a fancy rehab ward compliments of her well-connected Novan girlfriend. Ayaan made sure Kay had the best that money and influence could buy. And made sure no one used Kay's gene-line designation. She was Kay Deetchu, the made-up name she and Jax had used. Back in the day.

"Get a grip, you morbid Terran git." No one else was in the lap pool area to hear her rant at herself. Most wouldn't have understood it anyway, as Ayaan still insisted Kay practice her Terran Standard instead of speaking in Novan.

Kay tossed her damp towel in the laundry bin on the way to the locker room. This room had a couple of other rehab residents, but most of them had given up staring at her by now. Anyone who'd been here more than a day knew who she was and that she was dating one of the highest ranked Novans in the New China system. Freak was stamped on her naked ass as she hopped in the communal shower and then got dressed in black fatigues. She didn't know if she was still officially a Black March soldier or not, but the uniform was the only clothes she had.

Her datapad chimed out the five minute warning for her "reintegration" training session, and Kay double-timed it down the corridor. She stepped into the bootcamp arena right before the training Master Sergeant, a brown-clad Army man with a buzz cut so close to his tan scalp it was hard to tell if his hair was brown or gray. Ten other soldiers stood in line already, sporting Navy blue, Army brown, and Marine gray. She was the only one in black, of course. Most Black March soldiers rehab'd in the outer Rim, those that lived long enough to bother with rehab.

The Master Sergeant ignored her as she took her spot in line. "You've got a week to get your sad sorry asses ready for active duty again. I'm not here to decide who makes the grade and who doesn't. That's up to your rehab doctor and your branch physical evaluation board. I'm here to make sure you do your damned best, anyway. This isn't a free ride back to civilian life."

Kay took in the facility in a quick glance while he droned on with his drill sergeant inspirational nonsense. The arena had an elevated running track suspended above an obstacle course and a set of exercise equipment similar to what she used in rehab. None of that worried her. The persistent limp in her left leg was barely noticeable. She could make the grade there. It was the target range that got on her nerves. She clenched her left fist. That was the weak spot she hid from her evaluators, even from Ayaan. So far, she managed to schedule target practice in the morning, before the tremors showed up, but the timing of her shooting assessment test was out of her control. If it happened later in the day, she'd fail her marksmanship level for sure.

"Up to the track, single file," the Sergeant shouted. "Any slackers will give me an extra five kilometers."

Kay joined the rest, maintaining a pace in the middle. Running was the easiest as it involved no coordination, just raw endurance. She had plenty of that, and the benefit of a tall stature, for a Terran, with long legs that made it a smooth, easy pace. She worked up a good sweat regardless, a clear indication that her two months in rehab had eaten away at her muscle tone. She had just enough time to catch her breath before her turn on the obstacle course. The course emphasized agility and coordination for major muscles. High tech had its place, but not here. Tires, cones, a rope, and climbing wall were centuries' old traditions that drill Sergeants held onto with the zeal of ancient history majors.

Kay's pass through the course wasn't smooth, but wasn't the worst either. A junior grade Navy NCO ranked dead last, bested by an Army double amputee still learning control over her artificial legs, and then Kay. Wasn't a rank to brag about, but it kept her out of the drill Sergeant's eye, and that's where she wanted to be before the final drill—the firing range.

She lined up in her own slot at the range, with a standard-issue NC-8 rifle, simple Army peashooter. It would have been insulting if she wasn't already fighting to keep her left hand from shaking on the rifle barrel.

Her first shot was a miss, a freaking clear miss. *Shit.* She took a deep breath, gripped the barrel harder, and fired again. This time, she at least hit the target. Barely. The Sergeant paced behind the range, likely eyeing up the results. Kay's clenched jaw started to ache. This was not going well at all. She had one last trick. Wiping the sweat off her hands, she delayed her next shot until after the Sergeant passed her by. Then she picked up the rifle, but instead of balancing the barrel with her left hand, she rammed the gun into her shoulder with her right, positioned her traitorous left hand under but not touching the barrel, and took another shot.

Better this time, it was at least within the target. She fired off three more the same way, showing slight improvements with each. It wasn't marksman quality, but it was a decent score for a grunt. Too bad she wasn't just a grunt anymore. Too bad she wouldn't be able to use that trick with a real Black March rifle, or any of the firepower she was ranked expert on.

She released her targeting data to the automated range clerk which would add it to her record. She hadn't flunked out on her first day of reintegration, but it didn't matter. Ayaan was still officially her C.O. and there was no way that poor targeting data wasn't going to get Ayaan's attention and fast.

Why didn't rehab clinics serve alcohol? Or better yet, allow a decent traffic in illicit drugs? She could use a good hit about now.

COLONEL AYAAN NASSIEN-NOMANI entered Kay's rehab barracks at a brisk march, acknowledging salutes from subordinates with a slight nod. Ayaan's triple star rank beneath a red crescent bar on her black uniform drew almost as much attention on her first visit as Kay's blue eyes had. The Nassien Autonomy regulated a strict separation between military and religious affiliations, but Kay learned the rules didn't apply to the highest Novan castes. And the rest of the rehab occupants and staff learned fast enough who Ayaan was, and why she visited almost daily.

Ayaan stopped in front of Kay's rack and accepted her salute with a sharp nod. "With me, Sergeant," she said, and led Kay to an unoccupied office outside the small barracks.

Kay could have told her everyone knew what they were up to when they visited that isolated office, but she kept her mouth shut. What hadn't mattered during the Chagos mission mattered a lot more now that they were within a day's shuttle from Ayaan's family compound. Ignoring society's expectations was simpler when light-years separated them from caste and family.

Kay shut the door behind them but Ayaan didn't let down her icy edge. Instead, she took the seat behind the desk. She tapped a quick tattoo with her hands and that told Kay this was not a conjugal visit. She stood at attention, waiting, but not for long.

"What aren't you telling me?" Ayaan asked in Terran.

"Ma'am?"

"Don't Ma'am me. Your targeting scores. Even if you weren't ranked as marksmen, I couldn't ignore the pre- and post-mission differences in your accuracy. So, what aren't you telling me?"

Kay clenched her left fist and let it go. It was an involuntary reaction, but Ayaan's eyes caught the motion.

"It'll get better," Kay said, lifting her arm. "It's just fatigue."

Ayaan frowned. "Your doctor's report does not mention this."

Kay shrugged.

"He doesn't know about it, does he? Kay, how can we help you if you keep us in the dark?"

"They can't do anything about it anyway," she growled. "They are Novan specialists, with Novan cures for Novan injuries."

"Kay." Ayaan held out her hand but Kay ignored the peace offering.

"You know it's true. They've done as much nerve regeneration on me as an unaltered Terran can handle." Kay slapped her thigh. "The limp isn't going away. My grip isn't going to get any better. Shit Terran genes have healed as much as they can."

"Are you clean?"

"What?"

"Drugs. Are you clean?" Ayaan asked again.

"Yes, I'm clean." Kay wrapped her arms around her chest. "I damned well wish I wasn't."

"I'm sorry, but it was a logical question, given your history. You haven't been kind to yourself, what with the combination of drugs and the neurological damage from Chagos. There's only so much a human body can take, Terran or Novan."

Kay faced away from Ayaan and her tough love speech. "Either way, I'm screwed."

Nineteen Terran years old put her at the same physical maturity level as Ayaan, who was four years older, but emotionally, she couldn't hold a candle to Ayaan's rigid self control, and most often didn't want to. Whether it was the lack of drugs or getting her brain fried by hooking into a defense grid on Chagos meant for Novan brain wave patterns, Kay was a wreck inside, and she hated when it showed itself to her girlfriend of all people.

Ayaan let out a long sigh, rubbing her dark cheeks with her hands until they glowed. "So what do you want to do now?"

"I don't know. What do you do with a failed gene line clone facing discharge from the only military branch left for genetic misfits like me?" Kay winced. Even in her own ears, she sounded like a whining brat. She relaxed her arms and leaned against the desk. "I don't know. When the tremors started, I did inform the doctor. They ran tests, brain scans, and more tests, then sent me for more physical therapy. When that didn't help, I just got better at compensating for it." She smiled. "It worked for everything but shooting. Even that I can do well enough, if I'm not tired."

Ayaan stepped around the desk and took Kay's hand in hers. "You didn't have to hide this from me. When will you learn to trust me, trust us?"

Maybe never? How could she trust a three-month old relationship that broke every written rule and some of the unwritten ones? "Maybe when you're not my C.O anymore. So what are our options if I can't stay as a marksman?"

"Retirement."

Kay laughed. "Isn't that another word for euthanasia for a clone?"

Ayaan stroked her cheek. "You're not just a clone. And you're still my bodyguard, remember?"

Kay remembered accepting the Knife Oath and swearing her life to Ayaan's protection, before they fell in love, but not before she recognized her need to get the bastards who'd already tried to kill her and Ayaan twice. Their last mission changed everything.

Kay wasn't the only one out of place in this relationship. Ayaan was the result of an unapproved tryst between her Nassien mother and a man from one of the religious castes. That tryst ended in the murder of Ayaan's father, and twenty-three years of surviving assassination attempts herself.

"We make a hell of a pair, don't we?" Kay said. "What are my options besides a very shaky possibility of retiring?"

"Tactical specialist. You proved you have the skills for it, but you'd need more formal training."

Kay sighed. "Back to school, great. Would they even let me do that? How much pull do you have over my gene line?"

Ayaan lowered her head, breaking eye contact. "It's hard to say who controls your gene line right now, since Halabi disappeared."

"Disappeared?" The bastard was behind their last couple of assassination attempts, and responsible for setting Jax up to take the fall for it all. "When did that happen?"

"He was gone before we got back here. I'm sorry, Kay, but you needed to focus on recovery, not getting back at him." Ayaan looked back at her with a coldness in her eyes. "Trust me, my family will find him. It's only a matter of time."

"So, I'm in limbo then? There is no program manager for my gene line?"

"I didn't say that. Your interim program manager is significantly harder to manipulate, though."

Kay took a deep breath. "Okay, so who is it, and why is he harder to deal with than Halabi was?" Her experience was that all her PMs were one step away from incompetent. How hard could it be to pull this new guy's strings, especially for Ayaan?

"He is she, and she is Grand Madame Manji Nassien."

Kay's eyebrows bounced up. "Grand Madame? Nassien?"

It was Ayaan's turn to wrap her arms around her chest. "Yes. My maternal grandmother, and Premier of the Nassien Autonomy."

That's how hard it could be to pull her new PM's strings. If anything called for a night wasted in a drugged haze, that news did.

AYAAN AUTHORIZED KAY'S release from the rehab facility the next day on a special rest and recuperation leave. It left Kay's status as Black March, Inactive. Kay didn't know how long she could maintain that status before her PM took notice. Not that it mattered, since they were heading for a meetup with her new PM in a day. Kay shouldered her duffel bag, with a spare set of black fatigues and the few personal items she carried from mission to mission—minus her usual stash of drugs. Her time in rehab wasn't only for her Chagos recovery. Her system was as clean as the day she was born. She hated it.

Kay stepped out of the barracks door to a blast of hot air and painfully bright sunlight. She pulled out the archaic sunglasses she'd printed last night and put them on to protect her eyes from the glare. She should have fought harder against Ayaan's insistence that she let all of her illegal alterations fade out. Gene-doped black eyes were a great protection against an over-bright sun.

New China was the primary habitable planet in the star system that bore its name, with a massive eastern continent that stretched from the southern polar ice caps up to the northern ocean. The interior, where she found herself, was hot and flat, but the planet had a standard near-Earth gravity. Kay was glad for that as she hiked across the military complex, but she could do without the blazing sun that baked everything within a thousand kilometers.

A ground car waited for her beyond the manned gatehouse. She flinched when the corporal on duty saluted her. Shit, that Sargent rank was going to take time to get used to. She stepped into the ground car, glad for the civilian driver.

"Zeti Air Field," she said.

He turned onto the main road and the barracks and rehab clinic disappeared behind her in a dusty haze. She'd be at the air field in forty minutes, and then on a five-hour flight over the Nabian Sea to the western tropics. Ayaan would meet her when she landed and take her to the Nassien Compound. Meanwhile, Kay settled in for a long dull day of travel and ignored the nagging voice in her head that said she should be heading anywhere but where she was going. Ayaan had a way of making anything sound reasonable, even confronting the Premier of the Nassien Autonomy with her fragile status.

The road fed onto an automated highway where the driver became superfluous to the auto pilot that took them to the air field. He glanced at her through the rear view mirror a few too many times to be considered courteous but she ignored him. The last thing she wanted to encourage was curiosity about who she was. One benefit of military life is that most of the grunts didn't care who you were so long as you pulled your weight to keep your fire team alive. The outside world didn't look promising for an obvious unaltered Terran, even in a Black March uniform. Maybe especially in a Black March uniform.

"Airfield is the next exit, ser."

She acknowledged his comment with a curt nod. The car pulled off the highway and the driver took back control, keeping his eyes on the road instead of her. Five minutes later, she exited the car and stepped into the main concourse for Zeti Air Field. Given the isolated nature of the barracks, most everyone else in the small airport also wore military uniforms sporting the Nassien branch logo. She pocketed her sunglasses and inched from one processing line to the next until she finally made her way to the plane that would take her across the ocean. Her Sergeant chevrons earned her a few too many random salutes along the way, but she managed to respond to each, even if it wasn't quite military precision for each. Shit, she should have put on some civvies for this, but even on inactive status, she had to stay in uniform. How did officers deal with this crap?

The flight went from dry dirt to sea to the tropics, with a detour around some massive thunderheads that delayed her landing by thirty minutes. The lush green central plain grew in her window until the wheels touched down in an airport quadruple the size of the one she left from. Still, she exited the plane to a near-empty waiting room. The rest of the passengers passed through with surreptitious glances but enough common sense not to question the isolation, not with the foreboding presence of no less than five armed personnel in drab green uniforms surrounding one woman and another ten armed airport security personnel in gray uniforms lining the walls.

Kay walked up to Ayaan and gave a brisk salute from the outside of the security detail. Ayaan parted the security detail with a hand signal and Kay was allowed to step closer, separated from Ayaan now only by one obvious bodyguard.

Propriety in public won over emotion and Ayaan gave her little more than an acknowledging nod. She pointed to the over two meter human bulk beside her, dressed in a dark green flak vest and one of the drab green civilian uniforms. "This is Joris Tiburn of the House Guard. He is your secondary, responsible for my personal security."

Kay eyed up her new subordinate. He had dark brown hair and hazel eyes that could be real or doped, and towered over her in both height, girth, and most likely actual skill and experience in physical security. What she lacked in that category she made up for in motivation. Ayaan was her girlfriend and lifeline. She mirrored Ayaan's formality, giving Joris a stiff nod and slipped in next to Ayaan as the overtly showy detail marched out of the waiting room and through the airport. Heads turned but only briefly before turning back to their own business. This was Bahai, a megacity with bragging rights of its own, even if it was home to the ruling Nassien family.

The airport security peeled off once they stepped outside, to be replaced by more of Ayaan's green-clad house guard, lining up in front and behind a waiting row of ground cars. Ayaan and Kay slipped into the back seat of the middle car, with Joris in the front with the driver after he put Kay's duffel bag in the trunk. The lush interior of the car belied the extra-thick exterior frame. It was built as a moving mini fortress, with all the comforts of home, including a small wet bar in front of them.

Once the doors closed, Ayaan flicked a switch and the glass panel between them and the front seat darkened. Kay felt a tug on her shirt and she was pulled into a searing kiss. They separated as the car pulled out in the middle of their caravan.

"You don't travel light, do you," Kay said, catching her breath.

Ayaan rested back into the plush Moregian contoured seat. "Nana wanted to send a driver for you. When I said I was coming, she insisted on this fiasco." She gave Kay a brief smile. "On the plus side, she's still here in the capital for another two days, until the Legislature closes session. We should have relative quiet in the house for a while."

Nana. Premier of the Nassien Autonomy. This trip could very well fry what few functioning brain cells Kay had left. Still, a two day reprieve from facing that would give Kay a chance to get her bearings in this place. She glanced out the window as the competing tall towers of central Bahai passed by. As a military rat, she'd never made it beyond the Outer Rim planetoids. New China was vast, with a horizon that held no visible curve. That bothered her more than the flagrant displays of unmatched wealth as each pristine white and gray building competed with the next for outrageous size and architectural design. They passed more than one building where Kay couldn't understand how it stayed upright, given it looked more like an abstract sculpture than a building.

An hour later, their convoy sped past the outer edge of Bahai and into an area of rolling tree-covered hills and personal estates. Nothing prepared her though for where they finally turned off the main road.

She glanced at Ayaan. "This?"

"Is home, yes."

Home was not a term Kay would have used for what lay ahead. The outer wall was taller and more heavily fortified than most military sites she'd seen. Part of that wall folded in on itself as the lead car on the convoy passed through. When the car entered the main compound, the true scope of Ayaan's family's wealth and power opened up in front of her. Canals created a series of branch roads off the main road, each one stretching out a kilometer or more, and covered with buildings. The main road became more a central artery between these branches, covering another two kilometers or more before heading over an arched bridge across the lake that fed those canals. In the center of the lake stood the most extravagant mansion she'd seen yet.

"And this is your actual home?" she asked.

Ayaan stared out the window. "It's all home. I seldom got to leave here before I took up my commission in the Black March. Born, raised, educated, fell in love." She turned to Kay. "Fell out of love, took my place in the military."

Kay looked out the window. "I've seen smaller cities. Certainly less fortified ones," she added when she caught sight of the defensive drones hovering above the landscape.

The convoy split off, with their car the only one pulling up in front of the mansion. Green-liveried guards lined the steps from the car up to the massive cherrywood doors, propped open for the occasion. Joris popped out of the car first and walked to Ayaan's door.

"Do you ever get to come and go without the fanfare?" she asked.

"No." Ayaan stepped out when Joris opened her door. Kay got herself out and joined them for the silent march up the marble staircase into the opened doors. The two-story, sand-color foyer glowed in the sunlight streaming in from multiple arched windows. Beyond was a wide spiral staircase carpeted in dark red. Two steps up, stood an impeccably dressed older woman, her gray-streaked hair pulled back in a bun, both hands resting on top of a black cane.

Kay dropped her gaze instinctively. You didn't look Novan high caste in the eyes, not if you wanted to live long. Given the dominant scent of this woman's pheromones, Kay guessed she was highest caste.

Ayaan froze beside Kay, her scent shifting to a range Kay had never noticed from her before. Fear? "Nana?"

Shit. So much for two days to prepare for this.

CHAPTER 3

JORDAN PACED HER hotel room, her gaze bouncing between the clock and the hotel vid link. She'd logged two inter-system video requests in the past three hours—one to Varsha and the other to her mother, which would automatically route to wherever she was. Neither were getting through. In normal circumstances, she'd shrug it off as trans-system network delays, but this was anything but normal circumstances. Varsha was isolated at the edge of a poorly travel system. It could easily have a solitary communications node, but her mother should have been reachable by now, unless she was in transit herself.

Jordan did some quick mental calculations. She'd been out of Varsha for a week and then a handful of days here on station. Terrans didn't have the most advanced genetic facilities. How long could it reasonably take to analyze results and would they retest Dray before coming to some decision? Jordan grabbed her warm coat, hat, and gloves and left her room. She didn't have the luxury of depending on Terran bureaucracy.

The front desk clerk eyed her up as she give him her request. "Ma'am. It is the middle of the night in Ahki City. Wouldn't you prefer to travel down to the Gilgar homeworld in their morning?"

"Book the shuttle, please." She wasn't site-seeing. She had one call left to make, and that required a secure link not available on station.

She left the hotel without her respirator, inhaling the xenon-heavy air for the first time in a decade. Her Novan genes could handle it, though, and given her destination, it would help if she blended in with the local Novan population. She took a tram across-station to the planet-side docking bays. The station kept its own time cycles since its orbit around Giglar was not geosynchronous. She found her shuttle two levels up, boarded early, and took the first available seat. The shuttle had room for twenty, but only five other passengers joined her before the hatch was sealed and they undocked from the station.

Ahki City was a two hour ride, wrapping half way around to the dark side of the planet. Its city lights were visible shortly after the shuttle cleared the upper atmosphere. Ahki hosted some of the largest trading superfactories on Gilgar. Not the most interesting city, but one that had the resources Jordan needed. She linked to the airport and ordered a ground car, which was waiting for her when she disembarked the shuttle.

An icy Gilgaran wind stole her breath as she rushed to the car and sealed herself out of the cold night air. She keyed on the navigation system. "Dunhan Business Park," she said, her voice deep and raspy from the altered air quality. The autopilot kicked in and drove her the twenty minutes to her destination.

The parking lot bordered on one of the superfactories, bright light spilling across the otherwise deserted lot. Jordan rushed across the short distance between the car and the back door. She opened her datapad with gloved fingers and pulled up her Intel access code. She held it up to the door scanner, and the door hissed open a second later. She stepped inside and gave her eyes a moment to adjust to the low light before proceeding. Compliments of Kelvin Draybeck's forethought, her datapad held all the Terran Intel sites in Gilgaran and Novan-controlled space. According to the site record, this one should have a secure inter-system link.

She walked past darkened offices and down a flight of stairs. She found the com link in a storage room toward the back of the building.

"Thank you Kelvin," she whispered. "First of many favors you're about to do for me."

Jordan switched on the system and sank into the spartan chair. Terran Intel spent billions to create their own secure inter-system communications network. It took ten minutes for the system to come online, and another twenty after Jordan keyed in her code and her desired connection. When the video link came to life, she stared at the familiar red-head of Kelvin Draybeck, her brother-in-law. "What is Dray's status?"

Kelvin rubbed the sleep out of his eyes. "Good morning to you, too. I figured you'd know more about Dray than I do, being her wife and all."

Jordan tapped a finger against her lips. "Are you alone and do you trust the security of this link?"

His expression sharpened in an instant. "Yes and yes. What do you have to report?"

She leaned forward. "Dray's at Varsha station, or was when I left there two weeks ago. Her new implant was acting up so they ordered deeper genetic testing to fine-tune the match."

Kelvin smirked. "She called me long enough to brag about her latest prototype implant and the little glitch she had."

Jordan didn't think that medical emergency qualified as a glitch, but that wasn't important. "I know what caused that glitch, and Dray could be in trouble. I'm at the Massi clinic in Gilgar. The tests here on her genetic samples show she's got Novan modifications."

Kelvin shot forward in his seat. "That's not possible. I was there when she was born."

Jordan had hours to think that one through. "Your mother must have cheated on your father."

Kelvin was quiet for a long time before answering. "At one point, maybe, but years before Dray was born. My parents were separated for a year before my mother was captured by the Novans, but when she escaped from that prison, my parents got back together."

"Well it happened, somehow. And it wasn't just any Novan. The clinic here couldn't decode the genetic changes, but said it carried military enhancement markers."

"Military." Kelvin glanced to the side. "Military."

"Kelvin, you need to get Dray off Varsha."

He glanced back at her. "Yes. I can get her transferred to Intel. I'll have Jeffrey work on killing those genetic tests before the results come in."

"Good." Jeffrey was Kelvin's husband and Jordan's immediate superior in Terran Intel. "The next thing I need from you is a priority berth on the next ship back to Isere from here."

He rubbed his eyes. "From Gilgar? You're looking to cut short that six day journey."

"I can't do anything useful from here."

"And your visit there? Was it successful."

Jordan nodded. "So far." Her body had rejected implants before, within the first few weeks. "That berth?"

"Yes, I'll have it waiting for you when you get back to the station. Contact me when you get to Isere Junction."

Jordan disconnected the link and leaned back in her chair. She did all she could from Gilgaran space, but it didn't feel like enough. She gathered her datapad and coat, left the secure communications room, and walked back to the car.

It was a quiet night ride back to the airport, where she had a three hour wait for a shuttle back to the orbital station. She could worry, or she could meditate. She chose to meditate. Her mind chose to ignore her and spun on all possible outcomes for her and Dray. Few of them ended in their favor.

"MS. BOWERS?" THE hotel clerk called out as she passed the front desk. "Your call to Senator Bowers is available if you wish to take it."

"Yes, link it into my room please."

By the time she got into her room and stripped off her coat, the comm link was active. She engaged the call and a moment later, her mother appeared on the vid screen. Her mother's jet black hair was pulled back into a neat braid, highlighting the prominent cheekbones that Jordan had inherited.

"Jordan? Good to hear from you, dear. What are you doing back in Gilgar?"

Jordan took a long breath to formulate her thoughts into the code she hadn't needed to use with her mother in years. "Long story, mother." *Not important.* "Dray sends her regards, from Varsha." As smoothly as she could, she directed her mother's focus onto Dray.

"Is she recovering well?"

And now, the crux of the matter. "She's had some setbacks with her implant. They aren't sure what they've detected yet." *Implant, genetics. Discovered.*

Even her mother's long years of diplomatic and political life couldn't stop the quick frown of confusion before she smoothed out her features. Jordan was using all their critical code words to say the Terrans finally discovered Jordan's Novan genetics, but the conversation centered on Dray.

"Dray has never had problems before, has she?"

Yes, mother, it is Dray, not me. "Never. I spoke to Kelvin. He's certain the issue is minor."

"Sorry to hear that. Let me know if there's anything I can do to help."

Jordan drummed her fingers on the table that held the com link. Her mother had considerable pull, enough to get through to Dray if need be, but Kelvin was closer and less traceable. Her mother's talents were better suited to something else. "It's too bad Dray's mother died too young to tell if there were any medical issues on that side of the family."

Jordan saw the acknowledging nod from her mother.

"Medical issues could come from either parent." *Investigate mother and father.*

"True. Well, I'm traveling back to Terran space. I'll forward my itinerary, but I don't anticipate much for stopovers before I hit Isere Junction and Terran Customs."

"Call me again as soon as you get to Isere, Jordan." *Check in before reaching Terran space.* It made sense, though the itinerary would ensure her mother and Kelvin could leave messages for her before then.

They ended the call a few minutes later, after a series of idle updates on her mother's work and Jordan's next visit. Kelvin, true to his word, had a travel schedule ready for her thirty minutes later. She scanned the trip. A fast courier would get her back to Isere in half the time, with only one stopover on day two. It was the best she would get, far better than on her own connections. She looked at the clock and decided she had time for a nap and shower before she had to board the courier ship. Before that, she started a datadump of all Gilgaran records on Charles and Katherine Draybeck, and Helena Draybeck-Bowers. Gilgaran data would be limited, but it did replicate all open Terran and Novan records along with their own. She also sent a classified query to the Terran data warehouse on Isere. With luck, the results would be waiting for her at their lone stop over on day two.

Three hours later, she checked out of her hotel. The call to Dray at Varsha never came through.

JORDAN BOARDED THE courier at 08:00, local time. The pilot barely restrained the instinct to salute, even though she was still in civilian clothes. The kind of priority override Kelvin had to pull to get her on this ship meant the pilot knew who she was, and her rank, even if he didn't know the reason behind his Terran Intel passenger's rush.

"Welcome aboard," he said. "Your cabin is the second on port side. If you will prepare, we undock in twenty."

She nodded acknowledgment and carried her bag through the air lock. She heard the pilot close and secure the hatch behind her. The ship was the smallest she'd ever boarded for inter-system travel. A courier vessel held just enough room for minimal passengers. Its main cargo was critical data that could not be entrusted to the public networks. And few agencies outside of Terran Intel could afford their own private network. Data storage and hardcopy were stored below the one main deck. The ship bridge was comparable to an oversized cockpit on any other in-system vessel. The central passageway led fore to aft, a short walk before the rest of the ship was taken up by drive, fuel, and minimal defensive armaments. Whatever pirates they might encounter would be hard-pressed to catch this ship.

Jordan walked the short distance to the second hatch, left open for her. She stepped inside and scanned the small space she would live in for the next three days. A bunk took up the left side, with storage space underneath. A table, foldout chair, and data console took up the rest, the necessities and nothing more. She'd share the head with the pilot. At least she had access to the ship computer. She felt the data stick in her coat pocket, all the available information on Dray's family. Just the publicly available data took up most of the stick. She'd need the ship CPU power to crunch through all that.

She stored her bag and tore through a breakfast ration before the pilot's voice came over ship comm.

"Prepare for undock in five."

It was an old custom to announce that maneuver since undock and travel beyond the planetary gravity well went smoothly on all modern ships. It was six hours later when his voice broke in again, waking her from a short nap to announce the upcoming transition to FTL. "Jump in five minutes. Hold Fast. Hold Fast."

For that standard broadcast warning, she strapped into the lone chair and waited. Right on time, she felt the engines shift before the vertigo hit her in the gut. She'd have doubled over and slammed around the cabin if she wasn't firmly held in place by her harness. It wasn't more than a minute in transition, but she was rushing to unbuckle before the pilot announced the all clear. She made it to the head before she lost that breakfast ration.

The pilot interrupted her over ship comm. "Is everything okay, Captain?"

Jordan punched the comlink in the head. "Yes. Just a stomach issue."

"FTL transitions can hit people like that sometimes. This ship has a faster drive than most. Makes it that much worse."

She didn't bother to answer. Her Novan genes had protected her through all other FTL transitions. If she were traveling on a Tarquin vessel with its ultra fast Baeron drive, and even the Terran prototype version, she would have expected problems, but not on the courier ship. Maybe she was getting weak. Or maybe those embryo implants were making themselves known. In all her questions to her mother, she never thought to ask if morning sickness ran in the family.

She waited a few minutes to see if her stomach had finished its revolt. Realizing the lingering nausea wasn't going to get any better, she stood up and washed herself in the small sink. When she emerged, the pilot gave her a sympathetic nod as he made his way to the galley at the back of the ship. FTL flight meant he had few duties as well for the next two days. Her stomach ensured the galley was off limits for now, so she went back to her cabin. The small space would get on her nerves after a time, but for now, she was content to stay locked in there for a while.

By convention, the ship stayed on Gilgaran time through the first leg of their journey. When her stomach continued its revolt each morning, Jordan felt compelled to explain herself to the pilot, who gave her a brief congratulations, but otherwise kept to himself, for which she was grateful. She'd set the ship computer up for a series of queries on the Draybeck data she brought on board. Late on the first day, she sat down at her console to review the results.

The first set was a summary of what she already knew. Dray's father, General Charles Draybeck came from a long line of military commanders. He'd advanced steadily in the ranks up through the last Novan war. Nothing stood out in his background to suggest genetic issues. Dray's mother, Katherine Draybeck, had a more interesting history, having been both a hero and potential traitor in that same Novan war. Jordan studied the picture of Katherine at the top of the report. She was taller than Dray by a few centimeters, with long blond hair and eyes the same shade of blue as Dray.

Jordan paused in scrolling the results, her eye caught on one familiar name—Fenton. She pulled up the relevant data and was surprised to see a younger version of the woman who was her first instructor at the Buenos Aires Military Academy. Fenton was just as tall back then but not nearly as wide as she'd ended up decades later. The report linking her to Dray's mother revealed the details of their escape from a Novan prisoner-of-war facility. That's where Katherine Draybeck earned her hero's badge, for leading the escape and rescue of multiple of her fellow POWs.

The next data point proved more interesting. Jordan pulled up all related records. Katherine Draybeck had spent the six months before her capture at a separate home address from Dray's father. Did that suggest she could have been with someone else in that time? The dates didn't match though, since it was before her capture, which made it years before Dray was born. Jordan punched in the address for a separate query, but it was not mentioned anywhere else. She made a note to search on it once they dropped out of FTL. If someone else lived at that address, it could mean Katherine had an affair once, and possibly again. She flipped back to the younger photos of Dray's father. It was a long shot that they weren't related. Dray had a reddish tinge to her hair that would have come from him, and the same hard jawline.

She read one more report, this one written after Katherine's death. The report of her last mission repeated what Jordan already knew. Katherine Draybeck managed to complete her final mission against incredible odds, but every Terran died in that mission. The sentiment analysis of the data revealed a considerable percentage of people questioning Katherine's loyalties. Was it possible Dray's mother had been turned during her prison time? If she'd taken a Novan lover, that would explain Dray's genetics.

Jordan ran a hand through her hair. This was getting her nowhere. Maybe Dray's mother had an affair. Maybe either parent had some family skeletons of the Novan kind in their genetic closet. She didn't have enough data in the public records to tell on either case. She shut down the console and rubbed her tired eyes. Time for food, if her stomach allowed it.

By the time they made the nauseating transition out of FTL on day two, Jordan had enough of data analysis and the courier ship. They would only spend a few hours in system, but it was enough to say she could disembark on station and stretch her legs for something other than the few meters of the courier's central deck. Their stopover was at an Allied Defense Force installation. The station was positioned at the edge of the system's asteroid belt, far from the gas giants that made up the planetary system. The station itself proved to be less interesting that she'd hoped for, but it had a good restaurant or two.

The moment she synced her datapad on station she received a blast of data from her classified query. That might prove more fruitful on the last leg of her journey than the public records had. She also had a separate packet of data waiting from her mother, but no other messages. She didn't know if that was good or bad news. After eating the best meal she'd had in days, Jordan found the station's Terran Intel communications room and commandeered a video link to Kelvin. She was surprised when the call went through, and she faced her commanding officer, Major Jeffrey Franklin, instead.

"Sir?" she said.

"Jordan. Kelvin set a priority forward to me for any calls from you."

Jordan straightened. "What's wrong?"

"Calm down. We don't know the full details yet, but Dray was moved from Varsha two days ago. Kelvin was called in to join her so he's on his way there now."

"Have they detected the root cause of her genetic results?"

He shrugged. "Nothing that's been reported out yet, and if we don't know, I doubt they do yet either. It could be they want her at a better facility. Varsha is great for ships, but not state of the art for humans."

He had a point. Terran Intel would be one of the first departments to get involved if there was some Novan taint discovered. Well, second to the Terran Purity Standards department, but even that had Terran Intel resources. She took a deep breath and calmed her frantic brain. "I'll be at Isere in a little under a day. Leave a message for me there if you find out more."

"I can do better than that. I'll have an itinerary and berths booked for you to wherever Dray is." He rubbed a hand through his thinning hair. "Look, I know this will be hard on Dray, if the Navy gives her the boot for this. But you are in the best position to tell her, life as an Intel agent is not that bad."

Jordan smiled. "Try convincing her of that." She didn't voice her other fear, that Dray would take her Novan genetics as proof that her mother really had been some kind of traitor.

Jordan was back on the courier within the hour. She waited until after their transition to FTL and the inevitable nausea before digging into her latest batch of data. The batch from her mother included full genetic records for both Dray's parents, at least to the depth needed for their implants. Her father had nothing special, but her mother sported what was then considered state of the art implants for pilots. Her genetic data went deeper. Jordan had a better understanding of genetics than most Terrans, but even her detailed queries pulled nothing up from either set of records to suggest any nonTerran genes. Implants weren't as tied to personal genetics back then, so the data may not have gone deep enough to find whatever Massi found in Dray's genetic samples.

Her stomach rumbled, not a precursor to something vile, but announcing how long it had been since her last meal. She stepped out of her cabin and made her way down to the ship's galley. It was no bigger than her own cabin, a drab tan color instead of gray. Instead of a bunk, it had one short counter top with a drink dispenser, hot or cold, standard ration snack packs, and a stack of self-heating meal packs.

The pilot sat in one of the two chairs around a table attached to the opposite wall. He gave her a raised eyebrow. "Feeling any better?"

"Well, enough," she said.

He'd been mercifully quiet throughout the trip. Then again, courier duty didn't attract the extrovert types, not when they spent most of their time alone in space. Jordan scanned the meal packs and grabbed the less offensive looking pasta and vegetables.

The pilot stood up to make room for her. "We'll be at your destination in just under ten hours," he said on his way out.

Jordan snapped the heat element on the meal pack and left it on the table while she made herself a hot tea. When she sat down, the meal-ready strip on the packet turned green and she peeled it open. Steam rose, bringing with it a scent of steamed broccoli with a hint of spice that didn't cause her stomach any troubles. She had better luck keeping down the evening meals, though ship time had shifted to account for their pending arrival at Isere. The clock said 19:00 hours, but her body still felt like early afternoon. She ate the pasta slowly and managed to keep her stomach happy along the way. She tossed the remnants in the recycler and headed back to her cabin.

She should try to sleep, but it was too early according to her internal clock, so she pulled up another report, a classified one this time from her own Intel-based query. This one held the final classified report on the Battle of Turin, where Katherine Draybeck died. She'd read the report years before. Kelvin had given a copy to her for Dray, to prove definitively that their mother was not a traitor.

Turin was supposed to be a test run of a new off the line fighting wing, with Katherine Draybeck as wing commander. Each ship was equipped with a highly specialized artificial intelligence, and a failsafe kill switch, controlled by Katherine's implant. What wasn't known at the time was both the level of autonomy in the new AIs and that the failesafe worked in both directions. When the test battle faced four independent Novan Legion-class wings instead of the reported one, it became Katherine's final flight.

She didn't go down alone, though. With odds four-to-one against, Katherine accepted a battle plan suggested by her AI that inverted the failsafe, overrode local pilots, and ran the mission controlled entirely by her and the AIs. It was a masterful stroke that took out a full three Legion wings and crippled the forth. Turin was saved, but at the cost of her and her wing. The post-battle investigation cleared her of allegations of wrong-doing and secretly awarded her a posthumous medal of honor, but the political backlash from the families of her wing pilots killed the project and proved a major setback to the use of specialized artificial intelligence in battle.

There was nothing new in the report except a footnote that a more recent project, started by Kelvin a few years back, could not reproduce the results achieved by his mother at Turin. However she managed to control that many ships in simultaneous flight, it was a skill lost with her.

"TRANSITIONING TO NORMAL space in five," the pilot announced.

Jordan swallowed the anti-nausea meds she'd picked up at their last stop and strapped in. The transition five minutes later left her light-headed, but the contents of her stomach remained in her stomach. She unbuckled and flicked on the comm to the pilot.

"How long before we dock at Isere?" she asked.

It was a long pause before the pilot answered. "Sorry. I'm still waiting confirmation from traffic control. There's a hell of a queue in front of us."

Jordan frowned. Isere was the primary junction into Terran space from this quadrant. With significant trade links, it usually ran smooth. She went to her console and synched into local space to pick up any messages. She had two waiting before the pilot interrupted her again.

"We're going to be a while," he said. "The government's instated an emergency lockdown. Check the local news."

Jordan linked into the station news feed.

"Terran Purity Commission has detained over three hundred individuals in the past twenty-four hours. They are keeping the names and locations classified, but reports have leaked that it may be the result of a long-term Novan sleeper cell program."

Jordan shut it off and pulled up her messages. The first from her mother, urging her to stay out of Terran space. The second was a high priority video from Jeffrey. She played it on-screen. The first thing she noticed was his haggard expression. Then he spoke and each word sunk like lead in her stomach.

"Do not enter Terran space under any circumstance! The Terran Purists have effectively shut down all our borders and are instigating deep genetic scans on all returning Terrans. The news reports have most of the high level details, but the gist of it is, Dray's genetic results were passed up the line until someone with a purist bias detained the rest of the family. Kelvin and their father are clear and have been released. Cara isn't. She's being detained along with Dray. Given the split, the investigators are blaming Katherine Draybeck's Novan prison detention. They deep scanned all POWs from that time, and their families. So far there are over a five hundred people with nonTerran genetics in that list, all being detained."

He brushed a hand through his already disheveled hair. "I'm on my way to Isere. Kelvin and the General are pulling as many strings as they can, but given their link to Dray and Cara, they are likely under surveillance themselves for now. I'm sending you a data package. Use it. I'll look for you at Isere."

Jordan looked back at her messages and there was the data packet. She loaded it directly to her private datapad before opening it to find multiple sets of identification records for Intel undercover work. She chose one of mixed Terran origin. That would ensure she wasn't targeted for extra scans since it would already label her as unpure. She pulled a scanner out of her travel bag and uploaded the new ID. Then she placed it over her right hand and triggered the recalibration of her Terran chip implant.

She was now officially Jordan D'Escousse, rare artifacts curator.

CHAPTER 4

KAY TOOK ONE step back, mirroring Grand Dame Manji Nassien's bodyguard. She held her fist tight to control the tremor starting in her left hand. Damn if she wasn't tired of it firing off at the worst possible times. She wished she had even the ceremonial knife at her side, but she was bare. Some bodyguard.

Ayaan stepped forward and gave her grandmother a peck on the cheek. She towered over Manji but there was no denying who had the upper hand in this meeting as her grandmother gave her a dismissive nod. Ayaan stepped back beside Kay. "Good to see you, Nana."

"This is your pet clone?"

Ayaan's back stiffened. "She is my sworn bodyguard and more."

"So I hear. And yet she comes unarmed and unprepared. What have you to say, clone?"

Kay raised her eyes to Manji's light brown hands still resting on that cane. Her gaze was not high enough to give offense, but enough to take in the lack of ostentatious jewels or garments. The Grand Dame didn't use outward symbols of power. Something to file away for later, when Kay wasn't feeling like a mouse caught between the cat's paws. "I have yet to be briefed on house protocol, ser."

Manji took the final steps down and stood a pace away, barely shoulder height for Kay. "Leave us."

Kay moved, but it was Ayaan who backed up, squeezing her arm before she left the foyer. Kay swallowed down the sensation that she just advanced from the cat's paws to the cat's jaws. Questions she should have asked on the way here raced through her mind, all too late to help her now.

Manji continued to stare at her, until Ayaan's footsteps faded away. "Who are you?"

"Kay."

"An affectation."

Kay stared at a spot on the far wall where a moving seascape image hung over a flower pedestal. "I am gene-line designate KDTU--02128, fourth generation."

"And why are you here, clone?"

"At Colonel Nassien-Nomani's request, ser."

"Nomani, another affectation," Manji huffed as she started a slow circuit around Kay.

Kay gritted her teeth but remained at silent military attention. What was the woman after? If she was anything like Ayaan, she knew everything there was to know about Kay already, possibly even more if she dug into records not available to Ayaan.

"You have no training," Manji said.

"I have been in military service since I was eight." A bit of a stretch, since she started with an extended two year bootcamp for those unlucky enough to have no other option but the war.

"And what did that teach you about protection? Surveillance? Counter measures to protect my granddaughter?"

"Medals for close-contact fighting and marksmanship. I've survived longer than any other in my gene-line." That was a gem Ayaan had shared with her during her months in rehab. "And I kept Ayaan alive in our last mission."

"All before this!" Manji's cane whipped up and slapped Kay's left arm. The sting traveled down to the whitening knuckles of her clenched fist. Obviously, the old bat did her research if she knew about Kay's tremors already.

Manji stopped her circuit in front of Kay. "What stops me from ordering Bakri to kill you right now?"

"Nothing." Kay shrugged, letting go some of the tension. The woman was baiting her. Kay had years of experience with that one. "You've owned my life since I was created."

"Me?"

"You, your family, the Nassien Autonomy, take your pick . . . ser." Surly was one thing, but outright insubordination could end her in a coffin.

"Ayaan?"

Kay flinched but lowered her gaze, nothing to give overt offense. She caught Manji's smile out of the corner of her eye. The old bat was enjoying this.

"Hmm, bitterness," Manji said. "Freedom then. What if I grant you honorable discharge from service, full Novan citizenship?"

Sweat trickled down Kay's back. "That would be unexpected."

"But you will take it." Manji walked back to the staircase where her guard waited.

It wasn't a question, but Kay answered anyway. "Yes, ser."

"And you will leave here."

A grin tugged at Kay's lips. "When Ayaan does, yes."

The tip of the cane struck down on the marble step, sounding like a gunshot. "Enough of this." Manji turned to her guard. "Bakri, find my troublesome granddaughter in her quarters in the south wing. Slit her throat."

Kay's gaze shot up. The guard was older, but well-armed, and already heading away. Kay launched herself for the only weapon within her reach, the old lady's cane. With her left hand ready to shove the crazy old bitch to the stairs, she grabbed for the cane with her right hand. A surprise spin from Manji moved the cane out of her grasp. It was followed by a dizzying flip and Kay's head cracked hard on the step.

Manji stood over her with the black tip of the cane gone to show a hidden laser cutter. It would cut through bone and flesh like a hot knife through butter. Kay froze in place, trying to make sense of what just happened, and failing. Bakri was at Manji's side with no sign of surprise or expression change at all.

Manji stared down at her. "No one in this household goes unarmed. No one." She stepped back. "How was her reaction time, Bakri."

His voice came out as a baritone rasp. "Reasonable."

"Reasonable will end up with my granddaughter in an early grave." Manji replaced the tip to her cane. "Stand up, child."

Kay felt the back of her head for blood but her hand came away clean. She got to her feet, not sure what to think, other than Ayaan's family was completely nuts. "Your order to kill Ayaan?"

Manji waved her cane. "Simple reaction time test. I thought you'd react better to my original threat to have you killed."

Kay straightened out her clothes. "Sorry to disappoint."

"Hardly," Manji said, turning her back to Kay. "You show promise. It's the only reason you are still alive."

Bat-shit crazy and leading a multi-planetary autonomy with the largest military establishment in Novan space. How did Ayaan end up in a family like this? For once, Kay was glad she had no crazy relatives to deal with. "Are the tests done now?"

"Only beginning, child. Only beginning." She turned around to face Kay. "Twice a day, every day, you will come to my quarters and train with Bakri. You will do this until he and I think you are fit for the position you wheedled your way into. And until you can overcome that," she said with a final wave of her cane at Kay's hand.

Kay's tremor grew from a shaking hand until she had to clench her messed up left arm against her chest. Weakness wasn't a good thing, not in this household.

THE SOUTH WING didn't exist. Kay found out the hard way that the main building was one large circle surrounding the sizable interior garden she stepped into. Palm trees swayed in the humid breeze, providing shade to the patio chairs and table. That's where she found Ayaan, perched on the edge of one woven chair, with a drink in her hand, and a plate of untouched hors d'oeuvres on the low table in front of her. Joris stood to the back under a palm tree, out of Ayaan's direct line of sight but able to view all entrances to the garden. His eyes tracked to her the moment she stepped outside, but it was a brief gaze, as if acknowledging a new movement and marking it as no threat. What kind of home required constant personal security?

Ayaan put her glass on the table. "I'm sorry. I don't know why she's here and not in the capital. Did she behave herself?"

Threatening both their lives, did that qualify as behaving? Kay decided to ignore that bit and pulled a chair next to Ayaan's.

"I have this," she said, pointing to the holster and gun she now sported, compliments of Bakri. "And I have daily lessons with her bodyguard."

Ayaan laughed. "That's not her guard, that's her lover. He is the most singularly lethal person I've ever met, though." She took Kay's hand in hers. "Still, it's not the worst that could have happened, lessons from him. At least she didn't threaten to kill you."

Kay flinched, and Ayaan must have felt it through her hand.

"She did, didn't she?" Ayaan asked.

Kay recognized the cold hardness creeping to Ayaan's eyes and patted her hand. "I can live with training lessons twice a day."

"She may control the Autonomy, but that doesn't mean she gets to control me."

Kay popped a date into Ayaan's mouth. "I said it's okay. It's not like I have a packed schedule."

She was soon to learn that she did have a packed schedule. As Ayaan's bodyguard, she had to accompany her everywhere, when she wasn't in her own lessons with Bakri. And Ayaan had a lot on her schedule, from side meetings with representatives from the legislature, to welcoming ceremonies for visiting dignitaries, and discussions with branch commanders from the Nassien Army, Navy, Marines, and Black March.

Ayaan acted as representative for Manji in all of these engagements. All occurred within their home complex, surrounded by house guard, half-cousins, a bearded uncle, and more distant relations that made Kay's head spin, trying to keep them all straight. The schedule was relentless, with Kay tagging along as if she fit in, when at every available moment, there was someone to remind her just how much she didn't belong. It didn't help her nerves that the grandmother spent as much time at home as she did at the capital.

Days later, Kay, dressed in her new green Nassien civilian uniform, collapsed into a padded chair in Ayaan's residence in the compound. The residence boasted an expansive living room with private garden, office, gym, four bedrooms in case Ayaan wanted to throw some kind of party, a full kitchen, a basement with quarters for her staff, storage subbasement, and stocked bomb shelter—all the comforts of home. Over the days, Kay met most of Ayaan's private staff. All were trained in personal combat, most in intelligence and surveillance gathering. The main security office was also in the basement, with direct links to the Nassien compound security, Bahai security, and the orbital stations above the planet. Joris ran that office himself. Paranoia was the primary lifestyle choice in this place, and Kay had a whole lot to catch up on if she wasn't going to stick out as Ayaan's girl-toy forever.

The office they were in had a southern exposure that cast a golden glow across the real wood mahogany furniture. She stretched strained muscles after her latest round with Bakri. "Does your grandmother ever smile?"

"Rarely." Ayaan didn't look up from the console at her desk, where she spent most of the time between meetings and other official events.

The silence lengthened until Kay stood up and started pacing.

"Is that necessary?"

"Loosens muscles," Kay said.

She was bored. Bored with the complex, bored with her constant lessons, just plain bored. She was just as much of an oddity here as she'd been as a Marine, but at least then she had a real job and real assignments that she had to do, day to day. Here, she was the excess baggage, the bodyguard not really needed because Ayaan had four fully-trained and qualified guards in her household staff besides Joris, who was Kay's superior in everything but name.

She stood behind Ayaan, her hands working a light massage on Ayaan's tight shoulders. "How about a break?"

"Soon."

Kay leaned in closer, but Ayaan brushed her off. So much for that option for breaking the tedium of the day. "Can't we get out of this place for a few hours? Just the two of us?" And a half dozen of their closest house guard friends, but even that would be a relief.

Ayaan let out a poorly suppressed sigh. "Where do you want to go?"

Back to the Marines was on the tip of Kay's tongue but she settled with something more realistic. "You said there was a rain forest preserve about twenty kilometers away. How about a hike?"

Ayaan relaxed a bit, her frown disappearing. "Yes, that sounds pleasant."

The door to Ayaan's office swung open. Knowing two of Joris' qualified guards stood outside so the entrants were no threat, Kay simply dropped her hands and stepped back as two teenagers burst in.

"Ayaan!"

Ayaan stood up in time to catch the hug from the boy while the girl stood by waiting her turn.

"Zayn, Gemma, good to see you. Is your father here as well?" she asked.

"No, not this time." Zayn took a step back to give his sister a turn at swamping Ayaan with a hug. Both children looked to be similar in age, early teens if Kay had to guess, and both came up to Ayaan's shoulder. They had years of growth left.

Zayn turned to give Kay an open stare. "Are you Terran?"

Kay glanced at Ayaan who gave her a slight nod. "Yes. I am a sergeant in the Black March."

"You don't look like a soldier."

Kay clenched her fists. "On leave."

"Manners, please," Ayaan said. "This is Kay."

Zayn looked from Ayaan to Kay and back. "She's your girlfriend."

Ayaan patted the top of Zayn's head, messing up the black curls. "You see too much. So why are you here?"

"Your mother dropped us off on her way to the capital. She says Nana's caused another holy mess with the Terrans." Zayn turned back to Kay. "Do you know what's going on?"

Kay shrugged. "Sorry, no."

She kept to herself the silent hope that Ayaan's mother wasn't going to show up as well. There was only so much family bonding she could take, and she was already past her limit.

Gemma leaned on the desk, her hair the same curly black as her brother, but with hazel eyes instead of brown. Eyes that said she had a secret she was bursting to share. "I read about it in the Terran news download."

"Gemma," Ayaan said.

She lifted her chin. "'There is no shame in not knowing; the shame lies in not finding out.'"

Ayaan sighed. "'Small children give you a headache.'"

Gemma smiled. "No fair only using half a proverb, cousin."

"And is it fair that you break into classified transmissions on Terran activities?" Ayaan asked.

Gemma shrugged. "If they weren't meant for me, why do they make it so easy to get to?"

"Stop showing off and tell us what you heard." Zayn turned to Kay. "She pretends she's a genius but really she just steals our father's passwords."

"Again, if they weren't meant for me, why does he make them so easy to steal?" Gemma bounded to a chair. "It's got something to do with our great grandfather and something called project Troy."

That made Ayaan's frown return, but was it the project or the mention of Manji's dead husband? Either way, Kay didn't care. She'd already learned just how messy families were, and she'd had her fill of Ayaan's.

"You know something about it, don't you?" Zayn said.

Ayaan waved him off. "Sorry, I don't. I need to finish up here. I'll meet you both in the atrium in a few minutes."

As soon as the door shut behind them, Kay snapped. "Seriously? We can't get out of here for even half a day?"

Ayaan shut down her desk console. "It's family, Kay."

Kay threw her hands up. "It's always family. Meeting with them, being threatened by them, representing them in some function or other. Hell, I'm glad I'm alone if this is what it's like."

Ayaan pinched the bridge of her nose. "Now is not a good time for this discussion. I need to finish morning prayers and go spend some time with my cousins."

"Fine. Enjoy." Kay grabbed a light jacket from the closet.

"You're not coming with me?"

Kay opened the door. "Joris has you covered. I'm going to the gun range. Maybe I can get my Marine marksman grade reinstated." She left unsaid the obvious follow on to that, getting herself reinstated, and the hell out of this compound.

ANGER ALWAYS DID give Kay an edge, and it didn't fail her at the range. After a half hour of shooting, she got her best scores since the injury, and even her hand behaved itself with only a slight tremor. Too bad it did nothing to shift her mood.

She stepped out of the range, where the morning coolness was replaced by a muggy heaviness to the air and a light drizzle. At least she had the sense to grab a jacket, about the only sense she had as she made the short trek back to where she'd left Ayaan.

Stepping back into the main house, she found Bakri before she found Ayaan. Or maybe he found her. It was hard to tell given his general stoic nature. He nodded her back out the door, and she turned on her heels to comply. She knew a lecture in the making when she saw one.

He waited until they walked beyond the front steps. "Your duty cannot be compromised by emotional whims."

"Yes, ser."

"Idle words."

"I'm an idle guard."

"You lack purpose."

"I had purpose in the Marines."

He stopped. "You had drug problems, illegal genetics, and were written up for every mission. That was purpose?"

So he'd done his homework on her, too. She didn't know if that was good or bad, so she shifted directions. "Ayaan is my purpose."

"You cannot have purpose through another. Only through yourself. When you can answer the question of why you are here and alive, then you know your purpose."

Philosophy from a trained killer. What next?

"If you cannot perform, you will be replaced," he said.

"Yes, ser."

What Bakri lacked in pep talk skills, he made up for in cold hard reality. Shape up or ship out, potentially in pieces if Manji had her way.

He pointed her forward. "Your ride awaits. Stay at your post."

Kay walked around a set of tall broad-leaved bushes. She faced the helopad with a helicopter already prepping for takeoff. Ayaan walked toward her. "The rain forest on a rainy day."

If Bakri's speech wasn't enough, Ayaan co-opting a helicopter just for their afternoon jaunt put the screws to Kay's guilt. "Look, I'm sorry. We don't have to go out today."

Ayaan took her hand and led her to the copter. "Yes, we do."

They stepped into the least-civilian helicopter Kay had ever seen. The gun turrets weren't even hidden, and the stealth plating gave it an angular look that would never pass aesthetic design goals in ordinary civilian life. The inside though, was plush beyond belief. Two off-white sofas lined one side, separated by an actual table and lamp. The other side had two strap-in reclining chairs facing each other. Light filtered in through matching curtains on either side, covering up what Kay recognized from the outside as reinforced clear plasteen. There were just the two of them in the main compartment. Joris followed them in and proceeded to the copilot's seat, closing the cabin door behind him.

Kay looked out the window as the copter took off, but turned away when she saw three others lift off from surrounding helopads. Not quite a solo jaunt.

Ayaan pressed a button on her arm rest and a mini-bar slid open beside her. She pulled out a bottle of beer and handed it to Kay, the real stuff, not synthetic.

Kay popped the cap. "I'm not adjusting well to civ life, am I?"

Ayaan pulled out an orange Verali wine and waved the bottle as she spoke. "This is not civilian life. This is why I joined the Black March to begin with. It's hard to believe the military could be less restrictive than home, but it is."

Kay took a swig, savoring the bitter taste that no synthbeer could ever mimic. "Can we go back on active duty?"

"No. It's deemed too dangerous."

"Your uncle and mother are Navy ship commanders."

Ayaan stared out the window. "That's why it's too dangerous. Too much of the ruling family in harm's way. Besides, they were genetically destined for their roles. Two generations before them, the Nassien family depended on minor septs to control the military. Some of them proved disloyal. My grandfather started the integration of military genesets into his immediate family."

"Meaning your mother and uncle."

"Yes. We've all inherited that germline enhancement. Zayn and Gemma were taken a step further, folding in one of those loyal sept genelines with my uncle, along with improvements in leadership traits for executive functioning. Given how long-lived Novans are, my mother's generation would never be satisfied waiting for Nana's generation to retire, so they were literally born to take over the military."

"And your generation?"

"Will become the next Grand Dame or Master of the Autonomy. Or at least I was to follow suit as well, except my mother had a secret marriage with the Imam of Bahai and gave birth to me, an uncontrolled variant."

Kay had heard the story before, including the tidbit that Ayaan's grandfather had that Imam murdered. "Do you know what you inherited from your father, then?"

"Of course. I'm one of the most well-studied genomes in my generation. Every Novan citizen conforms to a base genome that is enhanced each generation, based on the cloning experiments you were part of."

"Am part of."

Ayaan ignored her. "The differences in clans occur on top of that common base. The Nomanis have been a religious caste for generations, and with that came a certain loose interpretation of the policy for strict genetic records."

"Kind of like the Terrans," Kay said.

"Some thought too much like the Terrans, especially given my caste and rank in the family. My mother survived two assassination attempts while pregnant with me, and we both survived a third, shortly after my birth. That was the one which led to my father's murder. Unfortunately my grandfather acted too soon, before my first genome analysis. Perhaps if he had seen the traits I'd inherited from the Nomanis, he would have reconsidered." Ayaan stared out the window. "Or perhaps not."

One hell of a family story. Kay caught sight of the virtual armada surrounding them in the air and wondered just how far up she was on someone's hit list for daring to date the Grand Dame's granddaughter. Time to redirect the conversation. "We need a hobby. Something more entertaining than who wants who dead."

Ayaan's hand paused as she was about to take another sip of her wine.

"What?" Kay asked, recognizing that look of concentration on Ayaan's face. She took another swig of her beer.

"Yes, a hobby." Ayaan put her glass down. "One that will get us out of the compound, and I have a perfect one. We can research your gene-line."

Kay choked on her beer. "I'm not sure that's such a good idea."

"Why not? We know so little about you."

"What's there to know? I'm an unaltered Terran clone. It doesn't get much more commonplace than that."

Ayaan waved a finger at her. "You are a fourth-generation unaltered Terran clone. Do you know how rare that is?"

Kay shook her head.

"It's rare. The clone program is expensive. It is set up for rapidly uncovering unique genetic traits and integrating them into select segments of the Novan population, usually the family funding the program."

"So the Nassiens in my case."

Ayaan nodded. "It's not a cheap program, and four generations is an unusually long lag time before isolating the genetic pattern for the target trait."

Kay leaned back, remembering some of the slip-ups from her meetings with Halabi, her gene line program manager gone rogue. "Situational awareness was supposed to be my superpower."

Ayaan frowned. "How do you know that?"

"Halabi let it slip once. Said we'd all failed miserably." She didn't have to explain that the "we" referred to all the clones in her gene-line, even if she'd never met any of them. And failed for the rest meant dead.

"Interesting. Well, it's a starting point. The records are held in a secure site, probably the Nassien Archives in Bahai."

"Isn't it all classified?" Kay asked.

Ayaan's lips curled into an icy smile as she raised her glass in salute. "Nana wants me more involved in the Nassien Autonomy's operations. I can't think of a better place to start, can you?"

Kay could think of a better place, yeah. Hell, she could think of a bunch of better places, any one of which wouldn't have put the knot in her belly like this one was causing. She returned the salute and chugged the rest of the beer.

Rain sleeted across the windows as the copter hovered over a lush, green rain forest. Kay could see the stream of aircars leaving the area, making way for the private use of one of New China's most powerful women. Power came with a price, and the next price might be Kay learning more than she ever wanted to know about her own genetics and just how much she'd failed.

She'd have grabbed another beer if they weren't landing already. Drug-free sobriety really had its drawbacks.

THREE DAYS OF politics and maneuvering by Ayaan after their rain forest jaunt got them a legitimate reason to go to Bahai. Manji was sequestered into some mess with the Terrans that even the news feeds wouldn't speculate on. That left her meeting attendance up to Ayaan, including renegotiating the neutrality terms with the Tarquins, a negotiation critical to the Novan war with the Terrans.

Rain poured down on their ground convoy as it entered the city limits. Kay got over her outer-rim gawker status after their fourth visit to the megacity. This being their eighth, she didn't even look out the car window anymore.

Given the Novan urgency to quell any disagreements with the Tarquins, they agreed to meet at the Tarquin embassy. The cars pulled up in front of a gated compound of muted proportions compared to

Ayaan's home. Two Tarquin guards stood on either side of a female Tarquin dressed in traditional light armor chest plate and arm cuffs. The Tarquin female waited for them at the steps of the main building, a two story flattened structure with few windows.

Joris and Kay stepped out of the car first, as the rest of their guard poured out and took up positions leading up to the main doors. Ayaan emerged last, wearing a somber dark green suit with the Nassien logo overlaid by her Nomani red crescent.

The Tarquin female stepped forward. "Welcome, Colonel."

"Ayaan, please. I am not here as a military representative."

"As you wish. I am Liason Sigan. Ambassador Tar Aspar awaits."

The Tarquin did a good job of ignoring Kay and Joris, a better job than Kay did in ignoring the Tarquins they passed en route. They were broader than Jax, her dead Marine partner, and a darker shade of red, but then Jax was an experimental Tarquin clone, and who knows how much Novan genes he'd had.

She was the first to step into their final destination and scanned the room. The Tarquin ambassador was impossible to mistake, his girth and raiment far more sizable than the two obvious guards that stood to either side of him. Two to balance Ayaan's two allowed bodyguards. Bakri's lessons helped her scan for the obvious and the non-obvious threat potentials in the room. After ensuring it was as clean as she could detect, she stepped to the side, letting Ayaan and Joris in next.

The conference room enjoyed one of the few windows in the building, looking out onto a central garden that held plants Kay had never seen. Imported Tarquin plants she wondered? She knew little about their culture beyond the briefing papers Ayaan shared with her and Joris for their security preparations. Tarquin was a warrior culture with an advanced technology that made them formidable enemies. They'd never been Novan allies, but Ayaan's meeting would ensure their continued neutrality in the Terran conflict.

Sigan closed the doors, leaving them alone in the room with Tar Aspar and his guards. He remained silent, seated in a highback chair, the only chair in the room. So much for social amenities. Kay stood to Ayaan's right, Joris to the left.

Ayaan folded her arms and stared down at the ambassador. "Do you expect me to kneel?"

His dark red eyes flicked between the three of them before settling on Ayaan. "You are the servant of the Grande Dame, are you not?"

Kay felt his voice rumble through her chest. Deep baritone couldn't hold a candle to that reverberation.

"I am her representative," Ayaan said.

"Her offspring," he countered.

"Her chosen heir."

"One of many."

Ayaan dropped her arms and stepped forward. "Stand as my equal, or prepare for challenge Tar Aspar."

A grin split his wide face as he unfolded himself to stand, towering over Ayaan by a good half meter. "Well met, Ayaan, Heir Apparent, Nassien y Nomani."

Kay made a note to ask about this heir, heir apparent business, later, when they weren't facing down the Tarquin equivalent of diplomacy. She'd read of Tarquin greetings equating to the old-Earth art of fencing. Had Ayaan responded to his verbal attack with anything other than parry-riposte, the meeting would have ended. Tar Aspar would not have respected her as his equal.

The door to Kay's right opened and Liason Sigan entered again, followed by another Tarquin carrying a chair.

Settled in their chairs, Ayaan wasn't exactly on eye level with her opponent, but that didn't seem to faze her.

"You have not responded to our request for Baeron-II drive technology," she said.

"And you have not released the details of your full use of Tarquin genetic material."

Ayaan pulled a data chip out of her suit pocket. "I'm authorized to present those details in return for the drive specs."

His eyes flicked to the chip in her hand and back to her face. "That depends on the depth of your records. Do they disclose any Tarquin material used as part of Project Troy?"

Kay saw Ayaan's jaw tighten, the only indication that she'd just been broadsided by the Ambassador's inquiry. "Your analysts can determine that."

Tar Aspar flicked his wrist and one of his guards stepped forward to take the data chip from Ayaan. "Your Terran opponents stole the original Baeron technology from us and lost our support in their alliance against you. I am glad to see not all branches of humanity act so blindly."

Ayaan nodded and stood. "We are integrators, negotiating the best, regardless of source."

"One last thing, Ayaan, Heir Apparent. Theft of our genetic material first brought us into alliance with the Terrans in their conflict with you." He accepted the chip from his guard. "Any other interference with our genetic material could bring us back."

Well, that was plain enough for even Kay to follow. Mess with us, and we'll squash you like a bug.

Their appointment at the Nassien Archives took far less fanfare and only a handful of guards besides Kay and Joris joined them in the ground convoy. The stone buildings that housed the government and foreign embassies passed by, giving way to less oppressive businesses and stately homes.

"Not that I'm complaining," Kay said. "But why is the Nassien compound so far out of the city. Wouldn't it be more convenient closer in like one of these houses?"

Ayaan glanced out the window. "No one living this close to the capital has any reason to fear assassination."

In other words, these were homes to the rich and unimportant.

"The capital buildings themselves hold residences underground," Ayaan said. "That's where Nana stays when she's not at home. With all factions housed within bombing distance of each other, there's no risk of significant attack. The human and electronic security detail takes care of the rest."

"Hell of a way to live," Kay muttered.

Their armored car turned a corner, and a vast stone edifice came into view, a light golden yellow four story building that seemed to defy all norms of architecture. Pieces of the upper stories jutted out over the first floor, held up by rectangular pillars. Overall, it was a building of lines and angles and reflecting windows.

Kay pointed out her window. "I take it that's it?"

Ayaan nodded. "The Nassien Genetic Archive. Well, one of them at least. There are dozens spread out over Novan space hosting the details from all of the major families. The architecture for each is unique, but the stone for all of them was imported from Earth as a reminder of our origins."

At one hell of a cost, Kay thought as their car came to a stop in front of the building, and Joris hopped out first to scan the perimeter. The remaining guards formed a short corridor between the car and the front glass doors to the archive as Kay and Aayan stepped out into the continuing light rain.

Kay relegated the ever-present security detail to the back of her mind as she stepped into the building. The front foyer was open for the entire four stories, showing each level had an overview back down to them. Two guards in Nassien livery stood at opposite ends of all three overlooks. So much for a lessened security presence.

Ayaan led the way up a winding staircase to the second level, where she greeted the Master Archivist, a youngish man, rail thin with curly black hair down to his shoulders.

"Your room awaits," he said, indicating an open doorway to their left.

With a brief nod, Kay entered the room first, followed by Ayaan, and shut the door.

"We're allowed in here on our own?" Kay asked, taking in the expansive view out of the window that looked back down the avenue they drove up from.

"Genetic records for the most part are a personal matter, even though the government tracks it all in minute detail."

"Except yours," Kay added.

"Except mine, which have been publicly accessible since I was born. The price I pay for being an unplanned accident." Ayaan took a seat in front of the console and rolled the pad of her index finger across a tiny indent in the desk top. "This extracts my DNA, which will match the archive search and pull up my full records."

The console came alive with an official photo of Ayaan, and a series of reports on her genetic makeup, as well has links to her relatives. "Every Novan citizen has open access to their genetic records, as well as high level links to all their relatives for five generations."

Kay looked at the links. "That's a lot of relatives."

"Given my position and approval level, I can link back twelve generations with full accuracy, and another five beyond that with partial records." Ayaan pointed to the screen. "My public record includes only the first four generations and the full genetic map."

"Sounds invasive enough," Kay said.

Ayaan stood up and waved Kay into the chair. "Your turn."

Kay sat in the chair and wiped her sweaty hand on her pant leg. This would give her a history of her genetic family, something she wasn't sure she actually wanted to learn. "Suck it up, clone girl," she mumbled as she placed her index finger on the DNA scanner.

She felt the slightest tug on the pad of her finger and a moment later, she stared at an image of herself with dyed black hair, taken from her military ID card. The report gave her designation, rank, and three links—clones (deceased), clones (living), and genetic donor.

"Try the donor link," Ayaan said.

Kay clicked on that link and the console paused, then pulled up a Restricted Access page.

"So much for full disclosure," she said.

Ayaan frowned. "What about the clones - living link?"

Kay backtracked and tried that link as well, getting the same result.

Ayaan waved her out of the seat and took over. "It's likely classified by the military. I can log in and override it."

A few deft keystrokes and Ayaan was in and searching for Kay by her official designation. She landed on the same page, with the same results.

"This doesn't make sense." Ayaan returned to the search page and typed in the only other designation Kay recognized, that of her former teammate and best friend, Jax. A page displayed with his image, sending a stab of regret through Kay. If she hadn't killed him, maybe he would have found his long lost family after all. The display showed multiple links for past and current clone programs, and with a few clicks, displayed full details on his genetic family.

Kay pointed to the bottom of the display. "What does it mean by 'project released'?"

"Part of our treaty with the Tarquins. We are releasing all Tarquin clones, Unaltered and Experimental. We disclosed all genetic Tarquin material that's been integrated into the Novan gene bank and agreed to stop all such programs in the future."

Kay sighed. "So Jax would have been released?"

"Along with Tejax, had they both lived."

Sometimes Kay forgot Ayaan had been fond of Jax's troublesome genetic cousin. "So is the Tarquin treaty why his record is an open book?"

"No. I should have full access to yours as well." Ayaan pressed the com button and an archive aide answered.

"This is Ayaan Nassien-Nomani. I have a gene history query here that isn't completing. Please investigate."

"Yes," he said. "The KDTU-02128 program. Let me pull up an access query report." The line went dead for a full minute before he returned. "My apologies for the delay. That record has been sealed by authority of the Grande Dame."

Ayaan's jaw tightened. "When was it sealed?"

"Five days ago," he said. "Is there anything else I can assist you with?"

"No, thank you." Ayaan switched the com off and stood up.

Kay recognized that tense stance. "It's not worth getting into a fight with your grandmother. I wouldn't know any of the people listed as my genetic family anyway. They're mostly all dead, according to Halabi. Let your grandmother play her games."

Ayaan enacted a crisp military turn and swung open the door. "This is more than a game. This is a direct curtailment of my access and authority. She will reinstate it."

<h1 style="text-align:center">CHAPTER 5</h1>

JORDAN MET JEFFREY four days after landing at the back of a busy cafe in the universal trade section of Isere Junction, the open access side of the Terran border. The ambient noise in the cafe guaranteed they couldn't be overheard easily by listening devices, at least not without a full audio scan and filter to separate their voices from everything else. Still, she wasn't surprised when Jeffrey placed his "wallet" on the table. The wallet was an Intel audio jammer, ensuring their voices could not be picked up beyond the half-meter radius that separated them.

"Where's Dray?" she asked.

Their server came over to get their order, delaying Jeffrey's response until they were alone, again.

"In a detention center on Nuevo Sonora with Cara. Near as we can tell, the government is gathering all suspect Terrans in one of five detention centers spread around Terran space."

Jordan drummed her fingers on the table top. "What is their status, officially?"

Jeffrey frowned. "That hasn't been decided. The Purists are calling for official charges of treason against all of them, upwards of two thousand at last count, from this war and the last one."

Jordan felt lightheaded. "Treason? How can they be responsible for what had to have been some kind of genetic experimentation by the Novans?"

"You're assuming rational mindsets here. This mess hits the deepest paranoia levels in Terran culture."

"Not just Terran," she said. "The last message from my mother says the Alliance Senate is calling an emergency session and demanding all Terran information on this genetic tampering be shared. Terrans aren't the only ones who worry about their genetic purity."

"No, we just turned it into a fine art."

Their food arrived, silencing their discussion for a time. Jordan wanted to push the food aside, but that might bring the kind of attention they didn't want. As she ate, she contemplated their options. Legally, they were in limbo until the government assigned an official status to Dray and the other detainees. She couldn't sue for release from an unlawful detention when there was no stated charges, yet. Still, the government could only procrastinate so long before basic rights prevailed and they had to all be charged or released. She did the mental math and realized that would be another three weeks at least, longer if the government dragged their feet to the end. Still, if the Alliance Senate was getting involved, that meant more political pressure on the Terran and Novan governments to resolve this.

Jordan paused in her eating. "Will the Terrans cooperate with the Senate demands?"

Jeffrey smirked. "Ask your mother. My guess is no, they'll consider it a local issue not subject to Alliance law. At least until another Alliance species provides evidence of genetic tampering like we're seeing."

She leaned back in her chair. "That brings us to why. Why would the Novans tamper with prisoners and then release them?"

"Well, officially, Katherine Draybeck escaped. That said, a number of the other families were freed based on prisoner exchanges, or at the end of the last war."

"Still, what's the point of all this? What is the benefit to Novans for going through this effort? The genetic changes had to have been very subtle or the Purity Standards checks would have picked up on it before now." She waved her right hand. "This chip ID would normally reject anyone not genetically pure Terran." Not that her original chip did, since it was altered on the black market to allow her to pass as fully Terran from the time she was a child.

Jeffrey put down his fork. "Maybe this is what they wanted? A holy mess that is crippling Terran space. The billions in lost trade profits alone is already creating whispers of a Terran-wide recession."

Jordan considered that while the server came back for their dishes. It didn't add up. Why put something in motion literally decades ago, only to have a minor financial impact now? And if the recession got severe, it would hurt neutral planets and impact Novan financial markets as well. No, it had to be something else, and she thought she had an inkling what it was.

Jeffrey paid the bill, and they left the cafe, joining the overcrowded causeway back to the hotel he was staying at. With the borders all but closed, it was a miracle he found a place at all. Ships were already being rotated off dockside to make room for emergency refueling for those left in a near-space holding pattern. It couldn't continue forever.

Jeffrey's room looked much like her own—a tiny studio with pull-out bed, side chair, and the luxury of his own bathroom. It was a significant step up from the crammed one-bed cubbies that many stranded travelers were grabbing up as soon as an opening occurred, for inflated prices of course.

Jordan paced in the tiny space. "How long do you think this could have gone undetected if Dray hadn't glitched from that experimental implant?"

"Years, maybe? Terran purity tests haven't changed much. Who thought there'd be a reason for them to?"

"Exactly," she said. "I'd go so far as to say this could have gone on for another generation or two. How many impacted people would there have been by then? Tens of thousands? The human population slowed down pre-space exploration, but once we found habitable planets, it exploded again and hasn't stopped. We found room to expand and we're racing to fill that void."

Jeffrey took the lone chair. "That actually matches what Kelvin found out. The impacted families have an exceptional rate of reproduction, more than the norm. The Draybecks may have stopped at three, but even Fenton, your old commander, managed five, and she never married. She was also detained, by the way. Her, five adult children, and twenty-three grandchildren. Add two more generations, and she'd be matriarch for over four hundred."

"And therein lies the reason. Left undetected, the modified population would be too much to ignore. Even today, a couple of thousand people are enough for one hell of a lawsuit if the government declares them nonTerran. After all, they all pass the current purity standards."

"And yet they have genetic differences that aren't found anywhere else in the Terran population so far. I don't think we'll win a lawsuit like that."

That still left the question of what the Terran government planned to do with two thousand and growing numbers of modified people. That question more than anything else was what kept Jordan up at night.

IT WAS THE middle of station-night when Jordan's com alarm woke her out of an unsatisfactory sleep.

"Lights on," she grumbled as she pulled herself out of the bed and picked up her com. The room lights came on at the same time as the most critical alarm she'd programed into her com flashed before her eyes.

"This cannot be happening." She rubbed the sleep out of her eyes and pulled up the traceback that had triggered the alarm. It had a convoluted trail that led back to her mother. It was real, and it was happening now.

With a settled calmness she didn't expect, Jordan clicked a voice-only call to Jeffrey. When his gravelly voice answered, she gave him one sentence. "We're leaving. Fifteen minutes, front lobby."

She disconnected before he could reply and packed her important belongings in one duffle bag. The rest would stay behind, leaving the impression that she still occupied the room. Her one last act was to autopay the room bill through the end of the week. The click of the door shutting behind her signaled the end of one chapter of her life.

Jeffrey was waiting for her in the lobby. He carried a backpack and pulled on a medium-sized luggage bag behind as she walked past him and out the lobby door into the stream of foot traffic that remained constant, no matter the time of day on Isere. He didn't question her until they'd traveled through two causeway intersections and down a level. Then she pulled him into a side passage.

"Dump the luggage," she said.

"Okay, but how about an explanation, now." He pulled out his Intel jammer and set it on the floor while he repacked his critical belongings in his backpack.

Jordan pulled out her com and showed him the details. "The Terran government finally traced my last-known whereabouts to the fertility clinic on Gilgar. The clinic refused to release my records, but Terrans put two and two together. I and my potential offspring are now listed as 'persons of interest' and subject to detainment."

"And full genetic scanning. Damn," he said. "Why didn't Kelvin warn us?"

Jordan pocketed her com. "Let's just say my mother and I have a faster network to monitor and trigger the alarm that woke me up."

Jeffrey picked up his jammer and stood up. "Because you're half-Novan."

"Because I needed to stay one step ahead of any investigation that might reveal that, yes. Are you ready?"

He stuffed his luggage down the nearest trash chute. "Where are we headed?"

"Catecombs, first," she said.

Every station had one, an underworld that lived in the structural recesses of the physical station, where the poor, the discriminated, and the not necessarily legal managed to survive and sometimes thrive. Given its prime location, Isere Junction had a strong network tangential to the upper station, and Jordan had all the details she needed to make use of that network.

A disjointed journey through station corridors and back panel ladders landed them in a dimly lit but well-populated series of tunnels that smelled of synth-oil, metal, and close-quartered sentient life.

Jordan paused. "This is where it gets tricky." She turned to Jeffrey. "I can't just disappear, at least not right away. I know how to do that, without an Intel trace. The question is—how far off-grid do you want to go? We can separate here, and you can remain in touch with Kelvin and Intel."

Jeffrey shook his head. "We stay together. I have IDs that have no records in Intel. They won't find you by tracing me. I can pull up an ID for you as well."

"That's okay, I have a plan for that." A plan she'd had for years and hoped she'd never have to trigger it. So much for that hope.

"And this is why we wanted you for Intel. Your skills are unmatched, you know," said Jeffrey.

Jordan led the way through the mass of people, human, and nonhuman, until they came to an obvious commercial center for the exchange of goods—material, living, and pharmacological. A query in the right ear got them a Chameleon guide with green hair and skin tone who led them through a different set of tunnels to a more upscale entertainment area. This district sold more than just physical entertainment, though. Jordan specified a certain illegal part of her required "experience" and the guide delivered the goods in the form of a younger woman, tall, dark haired, and obviously not a local resident.

The woman looked up at Jordan and Jeffrey. "Do I get to be a man or a woman, this time?"

Jeffrey raised an eyebrow but kept quiet while Jordan took the lead. She sat down in the chair next to the woman. "A woman, but that depends on who I get to be?"

The trade was simple enough. An illegal swap of chip IDs, and Jordan would become whomever this woman was. And the woman would become Jordan.

"I'm Sherin Val-Daxen, local to Isere, but I've been to over thirty planets, human and nonhuman."

Of course she had, probably using the same trick Jordan was about to do. Sherin was a flipper, someone who flipped IDs for fun with strangers and got to live different lives for a time. This time, Sherin would be in for a bit of a surprise, though, when Terran authorities caught up with her.

Jordan nodded her agreement. "I have access to a considerable flight budget and a hotel above that's paid in full through the next five days." Isere was okay, but she knew Sherin would hop the next flight off world. No one was a flipper to stay in a tiny hotel studio, not when there was a free flight or three in her future. That would give the Terran authorities a good chase and time for Jordan to disappear for real.

The agreement was sealed with a handshake and a simple confirmation of IDs through an illegal scanner that Sherin had in her shoulder bag. Jordan produced the chip ID re-coder, something that raised Sherin's eyebrows, but didn't garner further questions. That was a good thing, because this re-coder wasn't a temporary swap that would expire in the agreed upon two weeks. This swap was semi-permanent, at least until Sherin was detained and the authorities realized what Jordan was now doing and restored Sherin's original ID. By then, Jordan planned to be multiple planets and multiple ID swaps away.

KELVIN'S MESSAGE WAS terse, prerecorded, and lacking in actionable details when it finally caught up with Jordan and Jeffrey at the Basel Outpost, on the neutral border with Novan space. Jordan played the last part of message back again.

. . . It's a political mess, with no party willing to step up and move the process along, one way or another. The only details we have is some leaked messages from the Nassien Autonomy on New China, about a Project Troy. Your mother convinced the government on Gilgar to step in as a neutral arbiter, but even that's not getting any quick results. Without Novan cooperation to release details on Project Troy, it's unlikely the detainees will be released any time soon.

"There's no hidden code there," Jeffrey said, from the bunk above her.

They shared a cramped berth on the transport that had just docked at the orbital station above Basel. It would be at least an hour before they could disembark and determine the next leg on their journey, wherever that might be.

Jordan turned off the recording. "There's something about that name that's so familiar."

"Troy? Not very subtle if you ask me," Jeffrey said. "Infiltrate your enemy under the guise of a gift. Beware Novans bearing gifts, or prisoner exchanges, might become the new expression."

"No, not that. New China. What do we know about it?"

"Everything and nothing." The bunk above her creaked as Jeffrey repositioned himself. "It's one of the three biggest solar systems under Novan control. Originally populated by the Xiong Conglomerate but when they went bankrupt, the Nassiens bought up the colonization rights and added it to their power base."

Sounded like a dull history lesson in the making, so why was the name New China still rattling her brain? Jordan pulled up her datapad and punched in New China. The public records went into a bit more detail, but nothing worthwhile. She searched on Nassien Autonomy and got a similarly dry political and economic assessment.

"The Autonomy has an impressive military side," she said as she continued reading.

"Very clannish," Jeffrey said. "Even for Novans. It's a family business, top to bottom."

She clicked through the government structure, and the Nassien name dominated the results. "Head of Legislature—Manji Nassien, Major exporter—Nassien Industries. Military Chief of Staff—oh wait, not a Nassien."

"Maybe that Manji woman is losing her grip."

Jordan clicked on Manji Nassien. She scanned the woman's bio, from her marriage into the Nassien ruling clan to her offspring. Jordan saw a name there she never thought to see or hear from again. She stood up, forgetting the cramped space, and slammed her head into the top bunk.

"Jordan?" Jeffrey's head popped over the edge of the bunk.

"Hadro Nassien. That's why New China sounded familiar."

"Not ringing any bell here," he said.

Jordan rubbed the growing lump on the top of her head. "Remember that fiasco on Buenos Aries years ago?"

"When you tried to have me tossed out an airlock? No, forgot all about that."

"You're exaggerating. And I thought you were a Novan spy. Anyway, The Black March commander that came for the two Novan kids we rescued, he was Hadro Nassien." She tossed her datapad to Jeffrey. "The Commander of Nassien Military isn't a Nassien, but check out the names of the two five-star admirals right underneath her."

Jeffrey scanned the report. "Your buddy Hadro and another Nassien."

"Now check his bio."

Jeffrey let out a low whistle. "He's well connected. Manji's son. Great, how does this help us out?"

Jordan paced again. "I'm not sure yet. He all but gave me an open invitation to New China when I needed to escape the Terrans."

"Jordan, this will all get cleared up."

She stared at him. "Will it? My wife is in detention, there's an outstanding warrant out for me and my unborn children. Even if it all clears up, where does that leave us? I've been living illegally in Terran space since I was a child. They'll discover that when they deep scan me, and that's certainly not going to help Dray's case, to be married to a half-Novan."

"Okay, fine. But emigrating to Novan space isn't the answer. You could go back to Gilgar, or any number of neutral planets."

She shook her head. "I'm not thinking about emigrating."

"Then what are you thinking about?"

"About calling in a decade old favor from Hadro Nassien. If we can get him to convince his mother to release Project Troy details, we can get the detainees on better legal grounds for release."

Jeffrey rolled back over on his bunk. "Okay, fine. That almost sounds like a logical plan, except the whole getting to New China without being arrested by the Novan government as spies."

Jordan pulled out her bag and started packing. "For a man who's spent his career in Intel, you can really obsess over the minor details, you know." She poked the bottom of his bunk. "Dress nicely, we're going to an embassy on Basel."

"Gilgaran?"

"Tarquin." She zipped up her bag. "That alert I got on Isere also went to my mother. We've had a detailed protocol in place for years to handle if I ever needed to avoid arrest. She has the Gilgaran contacts, and through Red, my old classmate at Buenos Aries, I have contacts with the Tarquins. Either one can get us where we need to go, but Tarquins have faster ships."

IN TOTAL, THEY were in Basel space for less than four of the local thirty-hour days before a Tarquin ship was made available to take them on to New China. Baeron drives and human physiognomy didn't mix well, and they spent the bulk of their travel in deep sedation.

Waking up from that proved even more unpleasant than Jordan's persistent morning sickness. Groggy and nauseated, she waited in her berth for the all-clear signal from the ship commander. That took an additional two hours from when the ship had docked at the local orbital station above New China. Not that she could see anything, tucked away as they were out of sight of the other passengers.

The door to her berth slid open. Jeffrey looked even worse than she felt as he leaned against the bulkhead beside his Tarquin escort, a young lieutenant.

"I am commanded to shuttle you directly to the Tarquin Embassy in Bahai." With no further instructions, the Tarquin male led them through the now-empty ship to a shuttle craft that could seat up to twenty. It took off with only the three of them. Red's instructions obviously included a good dose of paranoid secrecy, for which Jordan was grateful, given the circumstances.

The trip down to the planet threatened to upturn what little Jordan had in her stomach, but eventually they leveled off to surface flight altitude, and her insides settled down some. Jeffrey had fallen back asleep, but she kept her gaze out the small window.

This was Novan space. Granted, only one planet among dozens, but still, it represented the culture of her father, someone she could barely remember at this point. It had been years since she'd been around other Novans, not since her time on Gilgar when her mother was Terran Ambassador there. Even then, she'd kept her distance from other Novans, as they would easily detect her from her pheromones, as she could detect them. Landing on this planet would be the first time she could truly walk free as who she was, yet it felt more constraining than liberating, given what she needed to accomplish here.

A brown landscape beneath them gave way to an ocean or inland sea. She had nothing on her datapad to help her with this geography, but soon they were flying lower, over another land mass covered in clouds, with the tantalizing hint of lush green breaking through. She felt the rumble of the landing gear as they descended through a final patch of clouds. The land beneath appeared as a broad expanse of high-rise buildings, mostly white or tan in color. The shuttle banked and the wings flipped to vertical descent mode as a landing pad appeared below them on the flat top of a broad two-story building, the Tarquin Embassy.

Jordan nudged Jeffrey awake in the seat next to her. "Welcome to Bahai."

"Huh. Thanks. Let's hope they don't arrest me on sight."

The shuttle landed with a small jolt and the engines revved down. She watched a tall Tarquin female approach from the roof doorway as Jordan unbuckled her harness and grabbed her travel bag. The lieutenant opened the shuttle door and a set of steps expanded down to the roof. Jordan was the first out, with Jeffrey right behind her.

The Tarqin female nodded to her and spoke in fluent Novan. "I am Liason Sigan, and I welcome you to New China, Ser Arbatova."

Jordan steeled herself against flinching at the sound of her father's name. She had never used it before, but traveling as a Novan, it made sense to use her legal Novan name, Jordan Arbatova.

Sigan paid little attention to Jeffrey and none at all to the young Tarquin lieutenant. Tarquin females had nothing but disdain for their male counterparts except when breeding time approached, and even then, it was more akin to a private battle than romance or seduction.

The Tarquin embassy decor was bold lines and hard angles, with the primary decorative motif of weaponry, modern and archaic, in strategic display cases that lined their route through the building. How Red, a near pacifist, came from such a warrior race remained a mystery, but he was a loyal friend and fulfilled his promise to her with perfect thoroughness.

They ended their walk in a side corridor lined with conference rooms. Sigan paused a few paces from one such room outside of which stood two armed Novan guards in green livery. "The ambassador regrets he cannot attend you directly during your visit. Given the nature of your request, he sent out queries on your behalf. Unfortunately, General Hadro Nassien is not on New China at this time, but we have managed to find you another contact we hope will prove helpful."

Sigan stepped between the guards and opened the conference door. It was a small room with a center table and cushioned chairs, all empty. The lone occupant stood staring out the window, her hand tapping restlessly on the side of her uniform trousers.

"May I present to you, Fleet Admiral Nailah Nassien, commanding the Flag ship *Lahore,*" Sigan said.

The woman turned to Jordan, taking her in with a quick snap of her brown eyes. She was shorter than Jordan, but older, with a touch of gray showing in her dark brown hair, surrounding a hard, olive skinned face. "Ser Bowers."

"Fleet Admiral," Jordan said. "I am traveling as Arbatova, my father's name."

"Hmm." Nailah pulled out a chair and sat. "You had specific requests of my brother, Hadro."

Jordan took a seat opposite Nailah, while Jeffery and Sigan chose to remain standing together by the door, bordered now by the two guards who stepped inside with them. The room was getting crowded. "Yes, we'd met years ago, and he'd offered his assistance should I ever need it."

"For rescuing my niece and nephew, yes, I recall the story." The barest hint of a smile lifted Nailah's lips before disappearing again. "That was for asylum for you, should your Novan heritage become an issue in Terran space. You come with a different request."

"Different but related. You have perhaps heard of the mass detainment of Terrans found to have unspecified genetic modifications, thought to be of Novan origin?"

A muscle twitched in Nailah's jaw. "Say that I have. How does that relate to you and Hadro?"

"My wife is one of the detainees. The connection to your family comes through Project Troy."

"The ambassador has made arrangement to share all Tarquin knowledge on Project Troy and Grand Dame Nassien's involvement with Ser Arbatova should she request such information," Sigan said.

Nailah turned her glare to Sigan for a moment, then back to Jordan, a cold smile breaking the harsh angles of her face once more. "Of course. Sigan, please see that Ser Arbatova is granted a visitor visa on my authority. Contact me when that is completed, and I will escort her to the compound directly to discuss the matter further." She stood up. "Ser, Hadro has vouched for you but I cannot extend that to your companion."

Sigan opened the conference door. "He can remain here as a guest of the Tarquin Ambassador."

Fleet Admiral Nailah Nassien swept out of the room, tailed by her two obvious bodyguards. Something in Nailah's swift decision to become helpful suggested to Jordan that she'd just become part of a different chess game, one she'd better discover the combatants of if she had any hope of helping Dray and the other detainees.

CHAPTER 6

KAY NEVER THOUGHT she'd be grateful for two quiet days at the Nassien compound, but with Manji hosting Ayaan's two young cousins in Bahai, there were no interruptions and thankfully, no political confrontations between grandmother and granddaughter over Kay's locked genetic records. It was only a matter of time before that all heated up again, but until then, it was her, Ayaan, and bevy of dull, but stress free meetings with various branch directors of the Autonomy reporting into Ayaan while Manji was away.

This all came screeching to a halt the next evening when a series of black armored sedans pulled up and poured out their contents on the front steps. A navy fleet admiral stepped out, surrounded by nearly as many bodyguards as followed Ayaan around.

Kay stood to Ayaan's right, and Joris to her left as they waited at the top of the steps.

The fleet admiral, an older woman, paused at the top step. "Ayaan. I didn't know you were here."

"I could say the same for you, Mother."

Too damn many relatives, Kay thought.

Ayaan turned to her. "This is Kay. I'm sure grandmother has spoken of her. Kay, this is my mother, Nailah."

Kay tensed, wondering if Nailah would prove to be as bat-shit crazy as her mother, but she was greeted with a tired smile instead.

"Can we take this inside?" Nailah asked. "I have a guest coming soon. Is Manji here?"

Ayaan stepped to the side to let her mother pass. "She's expected later tonight."

A smile that even Kay recognized as calculating spread on Nailah's face. "Good." She turned to Ayaan. "You and your friend may want to spend the evening in your residence."

Ayaan frowned. "In other words, you plan a fight with Nana. What is it about this time."

Nailah waved a hand. "Oh, I didn't start this one. This is Manji's own nest of vipers. I just stumbled across one of its victims."

"Less hyperbole please, Mother."

Nailah paused in the front foyer as her bodyguards dispersed, all except the requisite two that spoke of how little trust this so-called family had for one another. "That Project Troy she and Papa created years ago is coming back to bite her in the ass, and I want a front seat to that party."

Now this was a woman Kay could understand for once, though that damned Project Troy name caught Ayaan's full focus.

"What do you know about Project Troy?" Ayaan asked.

Nailah stared at her for a moment. "If you are that interested, then do come down for dinner. My guest will be here within the hour."

Nailah went on her way, and Ayaan led the way back to her residence, already spilling orders to Joris on the way. "Find out what you can of my mother's latest meetings, when and with whom and background on whomever you find. See if house staff has the name of her guest and any details on that person."

Joris split off from them as soon as they entered the security perimeter of their residence.

Kay waited until she and Ayaan were in Ayaan's office before popping her first question. "Is your mother a threat to us?"

Ayaan sat behind her desk, smiling and drumming her fingers on the table. "No. In fact, she may prove very helpful in our investigation into Project Troy. She has a way of getting under Nana's skin and squeezing out information my grandmother would rather not reveal. The real issue will be how far she pushes and whether Nana will shut down before we get any real information. I want as much background intel as possible so I can steer the argument in the best direction for us."

"So the two of them get along like a house on fire, eh?"

Ayaan's smile faded. "She blames Nana for my father's death."

"I thought Halabi was responsible for that?"

"Halabi's father arranged the assassination, yes, but he was my grandfather's man. My mother thinks if Nana had stepped in sooner, it wouldn't have happened."

"So she took out Halabi's father, setting you up as the scapegoat when Halabi came of age."

"She took out Halabi's father and my grandfather."

One hell of a family. "Still, it set you up as the scapegoat when Halabi came of age."

"I was a target from the moment I was born. The added security has kept me alive, but it hasn't eliminated the faction that wants me dead."

Joris knocked and stepped into the office. "Ser, the fleet admiral's guest has arrived."

Ayaan sat up. "What have you learned so far?"

"The fleet admiral has been meeting with military advisers for the past week, along with representatives of the legislature, from the opposition party. Project Troy has a strong military presence."

"And her guest?"

"Female. Novan, but required a visitor visa. No other details have been released."

Ayaan stood up. "Have security keep digging. You will accompany us to dinner. We will meet you here in ten minutes."

She swept out of the office toward their shared bedroom and Kay followed. They didn't join the family for dinner often, what with it entailing more bodyguards than actual dinner guests. And Kay, as a guard, had to stand behind Ayaan and wait to eat later. All in all, she preferred the quick meals Chef prepared in their private kitchen.

Dressed in a clean uniform, armed, and ready, she and Joris proceeded Ayaan into the reception room adjacent to the dining hall. Kay scanned the room as Bakri taught her, but there wasn't much to take in. Nailah sat on a sofa beside a dark-haired woman with light brown complexion wearing a black suit. Behind them stood Nailah's requisite two guards. The woman seemed to have none, making her a non-entity in Kay's mind. She focused on Nailah, who stood at their entrance.

"Jordan, may I introduce my daughter, Ayaan Nassien-Nomani."

Before Ayaan could respond, the woman, Jordan, stepped forward, staring at Kay. "Katherine? Katherine Draybeck?" she said in Terran. "How is that even possible?"

Kay stopped in her tracks. Joris and Ayaan did not, and she found herself the focus of their protective cover.

Ayaan spoke up first, also in Terran. "Who are you and what do you know of my companion?"

Joris's hand rested on his holstered pistol. Nailah's two guards were in front of her as well. The whole scene looked like some crazed standoff between enemies instead of the expected casual drinks before dinner.

Nailah pushed in front of her guards. "Can you all speak in Novan please? Some of us haven't the luxury to learn other languages."

"I know this woman," Jordan said in Novan, her eyes still glued to Kay. "Well, I know her exact duplicate. I'm married to her daughter. Her duplicate died at the battle of Turin decades ago."

JORDAN LET HER hands fall to her side and took a step backward. She'd never seen a situation escalate so dramatically as it just had. Add to that the Novan pheromone shifts overwhelming her system, everything was getting out of control. She needed time and information to reevaluate the family she was facing here.

"Apologies for my outburst Sers," she said, keeping to Novan. "Shall we sit, and I will explain myself better."

Some signal from Nailah made her guards step back into the background as she took her seat. Her daughter, Ayaan, seemed less-inclined to join them, but did after a pause. Her two guards arrayed themselves behind her.

Jordan tried not to stare at Katherine's lookalike but she did notice the younger woman was positioned as far from her as possible, with the taller male guard in the forefront. Whoever she was, she was more than a guard, based on how closely she was being guarded by both her peer and Ayaan.

Jordan took a sip from her drink, a red wine derivative but thankfully low in alcoholic content. She needed to be sharp to navigate these currents. "If I may begin, my wife is Helena Draybeck, Terran officer, and currently part of the detainees involved in the Terran purity sweep. Her mother was Katherine Draybeck. Had she lived, she would be approximately fifty Terran years old. While I never met her, I have seen vids and pictures, including her time as a cadet pilot." She turned to Ayaan. "She would have been similar in age to your associate. And their identical appearance is difficult to assume as a random coincidence."

Ayaan sat back in her chair, her fingers tapping a rapid rhythm against the chair arm. Like mother like daughter? While their complexions varied dramatically, Ayaan appearing more old-earth African than her mother, they had similar facial features and body types.

"Do you have any proof to suggest this isn't just a trick of your memory?" Ayaan asked.

"I don't have any pictures here, but I can request them. Katherine was a Novan POW during the prior war. Getting access to her genetic material would have been easy."

Ayaan turned to the Katherine duplicate. Whatever passed between them happened quickly. Ayaan turned back to Jordan. "Kay is a military clone, Terran Unaltered. Her records are, at the moment, sealed based on the classification needs on Project Troy."

"That damned project," Nailah said, turning to Jordan. "I've been dragged into that mess since your Terran purge started. My brother and I share responsibility for military issues within the Nassien Autonomy. And by share, I mean he conveniently gets himself assigned to active duty missions whenever the slightest whiff of controversy surfaces."

One of Nailah's guards bent down to whisper something to her at the same time as Kay whispered to Ayaan. While Nailah greeted the information with a cold grin, Ayaan kept her expression neutral as she said, "My grandmother has arrived. I suggest we postpone further discussion until after dinner. She is not tolerant of heated debates during formal meals."

"Given the mess she's caused, she can stand some indigestion," Nailah said.

"Mother."

Nailah stood and stretched. "Fine. I'll behave. Jordan, welcome to the Nassien compound. I hope you don't regret your visit."

Jordan agreed with that sentiment as she followed behind Nailah. She could see the one they called Kay watching her out of the corner of her eye but she refrained from attempting any direct conversation. Jordan couldn't imagine how the news was affecting the young woman. How was Dray going to react when she found out? Not for the first time, she worried about Dray's emotional state. Thanks to Jordan, she was more tolerant of Novans in general, but that wouldn't extend to being genetically manipulated. And icing on the cake? To find out her mother had been cloned as well. Though why Kay was so young was yet another mystery.

They entered the dining hall as the same strained group. A long wood table dominated the room, with place settings focused on one end that only accounted for four people. It seemed the guards would remain guards during this meal. Servants pulled out red cushioned chairs for each of them and Jordan was seated to Nailah's left, opposite an empty chair with no place setting. Ayaan sat across from her mother, and the head of the table remained empty. Each of the guards took up positions behind their respective responsibilities as the servants poured drinks for each of them.

Jordan turned as someone entered the hall from the opposite direction. A broad-shouldered man, tall, dark, with close-cropped gray hair entered with the same crisp awareness that said he was another guard. He was followed by a short older woman walking with a cane. Jordan recognized Manji Nassien from her official photos and stood when Ayaan and Nailah did.

Manji walked to the head seat. Her dark gaze fell on Jordan. "Welcome, Ser Arbatova. It is an unexpected joy to meet the woman who saved my grandchildren."

"Jordan, please, and I was only one of the two responsible for that honor." She wasn't surprised Manji knew who she was. She was equally sure the woman knew why she was here. This family was nothing if not thorough in the level to which they seemed to distrust one another.

Manji took her seat and that was signal enough for the rest to sit and the servants to return with the first course, a spicy vegetable soup. Jordan sat quietly as the meal proceeded, listening to the polite but empty discourse around her. Manji completely controlled the conversation, drawing her in now and then to ask about her travel and sites she should visit while on planet.

As the last plates were cleared, Manji shifted in her seat and faced Jordan. "So you know the gene-mother of my granddaughter's pet Terran?"

KAY STOOD AT her post, to the left and behind Ayaan. Joris had once again manipulated the positioning to ensure she remained as far from Jordan Arbatova as possible. She was already tired of the overprotective attention she was getting, and that didn't improve with Manji's confirmation that Jordan's story was true. Of course the crazy old bat knew, and of course she kept it to herself until forced to open up.

"Some respect, please, Nana," Ayaan said through clenched jaw. "Kay's position is little different from Bakri's."

Ooch, Kay thought. Ayaan had to be pissed to bring that up in front of company. Kay told her before she didn't give a shit what Manji said or thought, as long as she stayed out of their business. Of course their business was now the main topic of discussion, thanks to this strange woman showing up on their doorstep.

Manji huffed. "Bakri earned his position as a fully qualified guard."

"And Kay saved my life twice already. Imagine her skill set once she completes her training."

Nailah tossed her napkin down. "Take a break on the snark, Mother. What's so important about Ayaan's girlfriend that you had to lock her genetic records." She turned to Ayaan. "Yes, I know about that lock. I hit the same roadblock."

Was there anyone here not obsessed with her background, Kay wondered. If there was any kind of Higher Deity, now would be a good time for an assassination attempt, an air raid, an asteroid collision—anything to end this conversation and let her get back to anonymity.

Manji leaned back, eying each of them in turn. "Project Troy was one of my husband's many mistakes. I discovered the KDTU gene-line by accident as part of that project and have carried it forward since that time."

"Did you clone Katherine Draybeck before or after she was genetically altered?" Jordan asked.

"Before."

So much for that slim chance that Kay was something beyond vanilla Terran. The question she hoped wasn't going to be asked was the next thing out of Ayaan's mouth.

"What was so special about Katherine Draybeck?" Ayaan asked.

"She was a top pilot," Jordan said. "What she did at Turin has never been repeated in Terran history."

Nailah gave another of her cold smiles. "What she did at Turin happened after she was genetically modified. Care to elaborate on what those modifications where, Mother?"

Finally, the conversation going in another direction. Score another point for Nailah. As far as Kay knew, none of her gene sisters were pilots, so whatever that skill was, if it existed before the modifications, it wasn't top on Manji's lab rat tests for the rest of them.

Manji waved a hand dismissively. "I don't know the exact nature of each modification made. There were thousands of them."

"Thousands?" Jordan repeated. "Given the timeframe, there must be tens of thousands by now, including all the offspring."

"Hundreds of thousands," Manji said. "Your government is assuming Project Troy in Katherine Draybeck's generation was the first attempt to bypass Terran Purity standards. They will need to backdate that by decades. Troy was only the latest incarnation of a long-standing idea. It was one of my husband's first major initiatives when he was a young man, and he didn't act alone. The project spans three other Novan associations."

Hundreds of thousands of tweaked Terrans messing up their pristine gene-pool. Ayaan's grandfather must have been a complete jackass, but he was an ambitious jackass, back in the day.

"Ser," said Jordan. "That makes it even more critical that we find a way to release the records of those modifications. A few thousand people could have been re-labeled as nonTerrans and reintegrated into society. The number of people you are suggesting is beyond that threshold of possible acceptance."

"Call me Manji. Save the formalities for the Legislature. That's where you will have to make your case."

Jordan visibly paled, but seemed to recover quickly. "Will I have your backing?"

"Perhaps. But if your government has only found a subset of the affected population, you need to ask yourself—are you doing the rest a disservice by disclosing their so-called impurities?"

Damned if you do and damned if you don't, Kay thought, but nobody was asking her. The only thing worse than standing in the background while everyone discussed you like some interesting lab experiment, was standing in the background while everyone got their knickers in a twist about a subject that was even less important, and should have been irrelevant to the Terrans as well. Kay spent most of her youth wishing she'd had genetic enhancements, and here was a small city worth of Terrans crying foul because they were enhanced. There was no pleasing some people.

"Your point is valid, Manji," Jordan said. "Given the numbers the Terran government has uncovered so far, I can only wonder how long it will be before the rest are detected and detained as well. Whether all the information on Project Troy is released, it would be beneficial to be prepared for that eventuality."

Manji pushed back her seat and stood. "We can discuss a strategy in the morning. Where are you staying?"

"I am being hosted by the Tarquin Embassy in Bahai," Jordan said.

"You will stay here in the compound. Nailah, make arrangements."

Jordan stood as Manji did. "I don't wish to be a burden."

"It will be more convenient than traveling to and from Bahai." Manji spoke to Jordan but watched Kay. "Your direct involvement here has already proved . . . interesting."

The group went their separate ways, with Nailah escorting Jordan to her residence as a guest. Kay, Joris, and Ayaan returned to theirs as well. Ayaan was a tense ball of frustration for reasons that became obvious as soon as they were behind closed doors.

"My mother manipulated that conversation away from you on purpose."

Kay sank into a chair. "That makes her my second-favorite Nassien so far."

Ayaan sighed. "Kay, this is our chance to get the information we've been looking for."

"You've been looking for," Kay said. "I was perfectly happy being a no-name clone."

Ayaan smiled. "Now you have a name. Katherine Draybeck."

"No, she had a name."

"You have a family, here, now. Jordan is part of that family, and she knows about your gene-mother and her children."

Kay shut her eyes. Why was everyone obsessed with her genetic links? "Katherine Draybeck was genetically modified. Her children inherited that. Jordan is half Novan. Have you noticed that even my so-called Terran family isn't even Terran?"

"That's irrelevant, they are still family."

Family that will always be those few steps ahead of her. Because she was the last one standing that was Terran Unaltered. Bottom of the barrel in the military, bottom of the barrel in Ayaan's staff, and now bottom scraping with her own genetic relatives.

So, what was she going to do about it?

Kay didn't think the next morning would bring any relief from the enfolding fiasco, and she wasn't wrong. Breakfast consisted of an invitation to Nailah's residence and that meant more time being the center of unwanted attention. She dragged her feet as long as possible, waiting until Ayaan finished her morning prayers before getting up to get dressed.

Kay pulled out a fresh uniform, but Ayaan stopped her. "We're both invited as guests. You aren't my bodyguard this morning. You can wear something else."

Kay unfolded the green trousers. "I'm your sworn bodyguard, now and always." It was the sole identity she had that wasn't tied to her damned clone status. She wasn't giving that up just yet.

Nailah's residence was a short walk down the corridor from Ayaan's. Kay took in the surroundings with a fast glance, noting the stark differences to Ayaan's. Nailah's decor was minimalist, but then from the sounds of it, she came here only when necessary, and spent most of her time in Bahai or in active duty. Kay envied her that. The more time she spent watching Ayaan play politics, the more she itched to get back to a real assignment, just get to shoot something again.

Jordan sat at the breakfast table, waiting for them. Same shit, different day.

JORDAN STOOD UP when the guests arrived. She'd spent a good portion of the night thinking about how best to handle this new development, and really, there was only one option to dig herself out the hole she created.

"Kay, I apologize for my overreaction yesterday. I meant no offense, and had no idea you were not aware of where your cloning originated."

Kay eyed her warily as she spoke to her directly for the first time. "Officially, it's called a gene-line, and I am, or was only one of many. I don't know if any of the others survived."

Nailah walked in with a tray of sweet buns. "Leave that part to me. I have some ideas how to chase that information down." She set the tray down next to the juice and coffee carafes already on the table. "Sit, everyone."

Ayaan poured them both juice before she started in on Nailah. "We could have gotten that information last night if you hadn't redirected Nana."

"You know her better than that. She's working some angle here, and a frontal assault isn't going to work. No, we save that for what we can't get on our own. And Jordan here opens up a lot of locked doors for us now."

Jordan paused on the muffin she was about to eat. "How is that?"

Nailah smiled. "You are a direct relative to Kay, and a Novan citizen, through your father. Military clones don't have citizen rights, but since you do and you are related through marriage, you can get her records and that of her gene-line."

"They are under restriction," Ayaan piped in, "along with the rest of Project Troy's details."

"That," Jordan said, "is something I think I can help with. If I can convince the legislature to release those details, am I correct in assuming that would also unlock Kay's records?"

"What if I don't want them unlocked," Kay said. She sat with her arms crossed, not having touched any of the food.

"Sorry, I'm doing it again," Jordan said. "I'm trampling through your background without discussing it with you."

Kay shrugged. "So is everyone else."

Tread carefully. This was an edgy situation, and Jordan still didn't know all the permutations and personalities involved.

Nailah reached across and patted Kay's shoulder. "Hon, everyone here, excepting Jordan, has had her life trampled through. It's practically the Nassien family motto. It's in your interest to get those records unlocked. If you want to keep the contents to yourself, that's between you and Ayaan. But if you've learned anything in the time you've been with my daughter, it should be that knowledge is power in this family. And Jordan here, is the key to unlocking that knowledge for you."

"Anonymity is safety is my motto." Kay unfolded her arms. "I don't like this much attention."

Ayaan took Kay's hand. "You fell in love with the wrong person for that one."

Kay's grin looked so much like Dray's that Jordan had to look away. How would she introduce these two, and how would Dray react to a duplicate of her mother? And what if there were multiple of them?

A knock on the door drew Nailah away. Before Jordan had time to formulate her next steps, two young teenagers crowded in.

The boy locked his eyes on Jordan. "Gemma, you were right, it is her!"

Before Jordan could react, that same boy threw his arms around Jordan's neck. She looked up to see the girl frozen in place.

Nailah smacked the girl lightly on the back of the head. "I told you to stay the hell out of my personal communications."

Ayaan came over and helped peel the boy off Jordan. "Zayn, at least explain who you are before you accost a guest."

Zayn stood back up, wiping his eyes. "I just never thought we'd get to meet you again. I'm Zayn, and the stone statue over there is my sister, Gemma. You saved our lives when we were kids."

Of course, Hadro's children. Jordan had only thought of them as her way of getting access to those responsible for Project Troy. Now she saw two teenagers who, if she looked closely, did remind her of the two Novan children from so long ago. She stood up and held Zayn at arm's length. "I hadn't thought how much older you would be!" She stepped across and wrapped an arm around Gemma as well. "You were both so young."

"And you were the only one who seemed real to us," Zayn said.

Jordan laughed. "I was the only one with Novan pheromones, yes."

Gemma squirmed out of her grasp but her shocked expression was replaced by a smile. "It was written on your guest visa, as a secondary alias—Jordan Bowers." She pulled an old, rough patch out of her pocket and showed Jordan the name tag she'd given them so many years before.

Nailah nudged Gemma with her elbow. "And how exactly did you find that guest visa?"

"Your security stinks, Auntie," Gemma said, without even blushing.

Zayn rolled her eyes. "She thinks she's a computer genius. I think it's her only claim to fame since she can't keep up with me in inter-space economics or galactic history."

"Now that the bragging and reunion is done," Nailah said. "We have work to do here so you two need to go spy on someone else."

Zayn pulled up a spare chair. "If this involves Jordan, it involves us."

Nailah sighed and waved Gemma to the last seat.

And as easy as that, Jordan gained two new allies.

CHAPTER 7

KAY TYPED A message out to Gemma, short and to the point—*Teach me how you break into systems*. She could just imagine the kid's ear to ear grin. She was sure Gemma would agree, just as she was sure it was damned time she started taking back some control of her life. Her physical and combat training were improving, but her weak arm wasn't. What she couldn't accomplish physically, she could make up for with intelligence gathering. The whole Nassien Autonomy was a nest of vipers. With Gemma's training, she could find and squash a few of them.

The weather turned steamy four days later as Ayaan's convoy made its way to Bahai. Jordan followed behind them in a separate car.

"How many meetings did you set up?" Kay asked.

Ayaan pulled up the itinerary. "Two senators from the Centrists, a legal analyst specializing in genetics law who can double as a resource on what we can legally get released on your records, and a delegate from the New African Congress who is in town for trade negotiations. The New Africans are on Nana's list of governments with similar programs to Project Troy. It will be a good opportunity to get informal feedback on where their government stands on publicly or privately admitting complicity in international genetic interference programs."

"We're calling it genetic interference, now?"

"It's a term Jordan and the legal analyst adopted during their vid conference last night."

Days and nights rattling political cages, now that was Kay's idea of hell. The convoy pulled out with them as the second car, in the middle of three. The screen wipers kept the view clear on all sides, but there was nothing new to see beyond the drab rain-drenched highway. Even the high quality air filters in the car couldn't quite keep out the damp, not without deploying the emergency seals in case of a gas attack. Rolling green fields gave way to concrete and plasteel manufacturing sites and eventually to the stone buildings of central Bahai. After crawling through two checkpoints, the convoy inched its way along Xiong boulevard. Why they didn't rename the street after they took over the planet and system was a mystery Kay was too lazy to give a real damn about.

The cars pulled up in front of a massive metal gate with the gold star seal of the Nassien Autonomy in the center. One more set of guards scanned each car before opening the gate and letting them through. They were allowed ten guards, no more, and for any sane dignitary, no less. Only six were allowed in the building itself. It was going to be an interesting day of conflict avoidance with that many armed personnel marching about. At least the main legislature was not in session today. Kay couldn't imagine the coordination nightmare of marching hundreds of political figures and their personal armies around the complex without starting an internal war.

A broad driveway led directly to an imposing, multistory complex called the Ak Soray, the thousand-room home to upper and lower houses of the Nassien Autonomy's legislature. Each car in Ayaan's convoy pulled to the front marble steps and green-liveried Nassien guards poured out before she and Ayaan were allowed to exit their car. Joris stepped out first and opened the back door.

Kay stepped out and to the side, taking up her formal position as one of Ayaan's personal bodyguards. Despite all the security getting here, the legislative building posed one of the highest risks of assassination since their days in the Black March. The sources were varied, based on Joris's pre-trip analysis, but Kay recognized the names of Halabi's relatives as part of the lower house of legislature. Anything with his name on it sent red alerts in Kay's mind. She didn't have the benefit of a full military HUD helmet, but she did have an ear piece and one new, specialized contact lens to try out today. It would locate and track all potential threats—human and electronic. She set it up to put a special alert on any Halabi—relative or employee.

As she stepped out of the car, she blinked three times rapidly, to engage the display. Each of Ayaan's guards showed up as green dots. The building itself had a superimposed array showing the internal corridors. A handful of yellow dots showed up, but no reds, no deadly threads recognized.

It wasn't going to be a dull day, that's for sure.

Two guards entered the building first to verify their route and ensure no other armed guard contingent came in their vicinity. The itinerary and corridor access routes to every party in the building was mapped and coordinated to avoid any such interaction, but human verification was required at all times. Two more guards lagged behind to ensure no other party came into their corridors before Ayaan's party was secured in the next section. That left her and Joris to proceed with Ayaan and Jordan.

If Jordan was shocked by the security precautions, she hid it well. Kay gave her credit for that. For a military person, she had a keener understanding of politics and pressure far beyond what Kay ever hoped to have. She wondered if Jordan's wife was the same or had the good common sense of a soldier to stay out of these kinds of murky waters.

And what was Jordan's wife to her? Jordan suggested they would be considered half-sisters, perhaps. In a sense they shared the same genetic mother. And then she shut down thoughts about her genetic whatever and focused on her right-eye display.

The route to the first senator was clear until they came up to the corridor housing his office. Four yellow dots appeared, and one neutral gray, for the senator himself. Ayaan's lead guard saluted the senator's lead guard and negotiated positioning of their respective security contingents. The end result was she and Joris would of course accompany Ayaan and Jordan into the office. Two other of their guards would stand outside with a pair of the senator's guards. The remaining would split and wait at each end of the corridor until the meeting was over.

The first meeting and second proceeded with a dull litany of political fluff and vague non-promises of assistance that would have bored Kay to death if she didn't have the new contact display to play with. Blinks turned it on and off. Spastic eye flicks to left, right, up, or down, changed the display characteristics.

While Jordan spoke to the New African delegate, an ancient woman with dark complexion and short, tight curls that had gone completely white, Kay used her new tricks to do some digging. A couple of eye flicks to the right brought up the woman's complete bio. She was over 145. Another flick, and Kay scrolled through the New African Congress Intelligence report summary. Their claim to fame? The first group considered no longer homo sapien sapiens after using wide-scale genetic germline modifications on their population on the old Earth continent of Africa. They were the place where racial intolerance turned into species intolerance and led to the Terran-Novan split. And they were still primarily located on old Earth. There's some spit in your eye guts since they used their genetic knowledge to spread modifications across a wide swath of Asia and the Middle East.

And from the sounds of the conversation, The New African Congress had no interest in Jordan's problems. They poured out of that meeting and on to the last. None too soon as Kay's stomach was voicing its discontent that it was past lunchtime already. The legal analyst waited for them in one of the committee meeting rooms. Unlike the other offices, this room had no windows, few decorations, and according to Kay's overlay display, it was sound proof, bug proof, and guaranteed any security leaks were entirely human in nature.

The analyst sat by himself with no guards inside or outside the conference room. In other words, he was politically unimportant. Kay's display named him as Carlos Molina, dual doctorates in genetics and law, and, like Jordan, a child of Terran and Novan parents. She wondered if Jordan knew that little tidbit?

To Kay's surprise, he asked her to sit at the table as well. Three quick blinks and her display shut down. No way was she used to it enough to hold a conversation through the overlay.

"We'll start with your case," he said.

"If that's required," Kay said, gritting her teeth.

Ayaan sat next to her and took her hand. "I appreciate your assistance in Kay's case, but shouldn't we start with the more pressing Terran problem?"

At least someone recognized this wasn't her favorite topic.

"Actually," he said, "Kay's case fits in quite nicely with Project Troy and will bolster our legal standing there. Assuming we can prove Ser Arbatova's claim that Kay's genetic source was Katherine Draybeck, then we now have two litigants suing for release of Project Troy details."

Jordan slid a datapad across the table. "These are all I could get access to right now from my associate residing in the Tarquin Embassy. There is one video you should play."

He played the video, and Kay heard her own voice coming out, speaking Terran far better than she ever could. His eyes widened as he stared down and up at Kay through the whole, thankfully short video. "This is good. Very good."

He pushed the video to Kay. She didn't touch it, but Ayaan reached over and hit play. Once again, Kay heard her own voice. This time, she saw herself, maybe a little older, playing with a toddler. Katherine Draybeck looked like her twin, her exact twin. Except she smiled too much.

Kay pointed down, wanting and yet not wanting to know. "Who's the kid?"

Jordan smiled. "Kelvin Draybeck, your half-brother, so to speak. Katherine had three children." She took back the datapad and flicked to another image and pushed it back. "The one with the short hair is my wife, Helena. She goes by Dray. The other one is Cara. She's just a few years older than you and finishing up a degree in astro-engineering."

Kay looked down at the pair of them. She went from zero to full family in an instant. Not just a gene-mother, but three Terran siblings as well. No, not Terran. "All three are affected by Project Troy?"

"No," Jordan said. "Kelvin was born before Katherine became a Novan POW. So far, he's not being detained. Dray and Cara are."

Kelvin was like her then, Terran Unaltered. That fact wormed around inside her, and she wasn't sure just what to do with it. Luckily, Carlos took hold of the conversation again.

"This is good information, better if we had genetic details, but still, very good."

"We have genetic details," Jordan said. All eyes turned to her. "I was at the Massi Clinic on Gilgar for fertility treatment. During their genetic analysis of mine and Dray's eggs, they discovered Dray's genetic makeup was not entirely Terran. I have that report. The doctor couldn't identify the full genetic changes, but he did say they were flagged as military."

"Excellent," Carlos said. "I don't suppose you have any of your wife's eggs as well? We could repeat the genetic analysis here as further proof of both the genetic interference and the familial link to Kay."

Jordan shook her head, but Kay saw her hand go to her belly, a signal she'd seen more than once when one of her squad mates got knocked up.

"You're pregnant."

Jordan shot her an unreadable look. "Yes. Twins."

Kay's family was growing exponentially today. Twins, like Zayn and Gemma. Would they be as annoyingly clever as those two? Would she even know, once this Project Troy thing was settled, and Jordan returned to the Draybeck clan in Terran space?

"You should have said something," Ayaan said. "I will arrange for a doctor to stay at the compound and monitor your progress. Congratulations."

Carlos leaned forward. "I realize this is asking a lot, but would you be willing to undergo a DNA test on your embryos?"

"I'm not sure." Jordan looked away. "Let me think about that."

"Your children will have inherited the modified Draybeck genes. We could match that to Kay's unaltered DNA," he said. "It would seal the case for Kay and Project Troy. We could prove both links."

"She said she wanted to think about it." Kay glared at him. "It's not like we have the best track record on how we handle the family genetic material, have we?"

The guy had enough sense to switch gears after that. The conversation drifted back to legal filings and other cruft she wasn't interested in following. Thankfully, it didn't last long and they got up to leave. Joris stepped out first with Kay right after him.

Kay recognized the hiss of a shock grenade before she saw it. She threw herself back into the meeting room, colliding with Ayaan and Jordan. She had enough time to curse herself for turning off her intelligence overlay before the explosive concussion tossed them all down hard to the floor, forcing the air out of her lungs.

JORDAN'S HEAD SMACKED hard on the floor as she landed at the bottom of a pile. She heard nothing beyond the ringing in her ears for a moment, but years in active duty taught her to react, though not nearly as quickly as Kay, who was already at the door with her gun drawn.

"How many?" Jordan asked, but Kay bolted out the door and didn't answer.

If she was moving openly, the danger must be over. Jordan turned instead to help Ayaan, who was cradling her left arm. Carlos was huddled behind the table, already on a call with building security.

She would have stepped out after Kay but Ayaan held her back. To her surprise, Ayaan also had a gun in her hand.

"Never enter an attack zone until you know the threat has been neutralized." Ayaan pushed them both back against the wall and seemed to be listening to something from a well-hidden ear piece. She stood up. "Now, we move."

They stepped out of the room. Most of Ayaan's guards were down, unconscious from the shock grenade. Kay had her knee pressed into the back of a young woman on the ground.

"Halabi," she growled, looking up at Ayaan.

The woman squirmed beneath her. "Asylum! I seek asylum!"

Kay's eyes twitched to the left, then had that glassy look Dray got when she was accessing her implant. A moment later, Kay read out a report, ending in a curse. "It doesn't make sense. She looks just like him."

Jordan didn't know who "he" was, but obviously no one they trusted. "How did she get a shock grenade in here?"

"I will tell you," the woman said with her cheek still pressed to the floor. "Please, we have to get out of here before the building security arrives. You must realize their complicity in this if I got this far. I am Mala Halabi, and father set this up, but I chose to bring the non-lethal grenade. If we don't leave, we will all be killed."

Kay looked to Ayaan, who nodded silent agreement. Kay stood up and pulled Mala with her. The woman was centimeters shorter, and likely not even of legal age.

Ayaan stepped over to her other main bodyguard, unconscious in the corridor, and pulled out his weapon. She handed it to Jordan. "You have military training. I trust you know how to use this."

Jordan took the gun. "What about your guards?"

Kay pushed Mala to the front. "I contacted Nassien Security outside. It will be a race to see who gets here first, but either way, we need to not be here."

To Jordan's surprise, Ayaan took the forward position, still favoring her left arm. They ran down the corridor and cut through a side door that fed into another corridor perpendicular to the one they were in. A fast dash through that, and they were heading down a flight of stairs which should have been to the back of the building, by Jordan's reckoning. After the initial mad dash, Mala shouted for them to stop.

"All normal exits will be blocked by now. There's no way to tell who is loyal to the government and who to my father."

"How were you supposed to escape after the attack?" Jordan asked.

"I wasn't."

"Great, kid. That's not helping us get out of here," Kay said.

Mala glared at her, showing her younger years for the first time. "I have my own loyal friends. Get us to the sub basement, and they can get us out of here."

Ayaan, who had been speaking to her external guards, turned back to them. "No. What you say may be true or may be an even more elaborate plan to capture me alive. We leave here under the escort of my security alone."

"Do we leave her behind?" Kay asked.

"She stays with us." Ayaan switched places with Kay. "Access security lock code seven."

Kay's eyes twitched a short pattern again, then she grinned. "Now I see why we came here with such a large escort when most of them were supposed to stay outside the building."

Ayaan nodded. "Map the route and relay our coordinates to them." She turned back to Mala. "How did you escape detection from my security?"

"I didn't. My father erased my existence years ago so I could be used as a weapon for him at some point. If you are worried about other hidden attackers, I doubt there are any. It was hard enough getting me inside the building."

"Right," Kay said, but Jordan could hear the doubt in her voice.

Jordan pulled the clip out of her pistol and handed the ammo to Kay. "Send me ahead. Mala can carry the gun. If she has accomplices, they should come out of hiding if it looks like she's won." She handed the useless gun to Mala.

"Not the best plan in the world," Kay said. "Not the worst either. We're going to go down the next corridor and take the second exit on the left. Up a floor, then to the right until we get to the fire exit staircase. Nassien Security should be there by then to take us the rest of the way."

Jordan stuck her elbow out, and Mala grabbed it, a little too tightly at first. "It's okay," she whispered. "You've gotten this far. Let us get you through the rest of the way."

The girl loosened her hold, and Jordan found herself re-adjusting her age estimate, downward. Mala couldn't be much more than two years older than Gemma. Given the slower maturity rates for Novans, it was a wonder she'd managed to concoct a plan that had mostly worked.

Jordan set out at a rapid walk, with Mala keeping pace with her and keeping the empty gun in her side for show. Now if they could make it to Ayaan's guards before they ran into building security personnel with questionable allegiances, that would be a vast improvement.

NASSIEN SECURITY MET them at the fire escape, six heavily armed guards in green uniforms and no questionable allegiances. The first one jabbed Mala with a knockout drug and tossed her unconscious body over his shoulder. Wouldn't have been Kay's first choice on how to deal with the kid, but it worked, just like Jordan's plan worked, which upped Kay's estimation of the half-Terran woman considerably. Thinking on her feet in a crisis situation was a good skill to have.

Even with the added security, Kay kept a close watch on her overlay display, noting where the so-called neutral targets were. It bugged her that Mala showed up as a gray icon in the overlay with a false identity. She didn't know how that was possible, but she bet Gemma would. All she knew was Halabi was still in the game, and the bastard had some deep pockets to buy the loyalty of so many today.

A final set of staircases led them out of the building and on to an adjacent, flat roof. It wasn't meant to be a helicopter landing pad but it managed well enough. One Nassien copter landed as they emerged. Kay looked up to see two more of theirs circling the building, all with weapons ready. No enemy aircraft was in view. Halabi's pockets weren't that deep, or he wasn't ready to be that brazenly open in his attacks.

She hopped in the copter after Ayaan and Jordan just as Joris pinged her with details from inside the building.

"The stunned guards are safe," she said. "Joris will be in the land convoy. One casualty, nonfatal. Two dead in building security." There was going to be some serious shit flying over this incident, and Kay was sure a few government employees would disappear into a Nassien cell for questioning.

She strapped in next to Ayaan as the copter took off. "How's your arm?"

"It's the wrist." Ayaan flexed it and winced. "Likely strained."

"Sorry for that."

Ayaan smiled. "You'd better not be. I don't want to think about what would have happened if you hadn't pushed us back inside the room."

Jordan rubbed at what was probably a bruised knee. Nobody lands on the floor without some lasting impact. "This Halabi seems to take extreme measures, if Mala is telling the truth. Am I correct in assuming it's a personal issue and not just political rivalry?"

Kay answered to spare Ayaan. "He is, or was, my gene-line program manager, but I guess that was also part of his vendetta against Ayaan's family. Long and short of it is, the Halabi family killed Ayaan's father, the Nassiens had Halabi's father assassinated in return."

"My grandfather personally ordered the assassination on Halabi's father," Ayaan said. "Something like that sends a message. One Halabi is now trying to send it back."

"Through you," Jordan said.

"Through my dead body. This was an abduction attempt. The only reason for that would be to kill me himself. The good news is capturing me alive will be much harder than just killing me outright."

The bad news—he was expanding his reach if he could get into the legislature building security like he just did. Someone needed to off him and fast.

The copter returned to the Nassien compound, which had even more visible security in place as they landed. They each had orders waiting for them, compliments of Manji. Jordan to Nailah, Ayaan to Manji directly, and Kay to Bakri. Great, last thing she wanted was a combat lesson.

She rolled her shoulders as she walked into the building. Nobody landed on the floor like they had without some lasting impact, even if she had used Ayaan as a cushion.

Instead of meeting him in the gym, Kay was directed to another room, two levels below. She had to be escorted inside by another guard to where Bakri waited in front of a bank of computer screens. So this wasn't going to be a physical lesson.

Bakri turned to her. "Sit please. We wait for another."

Kay took the seat next to him and stared at the screens. She didn't expect to see visual surveillance feeds. Nothing that simple existed in the Nassien security offices. Video, audio eavesdropping, electronic eavesdropping, it was all handled through advanced security AIs that took in the bulk and analyzed it real-time. What she expected to see was summary reports, but even that wasn't what she was looking at.

The door opened again, and she turned to see Gemma enter, looking even more subdued than she expected from the girl. This should have been like a kid in a candy shop. With a nod, Gemma took the seat on the other side of Bakri.

"This is one of the interfaces to the main Nassien security AI. You have both worked with it before, but only through one of its ancillary AIs with limited capabilities. This is the master." Bakri turned to Kay first. "You will relate in detail what you saw, heard, and felt before and during the attack today. Every aspect is important. Our AI has a limited interface to the Legislature building. You will enhance that interface for today's attack. Your role is to teach it all you know and all you experienced so that it can learn what to look for in the future."

He turned to Gemma. "Your role is to learn how the AI learns. You will direct your security breaches toward Halabi targets and resources and feed that access to the AI. As a minor, if you are discovered, you cannot be prosecuted. Avoid getting caught as it will turn off an important flow of information in this case. You will also feed the AI information from sessions with Mala Halabi after her formal debrief, since you are closer in age to her. Your sessions will begin this evening."

"Who is Mala Halabi?" Gemma asked.

"She spearheaded the attack against Ayaan today. She's currently in a holding cell here in the compound until her status is determined," Bakri said.

So much for the kid's asylum. Kay looked at the banks of screens. "How do I turn on record for the AI."

"It is always on and listening," Bakri said.

And that wasn't the least bit disturbing. Kay rolled her shoulders to loosen the growing knot and began her report. The first time the AI interrupted her to ask for specifics, she learned this was going to be a long afternoon.

She and Gemma emerged from the security room two hours later. She was hungry, Gemma was bouncing on her toes as she walked.

"Do you see the kind of access I've got now? There's so many more places I'll be able to break into with the resources the house security AI has!"

"That's great, kid. Don't forget you still owe me some lessons as well."

"Oh sure, that's the easy stuff." She grabbed Kay by the wrist. "Come on up to our residence. My console there will have my new access available."

She would have preferred some food and a synthbeer, but whatever. She verified Ayaan was still with her grandmother, then followed Gemma up to Hadro's residence. Much to her surprise, it was considerably smaller than the others she'd seen. Hadro wasn't a space hog, that's for sure. Zayn wasn't around but the standard support staff were, and of course all had the bearings of trained security guards as well. Multi-talented workers all around.

Gemma turned on her console and flicked through a few screens. "Yes! It's all here. This is going to be great."

Kay pulled up a spare chair and sat. "How about we start at the basics."

"Sure sure. First thing you need to understand is that security always has a weakness."

She learned that the hard way today. "Like Halabi used our security protocols against us by converting his own kid into an alternate person years ago, just to sneak her into an attack someday."

That seemed to sober Gemma up. "Yeah, he did. I'll find out how he did that."

"Meanwhile," Kay said, getting Gemma back on track.

"Yeah, okay. So the weakest link. When it comes to a lot of people and places, the weakest link is human error. Everyone needs security, most people don't understand even the basics of how to keep their personal information secure. You are probably used to biometric scans. Even those can be tricked, with the right tools. But in the civilian world, biometrics aren't popular. The law states that any biological information can be used against you in a court case. That created an interesting legal loophole. If you secure your information with something like quad-level authentication with full data-at-rest time-shifting encryption, the government can't force you to open that up as it would be incriminating yourself. But, if you depend on say a retinal scan, that's biologic in origin. So the government scans your eye, feeds it into an access console, and boom—they have everything they want. So most people use some other form of external authentication, and that's where it's the weakest."

Gemma turned back to her console and Kay thought finally, she'd learn something she could understand. Alas, she was wrong as Gemma continued on her diatribe. "The authentication part is easy. Most people choose something simple that they can remember, and my old access could break the easy stuff within a couple of hours. But that left all the encrypted data, and that could take days to break, depending on how big the prime number was that they based the encryption on."

"Gemma, just show me something I can use."

"But, this is the best part."

Kay pinched the bridge of her nose. How to rein in this kid to something she could remember and repeat on her own. She looked up. "Okay, how about something tangible. Jordan has someone in the Tarquin Embassy. Can you find out who it is?"

"Oh, sure, that's nothing."

That nothing took another thirty minutes of flicking and poking and lecturing. On the plus side, Gemma did the lecturing but let Kay do all the flicking and poking so she could remember the steps better. Success came in the image of an older man, thin, with a name that was likely false. Still, one thing accomplished. Tarquin embassy security was locked down and unbreakable, according to Gemma. But true to her word, the weakness came in the form of external communications between Jordan and her Terran compatriot.

"Well done, kid."

When Gemma said nothing, Kay looked up at her. She was staring at the screen and looking pale.

"What's wrong?"

"He was there, on the planet back when we lost our mom."

"The planet where Jordan rescued you?"

"Yes. I remember him. He was Novan, but not Novan. He scared me more than the Terrans."

Novan, but not Novan. Kay stood up. Jordan had some explaining to do. Explaining that she could do right now.

JORDAN THOUGHT SHE'D get a quiet evening since Nailah had returned to Bahai. That disappeared the moment two serious guards turned up and escorted her out of the residence.

Jordan walked quietly between the two, analyzing the options of what went wrong. Armed guards meant she wasn't the honored guest anymore, so that meant someone felt she was a threat.

It wasn't Nailah, who was too straightforward to create a fake scene about Jordan's possible arrest. That left Manji and Ayaan. Manji could have decided Project Troy was too hot a topic in the legislature and thought it best to make it and Jordan disappear. Given the legal advice they got earlier, that would still leave Kay as a legal avenue to releasing Project Troy. So that left one Nassien. Did Ayaan resent Kay's new-found family? It didn't seem likely.

Jordan walked into an obvious interrogation room and sat down opposite of Kay and Joris. So she was seen as a threat to Ayaan, one question answered. The why came soon enough.

"Your counterpoint in the Tarquin Embassy has been arrested." Kay's blue eyes, deeper in color than Dray's held that same hard stare that covered for barely controlled rage. So Jeffrey was the threat, and Jordan was the link to him and the one who didn't reveal his background.

Jordan folded her hands. "He stayed there because Nailah would not grant him a visitor visa. His name is Jeffrey Franklin, and he is your brother-in-law, married to Kelvin Dreyback."

"By your account, I'm related to half the Terran empire. Why is he here and why has he tried to pass himself off as Novan in the past."

Jordan didn't know how they figured that out, but it was a risk he and she understood when he agreed to come into Novan territory. "As I explained to Nailah, I am a Terran Intel officer. So is Jeffrey.

Yes, he has represented himself as Novan on past missions. None of those involved the Nassien Autonomy."

"This is another fact that cannot be verified," Joris said.

"No," Jordan said, "but you will find him a cooperative prisoner on any details that do not involve Terran security. Neither of us are here as spies. We came for Project Troy. I never thought we'd find a genetic clone of Katherine Draybeck." She took a deep breath. "And that is one fact I can prove. I will agree to have a genetic test run on the fetuses I am carrying. It will show a familial match to Kay and prove out that much of my story."

"Agreed," Joris said. "Who shot down Falah Nassein's ship?"

"Who?"

"Zayn and Gemma's mother," Kay said. "You were on the planet and in the vicinity of her crash. Was that an Intel operation?"

"No. We were cadets when it happened. We escaped the Novan attack on Buenos Aries in an experimental ship. We had no control over the navigation."

Kay leaned back. "Did Jeffrey?"

"No. We thought he was Novan at the time and kept him as prisoner."

The door opened to another guard, an older woman and vaguely familiar. She stepped inside and both Joris and Kay stood at attention. Obviously a superior. She ignored them both. "Ser Arbatova, Manji Nassien sends her apologies for the overreaction of her granddaughter's staff and asks that you join her in the central common room."

Now Jordan recognized her as one of Manji's guards. She was getting too popular with the security staff in this compound, but at least this time it worked in her favor. She turned to Kay and saw that barely suppressed Draybeck rage getting closer to the surface. Time for a peace offering.

"No apologies necessary, ser. Kay's precaution is exactly what I would expect and hope for if I had security personnel on staff. She discovered a potential security risk in Jeffrey Franklin and investigated it."

"As you say," Manji's guard said.

Jordan didn't doubt that someone was going to get shouted at, but at least Kay didn't look like she was ready to explode anymore.

The walk to the common room was quiet, tense, and thankfully short. Jordan recognized the room as the first one she'd met Kay in. This time, the room looked more like a prelude to violence than a family gathering. Three potential combatants stood facing off. Ayaan stood for once in opposition to Gemma and Zayn. Manji stood in the middle, hands resting on the ever-present cane that Jordan knew the woman didn't need. Affectation or weapon? Jordan assumed the latter.

"Wonderful," Manji said. "More guards and glaring faces." She turned and sat in a large faux-leather chair. "Family and guest, sit. Guards to the far walls." When Kay moved off with Joris, Manji added. "Not you."

Jordan sat first, opposite Manji, on a rust colored sofa, and noted the seating pattern that formed between them. Kay sat to Manji's right, keeping herself between the matriarch and Ayaan. That as good as confirmed the cane was a weapon. On the bright side, Kay must have assumed Jordan was the lesser threat since Ayaan took the seat to Jordan's immediate left. Zayn and Gemma shared the sofa with Jordan, setting the initial stage in the battle ground. Now, how to diffuse this mess?

Manji took the lead. "One—Jordan is a guest under Nailah's protection. She is not subject to interrogation in my house unless Nailah orders it."

"My aunt isn't here to ask so I took responsibility," Ayaan said.

"As if you ordered this mess." Manji turned to Kay. "Your enthusiasm for my granddaughter's security is admirable, but misplaced in this instance. I let no one in this compound who isn't fully vetted by me."

Manji nodded to the one Jordan recognized as her primary bodyguard. He stepped forward, and Jordan listened to a near complete dossier on her, her mother, and details even she didn't know about her Arbatova relatives. He then extended his report to include Jeffrey and a summary of his presumed Novan assignments in the past ten years. She had no idea how accurate that list was, but it was impressive.

At the end, Ayaan still looked defiant, but Kay looked to Jordan and shrugged as a silent acceptance and apology in one. Jordan smiled back. She didn't look to Zayn and Gemma beside her but assumed given their ages, they'd both be wearing smug grins. At least she had a pair of consistent supporters in her camp.

KAY RELAXED IN her chair with the conclusion of another one of bat shit crazy grandmother's tests and how much she failed at digging out all the right information before jumping the gun on Jordan and her pal Jeffrey. Or maybe it wasn't a test, given Ayaan's continued ire. Whatever.

"If we can put all that behind us," Manji said, "there is a more critical matter pressing now. The Gilgaran Ambassador has been trying to reach Jordan for a day." She waved her guard forward, and he handed a secure data chip to Jordan. "I believe it impacts our efforts here."

Jordan accepted the chip. "You've read it?"

"No. You will see it still bears the embassy's crypto seal. We have received some disturbing reports through our own channels. I assume the urgency of this message, through a neutral channel common to both you and your mother, suggests it is related."

Jordan scanned the chip data into her pad and began to read. Kay didn't know her that well, but when she sat up straighter and then slowly slumped back into her chair, even Kay could tell the message was a shocker.

"How bad is it?"

Jordan looked up, her eyes brimming with what Kay hoped was just dust irritants and not tears. Jordan closed those eyes and took a deep breath. "It's bad," Jordan said in a kind of calm Kay could never emulate.

Must be some kind of political gene since Ayaan and crazy Manji could do it as well. Nailah on the other hand didn't seem to have time for it, from Kay's experience with her. Yet another tick in Nailah's favor in Kay's mind.

"The message comes from my mother," Jordan said, "and she's broken more than a few Terran laws to get it to me. At its core is a classified document authorizing the transfer of all current and future Project Troy detainees and their descendants to a refurbished Generation ship."

"The *Lazarus*," Manji said.

Zayn took Jordan's hand. "What's a generation ship, and why is this so bad?"

"They were originally used before we got FTL drives," Jordan said. "They are huge, slow, and can sustain entire viable populations for years, generations."

"Zayn, Gemma, hypothesize," Manji said. "Why would this be bad?"

Great, another lesson. At least it wasn't directed at Kay.

"Point, if the ships are that slow, maybe it's a delay tactic," Gemma said. "The Terran government won't have to decide what to do with them until they have all of them contained on that prison ship."

"Counterpoint," Zayn said. "The Terrans have already decided, at least at the highest levels of the government. *Lazarus* is a disposal vehicle. Gather them all and make them disappear."

Kay's eyes widened. "Would they do that to their own people?"

"It's not unprecedented in human history to take dramatic measures with a demonized population," Ayaan said. "The questions are—how far will they go, and what do we do about it?"

Kay tried not to stare at Jordan, but the woman was uncharacteristically silent through this mock debate. That spoke volumes about how possible this crazy Terran solution could be. It also suggested that dispassionate politician trait had met its end, for now. She leaned into Ayaan and whispered a suggestion.

Ayaan nodded. "Bring Jeffrey Franklin in. He's a Terran Intel officer with considerable experience. He may prove helpful in the discussion."

Manji signaled one of her guards to take care of it. She also ordered some food brought in, and that gave them a short break. It also gave Jordan time to recover.

Kay was munching down her third plate of salted pita chips and spiced dip when two guards entered. She looked up and realized it was one guard and Jordan's counterpart. He wasn't much to look at, short, medium brown hair and on the thin side. Still, Jordan looked relieved to have him present, so that was a good thing.

Jordan made the round of introductions, and Kay got the expected extra stare when it was her turn. In his favor, it didn't last long and he took the spare seat brought up by his ever-present guard. Kay guessed he wasn't fully free of suspicion yet.

Jordan brought him up to speed quickly, and his first question was a good one. "Do we know for sure it is the *Lazarus* that's being used here?"

"The information has been confirmed by two independent sources," Manji said. "Say it's correct, what does that mean to you?"

"It means the government isn't planning on shooting them all into a nearby star," he said. "The *Lazarus* is one of three surviving Generation ships. Of the other two, one is operational, but with original drive engines, and the other is a floating museum of old Earth colonization efforts. If the government just wanted the detainees contained, they could do it with the operational ship. Pack them in there and float it off-world until they could decide what to do."

"And what's special about *Lazarus*?" Kay asked.

"*Lazarus* was fitted with FTL drive a few years back. Someone's brilliant idea of an Armageddon escape option. A Generation ship is a self-sustaining environment. With a solid initial stock of plants and bio-nutrients, it could have taken the Terran government and their favorite lackeys off to rebuild the Terran empire somewhere else."

"And they would waste that on Project Troy detainees?" Ayaan asked.

Jeffrey nodded. "The idea that the government would up and run turned out not to be too popular at the polls during the following election. The project was dumped. The *Lazarus* has been used as a traveling tourist hotel since then. It has a tour route to major Terran destinations, and you book passage to travel in the style of our original colonists."

"And now it's on a special tour, picking up detainees," Jordan said. Finally, she was back in the game. "If this is being done at a highly classified level, there isn't a way to apply political pressure to end the plan. Not unless we can release the information we have so far."

"Possible," Manji said. "But broad-sweeping pressure based on humanitarian issues is a slow process."

"We need to stop the ship," said Ayaan. "Is it any place where we can send in a Naval strike force? I assume the *Lazarus* is unarmed?"

"Minor defensive weapons," Jeffrey said.

"No." Manji leaned back. "Overt Novan military intervention is not an option. As you have said, they are likely not planning to kill them. If we want to win this political battle, we cannot start a military campaign over this. Not until we have evidence to suggest they plan on injuring the population of detainees."

Kay was about to shout just how asinine that was, but Ayaan grabbed her by the wrist and shook her head. "Grandmother is correct. The political ramifications of first-aggressor in this scenario could do more harm than good to the detainees. We would have to declare them all as Novan citizens. That in itself would ensure none of them were allowed in Terran space again. We may have to do that anyway, but we need to consider other, less drastic options first."

Jordan leaned forward. "We infiltrate the ship. If we get a small party on board, we can use Dray and the other military officers to take over and pilot the ship to neutral space."

"That might work," Jeffrey said. "Two of us could do it, one as guard and the other as detainee."

"You and I," Jordan said.

"No. You're needed to help win that political battle. She would be the best option." He pointed to Kay. "Another Draybeck could slip in without question."

Kay stared back at him. At what point did the world turn crazy?

JORDAN SAT BACK in her chair as the arguments flew back and forth between Jeffrey and mainly Ayaan. Manji sat silent as well, a calculating expression on her face. She was waiting for something, but Jordan didn't know what. The idea was good, but it was more than she could ask.

"Jeff, can you get on board alone, as either a guard or detainee?"

He shook his head. "We need at least two people. One guard and one detainee. Given a disenfranchised population in the thousands, with a heavy military influence and unknown Novan modifications, we have to assume a prison-like setup. We need someone to work with the detainees and Dray, and someone on the outside of that environment to get them out and in control of the ship."

"Then we contact Kelvin. He can find us another supportive Intel agent."

Jeffrey shrugged. "Possible. It would take time."

Time they may not have. Jordan was about to end the debate on that point.

"I'll do it," Kay said.

Ayaan's look of shock was expected. The slight smirk on Manji's face was not. This is what the woman was waiting for, but Jordan didn't have a clue why.

"You don't have to do this," Ayaan said. "You are not a pawn in their game."

Kay shrugged. "We're all pawns in someone's game." She glanced at Manji. "Don't you agree?"

Manji smiled. "Some are more significant pieces on the chess board."

Ayaan turned on her grandmother with an anger Jordan had yet to see before. "This is your doing. Kay is sworn to me and I to her. She goes nowhere if I do not agree."

Manji's cold smile never altered. "That, child, is something you need to discuss with your Terran in private."

"If I may," Jordan said. "Kay, your willingness to help means more to me than I can say, but I won't ask this of you."

"You didn't," Kay said. "He did, and I agreed. End of discussion."

"Kay," Ayaan said.

Kay turned to her. "I'll guard you with my life, always. But this?" She waved her hand as if to encompass the entire compound. "This life is stagnating. You wanted me to discover more about my genetic background. Well, here it is. Instant family, and I can help them."

Ayaan looked at Kay and said to her grandmother, "Any sign of difficulty or risk to your life and we send in a naval strike force."

"I don't control the military," Manji said.

Ayaan turned to her. "Nailah and Hadro do."

"My father will assist," Zayn said. "Gemma and I will pledge for that."

Manji tapped her cane hard on the stone tile floor, but Jordan could tell her anger was fake. The look in her eyes still spoke of some subtle win. Jordan wasn't sure if she was that focused on separating Ayaan and Kay, but she doubted it. The Novan matriarch was far more complex than that. No, Manji had achieved some goal with this, and Jordan didn't like being the chess piece that helped her make it happen.

CHAPTER 8

KAY KNEW SHE'D have hell to pay for her decision. The first punishment came shortly after a strained family dinner. She accompanied Ayaan back to her residence, where Ayaan treated her to stony silence. That lasted a good twenty minutes past what Kay would normally have accepted.

"Out with it." Kay leaned against their bedroom doorframe and waited.

Ayaan stood on the opposite side of the bed, facing the dark window, tapping a slow beat on her leg. Well, that was a familiar sign.

"Tap. Tap. Tap." Kay kept beat until Ayaan stopped.

With fist clenched, Ayaan turned to her. "You're abandoning me for your new family."

Kay stood straight. "Never." She took a step into the room. "You heard Jeffrey's plans tonight. It will take a week to get onto the ship, then a few days to recruit assistance and determine who controls what. Then we take control and fly the ship to a neutral location and contact you."

"And then what?"

"Then back here to you. Won't be more than a month, tops."

Ayaan sank down on the bed. "You think you will just leave your family behind? I think you underestimate the pull they will have on you."

Kay sat on the opposite edge of the bed and took Ayaan's hand. "I think you overestimate it. I'm not like you. I've lived my life with no family ties. Seeing what you have here? I don't think I've missed anything. Sure, I'm curious, but you know, Jordan could probably fill me in on anything I wanted to know." She took a deep breath. "This mission isn't about them, it's about me and us. We've been together for every breath, waking and sleeping, since we got to this compound. And in that time, I've been your appendage. I don't exist beyond the orbit I'm in around you and your life."

Ayaan sighed. "It isn't an easy life, but it was what I was born for."

"And I was born to be a soldier, trained for action," Kay said.

"We don't actually know that. Nana hasn't released your gene study."

Kay shrugged. "You can work on that while I'm away."

Ayaan smiled, finally. "Any other orders?"

"Sure, figure out a way for us to be together, but not every waking moment. I don't think that's healthy for either of us."

"Agreed, but only if you also consider what it is you want."

"What's my purpose, eh?" Kay repeated Bakri's words. Something she'd have to consider during the long trek to the prison ship.

They ended up having four nights together before Kay departed with Jeffrey. She wasn't much for tearful goodbyes and neither was Ayaan. The real goodbye happened nights before, and the going away present was in the form of a covert Novan tracker that would hook into any local Terran network and convey her location back to the compound. It was surgically hidden under a skin flap on her shoulder and undetectable by any known Terran search.

Jordan's Tarquin connections got Kay and Jeffrey on a fast transport out of Novan space. Their first stop came at a Tarquin transfer station, where they changed over to a neutral planet's cruiser, slower than the Tarquin one, for which Kay was most grateful. She'd spent two long days on the Tarquin ship knocked unconscious on every jump. Baeron drives were beyond nasty.

Their first real stop happened a day later when they docked on a merchant trade station orbiting a neutral habitable planet. Jeffrey booked them on a ground shuttle, and Kay stepped out onto the first non-Novan world where she wasn't there to blow holes in something or someone. It left her feeling twitchy, her eyes naturally scanning for possible targets. There wasn't much worth blowing up, from a military perspective. The air field was reasonable in size, but not strategic in terms of the traffic it handled, mostly business people. Minor trade crates were visible, but the heavy trade traffic must go through some other air field.

As for personnel, the guard presence was again minimal and not particularly attentive. A pair watched the passengers disembark but stopped no one. Once through that sad excuse for security, Kay saw no visible security presence.

"You might want to tone that down a bit," Jeffrey said. "You're a Terran pilot now, remember? Not bodyguard to a high-profile target who needs constant surveillance to stay alive."

"Hard to turn it off. Situational awareness is supposed to be my superpower."

He turned back to her. "What?"

Kay shrugged. "They cloned Katherine Draybeck for a reason. Not that they ever told me that reason, but one of my project managers let slip it had to do with her high degree of situational awareness."

Jeffrey nodded, as if considering the option. "Dray got top marks in that for sure, but given Project Troy, who knows if she got that from her mother's Terran genes or Novan modifications."

"Interference is what they're calling it now, genetic interference."

He huffed and kept walking. He wasn't the most talkative of traveling companions, but that suited her fine. He did surprise her when he skipped the option to hire a ground car and boarded them on the public transport instead. Less traceable perhaps, definitely less conspicuous since only the business suits were driving off with hired help. Everyone else seemed more like the run of the mill worker types, and that's what she and Jeffrey were traveling as so far on this journey.

The planet had little to speak for it besides the obvious mines dotting the drab landscape. Black slag heaps rose to impossible heights as their train made its way through the first of three mining towns before they reached their destination, a gray crowded city with soot-stained buildings blotting the skyline all around her. It was a stark difference to Bahai's government-controlled desert stone building regulations and the visual contrast left Kay feeling grimy.

"First stop is for your implants," Jeffrey said as they stepped out of the station into the smog-filled city.

"Implants? I thought it was just a chip ID."

"Katherine was a pilot as well. That means a pilot implant, right about here." He tapped his left temple, just above the hair line.

Kay stopped in her tracks. "No."

Jeffrey halted and turned back to her. "What do you mean, no?"

"I'm not being injected with high tech junk all over. I agreed to a chip implant, and that's it."

He rolled his eyes. "Novans."

It was the only time she'd ever been called Novan and the irony wasn't lost on her as she was about to become as Terran as humanly possible on this trip. "Yes, and I'm not going back to my Novan position with a bunch of Terran tech wired to my brain."

"It won't be active. Just a dead device, for show."

She looked at him. "So if it's not active, how do they know it's even present?"

"It leaves a scar. They'll expect that when we get to the *Lazarus*."

"Fine. Give me a scar then. Keep your tech crap to yourself."

"Fine. You still need the chip implant to ID you as Katherine Draybeck."

She shrugged. "That's not in my brain, I can handle that."

He grumbled his way along the city sidewalk. Kay kept pace, trying to keep her visual scanning to a minimum. With some concentration, she could take in the same level of information without looking like she was a professional guard.

The landscape shifted from tall buildings to shorter, flatter manufacturing sites. At the same time, the flow of people around them shrank down to a few workers in drab brown coveralls that matched what she and Jeffrey were wearing. He'd done his homework to make sure they would blend in.

Kay also recognized the area as a perfect black market location. "How do you know the people we're about to see?"

"Long history of turning chip IDs on and off in my line of work." He turned down a damp alleyway between two buildings.

Runoff from the last rain trickled down the gutter spouts and across the cement to drains in the middle of the alley. With the closer confines, the air stank of machinery and rubbish. Two quick knocks on a door to the back of the left building gained them entrance from a broad-faced older man wearing the same coveralls.

"You're early," he said.

Franklin seemed to accept the man's words as verbal noise. "This is the one who needs a chip ID."

The man barely looked at Kay before leading them both deeper into the building. Ceiling track lighting lit the way for the first corridor before they ducked into another room with a confusing array of lab equipment on two benches that lined the opposite wall. No one else was present.

The man pulled up a stool and pointed Kay to the other stool opposite him. "Right hand, palm up."

She did as she was told. The man pulled out a needle and one quick jab later, she was a chipped Terran. She flexed her hand but could not see or feel any difference.

"Pilot implant next," he said.

Jeffrey piped in before Kay did. "Change of plans on that one. Just burn in a scar. Make it look real."

"Still need to charge you for the implant." The man smirked. "Recruited a Novan, eh? She looks the part well enough."

So Jeffrey had a history of turning Novans into spies. She sat silent as Jeffery exchanged something with the man. Payment she supposed. The man pulled out a small cylindrical instrument and held it to her left temple.

"This will sting," he said, right before it did.

It burned and then felt icy cold, before he removed the instrument. Kay lifted a hand but he smacked it down.

"Leave it alone. It will take a day to heal, and another three or so before it starts to scar over. You won't pass as a Terran pilot before that." He reached into a drawer and tossed a tube of some kind of salve at her. "Tomorrow, start rubbing that in three times a day. It speeds up the scarring."

Four days. Enough time to meet up with the *Lazarus* in Terran space. She waited until they were back on the main sidewalk before asking him the obvious question. "Why does Terran Intel need to create their own Novan spies that can pass as Terran?"

He smiled. "Always evaluating things, eh? Unlike Terran purists, Intel isn't as picky about its recruits. A Novan who can pass as Terran can get full Intel training and then be sent back to Novan space. Turn the implants back off, and your Novan security doesn't even know they've been turned."

"Devious," she said.

"Part of the trade. There are plenty of Terrans that Novan intelligence has turned and sent back to us as spies. It's what keeps it all interesting."

Someone certainly liked his line of work.

KAY LEANED AGAINST the door of the small communications room, waiting for Jeffrey to listen to his backed up calls and messages. They were one hop out of Isere Junction and their entrance into Terran space. She already wore a blue Terran pilot uniform, complete with shiny gold officer bars. The uniform was foreign, but the attitude she faked with it fit her more perfectly than she would have guessed. Maybe she had a future chewing her way up the command ranks.

Jeffrey slumped in the chair, drumming his fingers on the console. "I need to make a call before yours. Jordan's mother sent an update that the *Lazarus* was on the move again. We'll need to sync up to find out where it's headed."

He gave the console a voice command and coordinates and then waited. Less than a minute later, a woman came on the screen. She was older than Jordan, but the resemblance was there for sure.

"Jeffrey, where's your location?"

"We're outside of Isere and booked on a shuttle that leaves in three hours."

"Is that Jordan behind you?"

Kay realized part of her was in visual range but it was too late to shrink back out of camera range. Jeffrey turned back to her with a frown and she shrugged. Too late now to worry about it.

"No," he said. "She stayed in New China for now, working the political element. We're on a separate mission."

"Tell me," she said, with the same authoritative voice Ayaan used. Were all powerful families the same? She remembered the woman was a high profile Terran senator.

"Plausible deniability, Chandrika," Jeffrey said. "You don't want to know."

"There is no deniability left, my friend," Chandrika said. "Jordan will never be allowed in Terran space again. She won't pass the updated purity scans. You and I know she won't stay in Novan space if Dray remains in detention here in Terran space. I've heard from friends in Gilgar, I know she's pregnant. Trust me, motherhood makes you do crazy things."

"Like risk your senatorial seat?" he asked.

"Like risk my senatorial seat. If she has some half-baked idea, I want to know about it. I won't be a senator much longer anyway, but while I still am, I may have some pull to help out from here."

Jeffrey waved Kay forward and she stepped up behind him, in full view to Chandrika Bowers, Jordan's mother. "This is actually my half-baked idea. Allow me to introduce you to Katherine Drayback."

Chandrika's dark brows raised. "Dray's mother? Impossible."

"Very possible, given Project Troy, don't you think? We've known for some time that the Novans regularly take genetic samples from the Terran population, so it's not a big leap that they would do the same with their POWs. Kay here is the result of that, an identical genetic clone to Dray's mother."

Chandrika leaned into the camera as if to get a better look. "Your pardon, Ms. Draybeck, but I wonder how this all helps."

"It's just Kay," she said. "The Draybeck part is his bag of tricks. Mine is to get on your prison ship and work it from the inside."

"Hostile takeover? That's risky. What allies will you have."

"A good portion of that ship if they know they are effectively Terran refugees at this point," Kay said. "Terran patriotism has got to be wearing pretty thin for some of them by now."

"And," Jeffrey added. "Many of them have a military background. Perfect assets to turn this in our favor."

"Agreed," Chandrika said, to Kay's surprise. "You will need evidence to convince them their government hasn't got their best interests in heart. I can get you that."

"Appreciate your help, Ma'am," Kay said.

"Do you have the coordinates for the *Lazarus*?" Jeffrey asked.

"Better, I have its next three pickup locations. Sending that on now."

Jeffrey accepted the pickup locations and after a short discussion on when to check in and how to get the evidence from Chandrika, he ended the call.

Kay's turn now. He gave her brief instructions on how to make a secure, untraceable connection into Novan space, and then left her alone in the room. Kay took a deep breath, then made the call.

She wasn't at all surprised that it was Gemma who intercepted the supposedly secure, untraceable, private call. Jeffrey's bag of tricks weren't as good as he thought they were.

"You want to connect me to the woman I tried to call?" Kay asked.

"Sure, sure. But first, we need to verify your tracker." She looked offscreen for a moment. "I have you at one jump from Isere Junction, on Station JCS-77 orbiting Camden."

Gemma squinted and then read out Kay's exact location from the station map.

"Yeah, that's accurate. Now can I talk to Ayaan?"

Gemma waved good-bye and the screen flickered for a moment, before her grinning face was replaced by Ayaan. Kay felt a little pathetic that it had been just shy of a week, and she already just wanted to stare at her girlfriend for a bit.

Ayaan smiled. "Back in uniform again, I see?"

"Check out the bars," Kay said, leaning into the camera. "I'm an officer."

"I'll be sure to note that on your records for when you get back."

"I didn't think this qualifies as a field promotion," Kay said with a grin.

Ayaan sighed. "You're happy when you have a mission."

Kay shrugged. She wasn't about to start a million miles away argument on her last possible call back home. "Tell Jordan her mother's helping us out. Maybe don't mention she's going to give up her Senatorial seat over this."

Ayaan nodded. "We've made some progress here, but it's still slow. I'm a bit jealous you'll be in action soon."

"You love that politics stuff," Kay said.

"Maybe. But there is something to be said for blowing things up now and then." She leaned into the camera. "Be careful."

"Always am," Kay said.

That made Ayaan laugh. "Yes, well, at least come back alive, okay?"

"Deal."

CHAPTER 9

JORDAN HELD HER head in her hands. "If I have to give one more three hour presentation only to be given the brush-off, I might just scream."

Ayaan patted her on the back as she slid into the car next to her. "You're actually quite good at this. And trust me, these brush-offs are inching us toward a resolution, whether you notice it or not. We have two out of five governments agreeing to release details. One more, and the rest will fall in line."

"Your optimism is encouraging." Jordan stared out the window as they drove the now familiar route back to the Nassien compound. The sun was shining for once, and she watched as they passed beyond the yellow stonework of central Bahai and moved into the more industrial gray suburbs. The smooth ride and quiet atmosphere lulled Jordan to sleep.

She woke up with a start when the car's com link came alive. Wiping the sleep out of her eyes, she looked out at the green forested landscape and knew they were in close proximity to the Nassien compound.

"Mother, where have you been?" Ayaan said.

Jordan turned back to see Nailah on the vid-link, frowning at the camera.

"I'm sending someone to you, I need you to keep this quiet until I get there."

"Quiet from whom?"

"Your grandmother, of course, and her staff. This person stays in your residence until I arrive."

Ayaan frowned. "Security vetted?"

Nailah raised an eyebrow.

"Yes, of course," Ayaan said. "What else can I know ahead of time?"

"Nothing you won't figure out on your own fast enough. Is Kay with you?"

"No. She's on a mission."

"Hmm. Unexpected, but might be a good thing. You can fill me in when I get there. I shouldn't be more than a day delayed. I have one final loose end to tie up."

Nailah cut the link and Jordan looked to Ayaan. "Something I should perhaps not have overheard?"

Ayaan shook her head. "She would have expected we were traveling together. And before you ask, no, we're not in the habit of smuggling people into the compound. I honestly don't know how she expects to accomplish this without Nana knowing. Bakri has eyes everywhere."

Jordan stared ahead at the road stretched before them. "I'd guess it's either related to Project Troy or to Kay's genetic background. Seems the two main areas where she's in opposition to her mother."

"Oh, they are in opposition on more than that," Ayaan said, "but I agree. She wouldn't have spoken openly about anything else."

In front of me, Jordan thought. Given the complicated nature of this family, it wasn't unexpected that more intrigue would creep in on them. She counted herself lucky there'd only been that one incident so far that involved armed conflict at the legislature. It certainly wasn't a dull experience so far.

Jordan separated from Ayaan once they reached the compound. She had a doctor visit that Ayaan had set up for her. A short walk from Nailah's residence and she was in the compound's clinic. She walked into the facility expecting a small affair, a nurse and perhaps a visiting doctor. What she found was a working hospital to envy those at any small Terran city. The modest two story building masked the five stories that existed underground. While she didn't get to see the full facility, the floor maps on her data pad showed her surgical facilities, triage and trauma, and a multitude of other specialties all in this building. She hadn't seen most of the Nassien compound, having spent more time in Bahai than here. It was far larger than she imagined, and unlike the hospital, it did not provide her with a full site map on her data pad. Some things remained classified and for good reason, she supposed.

Her wait in the hospital room was thankfully short when a young doctor entered.

"Good afternoon, Ser Arbatova. I'm Doctor Addy Nassien-Dasti."

Another branch of the Nassien tree. Jordan shook his hand. "Thank you for taking the time to see me."

"It's a pleasure. I did my understudies in Terran physiognomy and genetics. It was quite unexpected when I got the call from Auntie to come here."

So he wasn't the local doctor. Given his age, she expected Auntie to be Manji, but she didn't ask.

"Thanks to your release authorization, I've pulled your records from the Massi clinic in Gilgar. Most impressive what they and you have achieved. And twins no less! Have you been having any difficulties?"

"Just morning sickness."

"Unusual for Novans, but not unheard-of, especially for someone with such close Terran heritage. I can prescribe something for it if you like."

"No, it's not that bad," she said.

"Fine. I'd like to run a quick scan on you and the babies."

Jordan lay back while he verified her vitals and did a remote scan across her still-flat stomach. He flicked on a monitor overhead and she got to see a very accurate video of her two children.

"At eight weeks, they definitely look human, but visually at this point, we can't determine the biological male or female state of the babies. As you can see, both are developing on target for the first trimester."

Jordan looked closely and he manipulated the scan to show each embryo. She could see arms, legs, and what might have been an eye on one of them. "They are healthy?"

"Very much so." He turned off the monitor. "Terran and Novan physiognomy are nearly identical, as I'm sure you know. Under normal circumstances, you could expect an easy pregnancy."

She laughed. "Twins and easy don't seem to go together."

He smiled. "Relatively easy. That said, you've had issues in the past, so we'll want to keep a close eye on things. I'd like you to come in every three weeks so we can monitor their progress."

She felt a lead weight in her stomach that had nothing to do with the babies. Would she really still be here in three weeks? Given the slow crawl of politics and the increasing intransigence of the Terran government, it shouldn't have been a surprise to her.

What she didn't know, or want to know at this point, was how long it would be before she could see Dray again.

JORDAN FINISHED HER evening meal in Nailah's residence. The woman's staff ran the home impeccably in her absence, though Jordan would have preferred some company when she wasn't busy negotiating in Bahai. Like any first-time pregnant woman, Jordan wanted to talk about it and what to expect, and Nailah would have been a good choice for that. Ayaan was a few too many years her junior, and had not, as far as she knew, any experience with babies.

The com link buzzed her out of her reverie, and she answered the call from Ayaan. She seemed, for one of the first times, rattled.

"What is it?" Jordan asked.

"The package from my mother just arrived. You'll want to see this. Come in directly, security is expecting you."

Jordan slipped on a pair of shoes and hurried to Ayaan's residence. It was a short walk and true to her word, Ayaan had forewarned her security staff of her arrival. A sizable opened crate crowded the usually pristine front security office. She was let in with a minimal body scan and directed to Ayaan's central living room.

Jordan walked into the room and took in the scene. Ayaan was standing by an arm chair, facing Jordan. She had one bodyguard, Joris, who seemed to be holding back a grin, poorly in Jordan's mind. And the object of Ayaan's consternation stood in the middle of the floor. A youngish girl with shoulder-length blond hair, wearing a military cadet uniform if Jordan's guess was right. And if Jordan's other guess was also correct, the face of that young girl was going to look remarkably familiar.

"Who is our young guest?" she asked, stepping into the tense triangle.

The young girl turned to her with a face that matched the images she had of a twelve-year-old Katherine Drawback.

"This is—" Ayaan began.

"I am KDTX-02128 Generation 1, creche A, Replicant 3," the girl said.

Jordan shot a quick look at Ayaan, but the woman wasn't adapting well yet to Nailah's surprise. Jordan held out her hand. "Nice to meet you. I'm Jordan."

The girl gave a crisp shake. Now Jordan found it hard to hide her own grin. The child was nearly identical to Kay, except for one detail. "You have brown eyes."

The girl just frowned at her.

"X is for experimental," Ayaan said. "She isn't an exact duplicate of Kay."

That got the girl's attention. She whipped her head around to Ayaan. "You know one of my replicants?"

Ayaan smirked. "Yes, I do. KDTU-02128, sorry, I can't recall creche and replicant number. She goes by the name Kay."

"Terran Unaltered," the girl said in awe.

"Do you have a name for yourself?" Jordan asked.

"Nicknames are not allowed," she said.

Ayaan sat on the chair. "Have you heard of the Black March?"

The girl's eyes widened. "Yes, ser."

"I am a retired Black March officer. I've worked with many gene lines. I can assure you, they all have nicknames." She smiled. "Regardless of protocol. It's very difficult to say your full gene-line designation in the mess hall when someone wants you to pass the salt, isn't it?"

The girl ducked her head, her blond hair cascading to cover her face. "Sometimes they call me K-D."

"Katie, that fits well," Jordan said. She looked to Ayaan. "Did your mother send any details at all?"

Ayaan shook her head. "Nothing at all. And you don't want to know how our dear Katie arrived."

Jordan remembered the crate in security. "And that passed through Compound security?"

"Kitchen supplies," Ayaan said. "And a good portion of it was. Katie, the shower is down the end of the right corridor. Make use of it."

"Yes, ser." Katie left.

Jordan watched her go. "So your mother sneaks one of Kay's gene line in here without your grandmother in the know. Seems more directly involved with Kay than with Project Troy."

"Most likely, yes. My mother was never one to be predictable."

Jordan hid her disappointment. She'd hoped for more help from Nailah, but then the woman wasn't politically involved like the rest of her family. "What do we do now?"

Ayaan got up and stretched. "Now, we wait."

The wait lasted the rest of that day and night. Jordan woke up the next morning to an urgent summons from Ayaan to meet in the main hall before breakfast. Jordan threw on clean clothes and rushed out. She could hear the shouting match long before she entered the room to see yet another standoff happening between Nassiens.

Manji tapped her cane on the floor, emphasizing every word she spat at her daughter, Nailah. "You broke protocol and possibly destroyed years of work!"

"That work is one child, and I saved her life."

Ayaan joined Jordan as they both entered the room and caught the glaring eye of Manji. "You, bring that child here."

Ayaan signaled her guard who spoke softly into his com link. Jordan looked at the other guards aligned around the room and took her cue from them to relax. Whatever this scene might be, it wasn't as volatile as all the shouting suggested. How the guards could tell the difference, she didn't know, but at least it wasn't going to literally end in violence.

Katie came in, escorted by another of Ayaan's guards. She took in the room in a rapid scan, but otherwise, she seemed calm. The guard stopped at Ayaan but Manji waved the girl forward and she complied.

Manji lifted the girl's chin and studied her a moment, then let go. "Name."

"Designation is . . ."

Manji cut her off. "Name."

Katie glanced back to Jordan and Ayaan. "Katie."

Manji dropped her hand back to her cane. "She goes to Zayn and Gemma's residence."

"She stays with me," said Ayaan.

Manji's cane slapped down with a sharp crack. "With the other children." She turned away. "One stolen clone is enough for you." With a flick of her wrist, one of her guards stepped forward and escorted Katie out.

Jordan could sense the anger surrounding Ayaan, right down to the rapid tap tap tap of her hand against her thigh, so much like her grandmother's cane tapping, Jordan almost smiled. Instead she caught Ayaan's eye and shook her head. Now was not the time for a head to head clash. They lacked any real information on what was going on here.

"Are there more Draybeck clones?" Jordan asked, emphasizing her legal familial link with them all.

Manji scowled at her as she sank into one of the chairs. "Nailah? Since you've seen fit to take over the project."

"Spare me your dramatics, Mother." Nailah took a seat on the sofa and waved them forward. "Have a seat. I'm sure she has breakfast on the way."

A door opened to Jordan's left as if some silent signal had transpired, and in came the expected breakfast, set out as a buffet on a central low table between the chairs. She considered asking her question again when the staff left, but Nailah hadn't forgotten it.

"The sad fact that my mother doesn't wish to acknowledge is that there's been a systematic effort to eliminate that gene line in the past few years." Nailah held up a hand. "Nothing against Kay. It's a personal vendetta against my family, and it's not the only gene line targeted by Halabi."

That name again. "So, are there any other of Kay's gene line left?" Jordan asked.

Nailah shook her head. "That girl was the last I could find. Even before Halabi joined the program, the survival rate had been exceptionally low."

"You accessed classified records," Manji said.

"Gemma. You really should raise her security clearance. She's quite exceptional at what she can do." Nailah sipped her tea. "The real question I'd like an answer to is why so few clones survived, Mother."

"So would I," Ayaan said. "If the gene line was being tested for situational awareness traits, there should have been more survivors."

"It wasn't," Manji said.

"That's what those classified records stated," Nailah said.

"Those records also stated the gene line was begun by your father. Don't believe everything you read in stolen records." Manji dabbed at the corners of her mouth with a napkin. "The gene line was mine from the start, and believe me, I had no long-term interest in situational awareness, no matter how good the genetic original was as a Terran pilot."

"Then what?" Nailah asked.

Manji turned to Ayaan. "Ask her. She's intimately familiar with the last unaltered clone."

Ayaan stared blankly at the table for a moment and then looked up at Manji. "Loyalty."

"That's crazy, you can't isolate a set of genes for loyalty," Nailah said.

"Says the child who barely passed her genetics courses," Manji said.

"It's an emotional and environmental reaction in a person," Ayaan said. "How can you isolate that into a set of genes to inject into the Novan population?"

Manji waved her hand dismissively. "That was never the point. Look at how long the gene line remained Terran Unaltered and at considerable expense no less." She leaned forward. "So many gene lines waste money on finding that tiny set of genes that can bring a desirable trait into the overall population. Why bother? Project Troy was a mess for many reasons, but one reason in particular has made it worthwhile. Or I hope it has. Jordan, if you had to describe your Draybeck wife in one word, what would it be?"

Jordan leaned back in her chair, her brain spinning on all that was being disclosed here. What was Dray's top trait? She turned back to Manji. "It hasn't changed. Loyalty."

"Exactly. The gene line was never a failure, even with Halabi's interference. The clones death rate is dramatic because they consistently put themselves in harms way. Every time." Manji turned to Ayaan. "Even your pet clone has proven the gene line so far."

"So far?" Ayaan asked.

"So far. The gene line has never interacted with itself. No familial ties, until now. The psychology of clones is a fascinating study. Socially, they have no real mother or father, yet as all humans do, they search for their own identity. With the introduction of the Draybeck family, will Kay alter how she self-identifies now? And thanks to my daughter's interference, will this experimental clone stay true to her gene line, or also self-alter based on either Kay or the Draybeck family?" Manji stood. "You've all done an excellent job of muddying the waters on a genetic study that has gone on for two generations. I've yet to determine if I owe you thanks or a slap in the face for that."

Jordan watched her leave, feeling it would be a bit of both in the end. You don't try to predict a Draybeck with conflicted loyalties.

CHAPTER 10

KAY LEANED ACROSS the console table, staring down at a map of the interior of the *Lazarus*. "It's big."

Jeffrey sat next to her in the cramped travel compartment they shared on Isere. "Big enough to house fifteen thousand, over time. The original generation ships set out with a populace of five thousand and room to grow before reaching their destination in a century or more. If Chandrika's leaked reports are correct, we are nearing five thousand already on this ship. It won't be easy to find the Draybecks in that mess, and that's not even the bad news."

"What's the bad news?"

"Getting a population that size to agree to redirect the ship out of Terran space for now."

Kay shrugged. "We don't. Crew size must be significantly smaller. Overtake them, then use the same containment they use to keep the Project Troy populace under control until we're in neutral space. Then we pull the Draybecks off ship and let the rest decide what they want to do with themselves."

Jeffrey scratched his three-day old beard, an affectation to ensure he wasn't easily identified now that they were in Terran space. "I wish I had your simplified philosophy." He turned to her. "You have to remember you're Terran now, in Terran space. These aren't your enemies anymore."

Easier said than done. She hadn't managed to stop scanning everything and everyone for their relative threat potential, but she had gotten better at masking that's what she was doing. At least Jeffrey hadn't noticed it lately. Then again, he'd been preoccupied with shifting their identities and ensuring she was back in the Terran databases as an alive and young Katherine Draybeck.

"Did your contacts specify crew size?" she asked.

"Ship crew itself is under twenty, but then there is an additional thirty armed guards to monitor the detainees. The ship isn't set up as a prison, so they have to rely more on isolating the population from the rest of the ship." He pointed to the map. "If they modified these few access points, they would be able to cut the general living areas away from the crew quarters and the overall operation of the ship. Put guards at those points, and you have good control."

"Too good control," Kay said. "Unless you can compromise some of your new guard buddies to join our revolution."

"That's where Kelvin comes in. His last communication gave me the names and post descriptions for fifteen trusted Intel agents already on board the *Lazarus*. It's not much, but enough to say we could gain control over at least one access point, if not more. If you can convince a few of your new Project Troy buddies, we'll have a viable fighting force, if needed."

He turned to her. "Last chance to back out."

"And why would I want to do that now?"

"Because you're in Terran space with a Terran ID. Maybe you just wanted to escape Novan space?"

"Maybe I was just shit-ton bored and needed something interesting to do." She stared back at the map to memorize as much as she could. They had less than a day left to find any weaknesses in the overall structure that could help their plan, a plan that seemed a lot more solid when they were still in Novan space.

They left the compartment two hours later, as prisoner and guard. Jeffrey wore a drab gray uniform with the name Weber on the front and rank of staff sergeant. Kay had her same blue Terran officer's uniform on, name Draybeck and rank first lieutenant. She also sported an ankle band that, had it been operational, would allow Jeffrey or any other guard to zap her with enough juice to flatten her if she tried to escape. Just like the scar on her temple, though, it was a fake with just enough authenticity to get her past the Terran security checkpoints. They both carried duffle bags with the rest of their meager belongings. For Kay, it was a second uniform, toiletries, and some fake personal items.

Isere Junction was a squirming mass of Terrans and their allies. Most were civilians, dressed strangely to Kay's eyes, but dotted amongst them were Terran military in familiar uniforms, uniforms she'd shot at for years. And a few aliens. One set in particular caught Kay's eyes, a clustered group of nonhumans with matted brown and green, something sprouting from their heads.

She nudged Jeffrey. "What are they?"

He glanced to where she pointed. "Aquarans."

"Never seen them on a mission."

"You were ground troops, right? Aquarans are nearly always deployed on naval vessels. They require a controlled atmosphere with a very high level of humidity."

She turned away from the group as she and Jeffrey approached their first important checkpoint. Unlike the other transit points on their journey, this one had a heavy military presence, with armed guards on each side of the passageway leading to the checkpoint scanners. Also, unlike every other transit point, this one was nearly empty. As they approached, only one other pair were in front of them, another guard escorting an older person in civilian clothes.

"Prisoner or detainee?" she asked Jeffrey.

He looked ahead. "Impossible to tell, really. This military shuttle is making multiple stops."

The checkpoint scan was thorough. Jeffrey was taken to the side by one guard while two others, both female, scanned Kay and her luggage. The chip ID worked perfectly, as it had previously, but this time it had the added change of identifying her as a detainee. Like the civilian in line before her, that tidbit got Kay even more fun scans, including and extra body pat-down and dental check. As if she were hiding Novan secrets in her teeth.

Then again, maybe someone had hidden something in their teeth. Anyway, after a full thirty minutes, she and her bag were released back into Jeffrey's custody. His demeanor changed to one of pure indifference, full on guard duty mode. She marveled at how well he carried it off, but then again, he was a Terran spy with years of experience at this.

The only demeanor she had to carry off was one of sullen discontent. She didn't linger on how easily that came to her. Instead, she took the opportunity to glower at every Terran she passed, most of whom were easy to glower at as they were Naval personnel, and she'd lost enough squad mates to Naval overhead fire to be able to channel some real anger out. It felt great.

Jeffery took a quiet opportunity where no one else was around in the passage to nudge her in the elbow. "Tone it down before you start a fight."

Kay considered how much fun a fist fight might be right now, but rejected the idea and took his advice. Her glower simmered down to an annoyed frown by the time they were escorted onto their final transport shuttle that would take them to the location of the *Lazarus*.

She wasn't assisted to her chair and buckled in so much as locked and restrained into place. A glance at her fellow shuttle passengers answered her prior question. Too many wore military uniforms and had that look about them that said criminals. Of course, she likely looked the same to them, but she and the older civilian person were the only two with their own pet guards. She glanced at her fellow detainee—tall, thin, with a weathered brown complexion and a curious gaze that winked at her when their eyes met. She nodded and turned away.

The ship itself wasn't much different in design than some of the others they'd travelled on, except it was smaller. The cabin could have held twice as many as it currently had. She'd counted nine prisoners, three cabin guards besides Jeffrey and the other detainee guard. As for ship crew, none were visible. Given the small size of the ship, she guessed only two at most on crew.

The engines came to life beneath her boots. She leaned back into her seat and shut her eyes. It would be a long, silent flight since Jeffrey's guard persona wasn't going to be the chatty kind. In seven hours and two FTL jumps, they would arrive at the transfer station where the *Lazarus* sat in orbit, waiting to pick up more like her.

In seven hours, the real fun would start.

GATE ACCESS SPOKE five, D-stack.

That was Jeffrey's last command, hand-signaled to her after he got his assignment, right before guard and detainees were separated. Unlike the other guards who were mere bounty hunters, Jeffrey was assigned to the *Lazarus* itself. The last she saw of him was the back of his head as he disappeared down a corridor with two other guards, hopefully not new ones or that jumped their estimated opposition numbers up higher.

Kay was on her own now.

She pictured the toroidal shape of the *Lazarus*, with crew in the central hub and multiple access spokes connecting to the outer rim that housed the living space for an entire mini population. Jeffrey was stationed in the fifth spoke, controlling the population from the D-stack living quarters. Unlike a standard military transport, the living quarters were formed in a staggered stack, each with access to the spokes. She knew where he would be, now she had to find out where she would be, and eventually, where the Draybecks were.

Before that, they had a sixteen hour trip from the station out to where the massive generation ship sat far from the normal traffic lanes in and out of the system. Kay stood beside a cluster of other fresh, new detainees—three in military uniforms like her, and four civilians, including the older person from the prior leg of her journey who hovered near her like they were old buddies. Then again, on a trip like this, maybe they were.

"Ex-pilot?" the older person asked in a smooth gender-ambiguous voice.

"Yeah," Kay said. "How'd you guess?"

"The uniform and the scar on your temple. My wife was a pilot as well. Died in the first Novan war."

"Sorry about that," Kay said, then corrected herself so it sounded less like an apology for her part in the current war. "I mean sorry for your loss."

"Ages ago at this point. Marry into the military, and you have to expect something like that might happen."

"If you don't mind my asking," she said. "How did you end up here, I mean if you were a civilian back then, too?"

"Unlucky enough to have been traveling in a district with a distinct Purist bent when the mandatory scans started." The person waved a hand at themselves. "Gender non-binary. I didn't fit someone's mold of the ideal Terran."

Kay widened her eyes. "That's barbaric."

"I'm a retired sociology professor. Believe me, I won't be the only illegally detained person on this new ship. That is reality when a society decides some people are not fit to remain in the general population." They held out a hand. "I'm Desi Aguilar."

"Katherine Draybeck," she said aloud for the first time. "Legally detained." Ironic that she'd be the only one lying about that on this mission.

Their chitchat died down when a pair of guards came up to the group. One remained alert with a shock rifle resting in his arms while the other bent down and detached the ankle restraint from each of them. They were beyond the point of any escape. Kay didn't have to watch the pair for long to realize only one was present to police them. He was dressed in gray as Jeffrey had been, while the other was in a drab green uniform with the *Lazarus* ship logo stitched to the front of her shirt.

The armed guard led them down a different corridor from the one Jeffrey had taken. Kay fell in line near the middle of the group and followed along as they progressed down a ramp and out into an open bay area.

Her first sight of the *Lazarus* shuttle was less impressive than she'd imagined. There was a large expanse of open space in the bay in front of them that ended in a broad hull of carbon nanotube alloy, instead of the stronger plasteel that had been in use for ages. She knew the ship was old, but that old? And couldn't they have given it a more modern shuttle craft?

The bay itself was filling up with massive crates slowly being hauled into the shuttle's cargo hold to their right. They on the other hand were headed for a smaller open hatch on the left, meant for the human cargo.

Each detainee was scanned again as they entered one at a time through the hatch. Their luggage was taken from each of them for a separate investigation. Kay handed over her bag and paused for her scan, no longer nervous that they would detect her Novan tracker at this point. She then stepped through the hatch and smelled that distinct scent that must be universal on all ships—sterile air and sanitizer. It would have felt like home if she wasn't surrounded by Terrans and not shooting any of them.

Then again, their sole armed guard could do with a bullet grazing to wake him up from whatever stupor he was in. If this was the best the *Lazarus* had, then a takeover would be a piece of cake.

The hatch led into a short passageway where they were shifted into groups of three. The woman in the drab green *Lazarus* crew uniform coordinated the groups.

She looked at Kay, took in the uniform at a glance. "Stand to the right."

Kay moved to the side as the woman picked Desi next, then skipped over the next in line, another military person, to grab a third civilian for Kay's little group. Keeping the military personnel isolated from each other—smart.

"Name and Chip IDs," the woman said.

Kay and Desi held out their hands and she scanned them as they said their names. The other civilian, a middle-aged man who spoke Terran with an accent thick enough that Kay couldn't understand him, sounded like his name was Enzo.

"You are in temporary berth 2-15. Your luggage will meet you there."

And that was it. Another bored crew mate led them down the passageway to a stairwell that took them down a level. Then it was a long walk down a narrow passageway with closed hatches on either side until the guard stopped outside the first open hatch. Kay stepped into their berth first. It was a tight space with four bunks bolted to the bulkhead and just enough space in between to get in each other's way. On the plus side, there was only three of them so far. Kay peeled off her uniform jacket and tossed it on the bottom right bunk, claiming her spot. She turned back to the crew mate.

"Where's the closest head?"

"End of the passageway." He glanced at Desi. "Universal. Full details on this shuttle and the *Lazarus* has been sent to your data pads."

He left them there, Desi and Enzo staring in at her but not yet stepping across the open hatchway.

She sat down on her bunk. "Might as well pick your spot."

"It's tiny," Desi said, stepping inside and doing one tight turn. "They expect four people to travel like this?"

Kay shrugged. "You get used to it. And it's temporary." She pulled out her data pad and scanned for the new information she had on the *Lazarus*. It was a familiar layout, but the overlay was new, detailing where the detainees were located. She zoomed in on that and handed it to Desi. "See? Says we'll be living there eventually."

He looked at it, zooming in and out. "Well, better than this I suppose."

Enzo stepped in and glanced over Desi's shoulder. "Is that a river? On a ship?"

Kay accepted her data pad back from Desi. "Controlled waterway, yes. The ship we're headed to is set up for long-term civilian living, like centuries."

Desi put a jacket on the bunk above Kay. "It's why they picked this ship for us. All the comforts of a sizable refugee camp, without worry of any escape or spill-over into the pure Terran population. No Terran planet was willing to take us all in is what I hear."

Kay wasn't surprised by that. Still, a short-term fix to a longer-term Terran problem that gave her and Jeffrey the chance they needed to free the Draybecks.

After that, it was the Terrans problem what to do with the rest.

MUCH LIKE THE shuttle, the actual *Lazarus* failed to impress on first arrival. The same ancient carbon construction greeted them when they disembarked into the central crew hub of the ship. Reunited with her duffle bag, Kay scanned the open docking bay. With Desi standing next to her, staring wide-eyed at their surroundings, Kay had no trouble using the same awed tourist approach to study as much of the crew area as she could and match it to the schematics she'd memorized with Jeffrey. With a crew of only twenty, most of the people she saw now were the guards that would keep the detainees under control.

Still, it was neither a drab green *Lazaurus* crew member nor a gray armed guard who greeted them in a meeting room adjacent to the docking bay. Instead, it was a young civilian man a little too perky for his role.

"Welcome to the *Lazarus*! I know your trip has likely been stressful, and while none of us want to be here, I can assure you this ship is fully equipped to make our stay here as comfortable as possible."

"Happy for a detainee," Desi whispered to her. Too damned happy for someone who just had all their legal rights stripped from them. "But does he work for us or for them?"

Kay turned to Desi and frowned.

They patted her arm. "Don't let the pleasantries fool you. There is always an us and a them, and those who think they benefit from collaborating with the 'them' who control the rest of us."

Kay smiled. "Contemplating the revolution already?"

"Always, child. Always."

Chock up one civilian ally. Kay focused back on the litany of noise that came out of their welcome party's mouth. Did civilians always have to put up with this much bullshit wrapped around their commands? If this were a marine sergeant, it would have all been shouted out with a simple "find your bunk, mind the rules, and shut the fuck up about your personal problems."

Right about the point where Kay was ready to start the revolution early just to shut the guy up, the welcome speech ended and they were assigned quarters in the same groups of three or four that they'd travelled with on the shuttle. She and what seemed to be her semi-permanent bunkmates were led with the rest of their shuttle passengers down a corridor, past the intersection Kay knew would lead to crew quarters, and to an elevator that took them down two levels. The sign above a central tube said Spoke Three. So she was half a ship away from Jeffrey's post. That was inconvenient but not impossible to deal with. They boarded the spoke tube transport in groups of ten and were whisked out to the rim in less than a minute. Detail one to discover—were the spoke tubes pressurized and oxygenated? If so, they wouldn't need the transports to gain access to the crew hub. If not, that complicated things and would make it easier for the crew to shut them out if their coup didn't succeed fast enough.

Disembarking from the transport was like getting off a ground shuttle. There was a breeze, an actual breeze in the air and the scent of something besides artificially sterilized air. This time, Kay's expression of awe wasn't faked, and she had to remind herself to look back at the signage to realize she was on C-stack. A few steps down from the transport tube and their perky young welcomer left them in the care of a pair of less perky teenagers. Now the litany felt more realistic in the bored monotone of one of the teens.

"Welcome to Three-C. Three is our spoke, C is this stack. Remember that if you get lost." She waved a hand behind her as if to take in the entire visible portion of the torus. "We have a sustainable living ecosystem here, with planetary-like atmospheric conditions, including clouds and rain, so pay attention to your weather updates. The stacks are laid out in a vertical grid. Your party is on," she glanced down at her data pad, "the seventeenth block, building two, apartments five through twelve."

She turned and started down the walkway. Her partner, equally bored, waited to follow behind them and prevent any strays. They passed their first prefab modular house where the girl paused and pointed to the sign on the building. "Each building number is clearly visible, and each block corner is marked as well."

They crossed two intersections before the housing section opened up to include a grassy openspace area. "Designated open space occurs every two blocks and are open to all residents regardless of your block designation."

Another quiet march along before they hit one more sizable intersection, with access to the stacks above and below, and an opening to see the controlled waterway that spanned the entire length until it slopped up with the curve of the rim and out of sight. Kay could see agricultural plots with what appeared to be the bright green of early seedlings growing in some of them while others remained patches of brown dirt.

The tour ended abruptly at their designated building. "Your chip ID gets you access to the building and your apartment. See your data pad for your assigned apartment number. Each apartment is furnished. Watch the intro vid before you leave your building. Welcome to the *Lazarus*."

And that was it. The two teens walked away with more liveliness than they exhibited for the length of their short tour. Kay deliberately slowed herself down, pulling out her data pad to check her assigned apartment, then followed the others inside after the first person palmed the access panel beside the front door. Seemed simple enough, but Kay watched again as Enzo palmed access to his apartment two doors down from hers.

Desi gave her an encouraging nod before disappearing into their own apartment. Kay stood in front of her own door, apartment four, and slapped her right hand on the access panel. The door clicked, and she pushed it open. First time she had to use her Terran chip ID other than to pass security checkpoints, and it worked fine.

She stepped into the studio apartment and took it in with a quick glance. Tiny kitchen with built in counter and stool were on her right. Facing her was a small sofa on the right with a low table in front of it, and the far left wall was blank where the pullout bed would be. All the comforts of home, including a broad window on the opposing wall that looked out onto the stacks below her and the open fields surrounding the waterway. Not a bad view if you had to live here for a long time.

That wasn't the plan though.

Kay dropped her bag by the door, sat on the sofa, and flipped up the vid screen. It opened to a welcome video that she cancelled and then checked the screen menu for more important details. Ship time read 19:00 hours, past normal meal times. She flipped back to the amenities menu and discovered they had a communal kitchen where they could share main meals. What she was looking for wasn't present—no ship directory had been assembled. So much for an easy way to find the Draybecks. She flipped a few more screens before there was a knock on her door. It wouldn't be Jeffrey, and she had only one other associate so far, so she wasn't surprised to see Desi standing there when she opened the door.

They brushed past her and sat on the sofa. "I assume you have no plans for the evening so I thought I'd invite myself to a far better Welcome to the *Lazarus* party."

Kay grinned. "Well, I do have a task. I have family aboard here somewhere, but there's no directory listed."

"Ah," Desi said, sitting up. "Finding relatives in a refugee camp. Funny how the powers that be never bother helping with that one." They stood up. "Let's head for the main dining hall."

"It's past meal time," she said, stepping out of their way as they walked out to the hallway.

"Food and community go together at all hours. And more importantly, so does the information network. You have relatives, someone down at the dining hall will know how to find them. Come."

Desi walked on with the assumption that Kay would follow, and she did. Kay hadn't thought to what extent a civilian friend would benefit her, but she was realizing the perks of that already.

The dining hall was set up cafe style, and true to Desi's word, it had more than a few detainees mingling about, drinking and talking. There was one cluster of military personnel in a variety of Terran uniforms off to one side, but Desi led them to the more boisterous group hanging around the coffee machines.

A broad-faced woman greeted them first. "Newcomers? Grab a cup, pull up a chair, and tell us your tale." She waved a hand at herself. "I'm Greta Dunen, mother of four, grandmother of fifteen Terran undesirables." Her words were harsh but her smile real and Kay grinned back. "Katherine Draybeck. And I'm looking for my family."

There were a few more welcome greetings before a hand grabbed her arm and twisted her about. She looked up into a pair of dark blue eyes on a cold pale face.

"Draybeck," the man growled. "Didn't a Draybeck start this mess?"

He was the front man for a party of three other goons, all who looked drunk or high, take your pick, but Kay had seen more than her fair share of the likes of them. She twisted out of his grip.

"Yeah, Draybeck," she said. "And this shit started decades before she was born." Weight on the balls of her feet, hands already clenched in fists, she was ready for this fight. Hell, she'd been ready for weeks to let off a bit of steam, and this guy's ugly face seemed as good a place to land the first punch as any.

Her adrenaline rush was left high and dry when the group of military personnel surrounded her.

"Call it a night, buddy," the lead NCO, a Terran grounder sergeant, said. "We won't be pounding any Terran officers tonight."

The guy glared at Kay but backed down. She glanced at her own lieutenant stripes and tried to think how an officer would respond to her rescuer.

"Thanks, sergeant," she said.

The sergeant, a woman a good decade or more her senior, saluted her. "No problem, Ma'am. That said, with your name, you may want to keep a low profile, or come get one of us before you wander around. Your relative isn't the most popular person on board right now."

Great. Not only was she a Novan spy, she was sporting one of the most hated names on the ship. Wouldn't that just make things that much more fun?

CHAPTER 11

JORDAN'S INTERACTION WITH Gemma and Zayn in the past weeks was enough to tell her the two teenagers that rushed into Nailah's residence were terrified. Nailah sat at the breakfast table finishing her coffee when the two came in, both talking at once.

"One at a time," Nailah said. "And with less panic please."

They gave a silent nod between them.

"Mala Halabi is gone," Zayn said.

Nailah put down her cup with a harder clunk than normal. Both teenagers flinched.

"Security is aware and is pursuing the matter," Zayn added.

"Fine," Nailah said. "No tell me exactly how this happened."

"It was my fault," Gemma said. "I was assigned to her for additional information gathering in a less formal environment. We've been meeting once or twice a day for the last three days. When I went into her cell today, she was unconscious on the bed. She'd cut her wrists."

Nailah raised an eyebrow.

"I called for medical to transport her to a hospital," Gemma said.

"Which hospital," Nailah asked.

"Nassien Military," Gemma said. "Mala's still a prisoner. Halabi's forces attacked the ambulance as soon as it left our compound and took her."

Nailah stared at her half empty coffee cup for long enough that Jordan stepped in.

"Do you remember how she cut her wrists? Was it vertical, or horizontal?" Jordan asked.

Gemma held up her wrist and made a horizontal slash. Jordan noticed the blood on her sleeves. "It's unlikely Mala would die from those kinds of wounds. Meanwhile, you should probably get cleaned up."

Gemma turned to Nailah. "Nana will find out."

Nailah looked back up. "Nana likely already knows."

"Auntie, I'm sorry." Gemma looked one step away from tears.

"Not your fault. If it was a legitimate suicide attempt, Security would have done the same thing. Go, wash up. I'll deal with my mother when the time comes."

Both kids left the residence in subdued silence. Jordan waited until they were gone to ask the obvious question. "Do you think it was a real attempt?"

"You said it yourself. That kind of cut wouldn't have been fatal. Given that Halabi's forces were ready and waiting to rescue her . . ."

"Or recapture her."

Nailah nodded. "Either way, it was expected and well-played. The question now becomes, why."

Jordan sat back at the table. "Either the attack on Ayaan was real, or it was staged. If it was real, then Mala was telling the truth and has likely just gone to her own real death."

"And if it was staged," Nailah said. "What was the purpose of it all? Mala's internment here was short and ineffective. It doesn't make sense."

Jordan wasn't convinced. Mala was too expensive a pawn to waste on this deadly chess game between the two families. If the attack had succeeded, they'd all be dead or captured. Given the attack failed deliberately, Mala must have had some other primary goal, as deadly or more if she'd been captured. Jordan remembered the stain on Gemma's sleeve.

"Blood-born pathogen," she said, looking up at Nailah.

To her credit, Nailah understood instantly and shouted the residential AI alive. "Message the twins. Do not launder that shirt and stay in their residence. Accept no visitors. Enact Second-level bio lockdown procedure for the compound."

Amber lights flashed within the residence and along the outside pathways. Even from a distance, Jordan could see the uniformed guards marching at double-speed. The efficiency was admirable. The life that required such preparedness, she could do without.

Her hand went to her stomach. And so could her unborn children. "What happens next?"

Nailah went back to her coffee. "We wait. If it's blood-born, we're minimally at risk. Gemma is first priority, along with the guards and cleanup crew for the cell Mala was in. It isn't the most efficient way to kill us off, so long as it's contained."

Nailah's words were calm but by now Jordan could recognize the barely restrained anger in that calm facade. It was another attack on her family, a well-planned one at that.

Within ten minutes, they had their own visitors in full biohazard suits and were instructed to strip down, put their clothes in a sealable bag, and were then led out of the residence wearing thin, disposable top, pants, and padded slippers. A short ride in a site shuttle brought them to the medical wing that Jordan was already familiar with. This time, instead of seeing her doctor for a checkup, she and Nailah were brought into a separate entrance, stripped, and showered down, then set up in individual, sealed hospital rooms.

Poked, prodded, and left on her own, Jordan went over the scenario again in her head. She was reasonably good at recognizing character traits, and to her, Mala was genuinely afraid when they were escaping the legislature. Then again, if she was a disposable pawn, she'd have plenty to be afraid of. Either a willing conspirator or a victim, either way the girl was out of their reach now.

Two hours passed before the nurse came in, this time without a biosuit. "You are free to go, Ser Arbatova. You're blood tests have all come back negative to the pathogen." She handed her a sealed package with her clothes, presumably sterilized as well.

"It's been identified?" Jordan asked as she got up to dress.

"I'm sorry, that information is classified at this point."

Dressed and released, Jordan went back to Nailah's residence, not surprised to see the older woman there already. She didn't have to ask the obvious question when she stepped in.

"Hemorrhagic bio-weapon," Nailah said. "We are so very good at assassination options around here."

"Gemma?"

Jordan noticed Nailah tapping her side just as Ayaan did.

"Gemma is in isolation, along with two of the guards involved in helping Mala into the ambulance."

Nailah stopped as the door to her residence opened and Ayaan came in with a rush of air. As mother and daughter stood face to face, the resemblance was unmistakable, as was the tension. For once, the tension wasn't between them, but directed at their common enemy.

"We have eyes on the rescue vans last locations."

"Multiple locations?" Jordan asked.

Ayaan turned to her as if just realizing she wasn't alone with her mother. "Yes. We have planet-wide access to all video surveillance fed into our AI. Within minutes of the rescue our drones were in the air hunting them down."

"Put a feed of each location up on the living room screen, please," Nailah said to the ever-listening security AI.

They walked into that room just as the wall came alive with three individual shots. The first was of a waterfront dock, isolated from any other buildings. The second and third screens showed what looked like an office building in the center of Bahai, and a park of some sort, bustling with people.

"What next," Jordan asked. The first screen lit up before she got an answer. Whatever was at the dock was obliterated. Her eyes widened. "You can't blow up the other two."

Nailah turned to her just as the second and third screens showed flashes of light and then smoke. "We aren't known for our subtlety, but you are correct. What you are seeing is the deployment of large-scale shock bombs." She looked back at the screen as multiple helicopters landed at the park and soldiers in full hazard gear poured out. "Bahai police will arrive shortly as well, but our teams will have ID'd and detained most people present at these sites for questioning."

"And Mala?" Jordan asked.

"It won't matter, really," Ayaan said. "If she's survived this long, she will likely be dead by the end of the day. The progression of this bio-weapon is rapid. Most of the round up will be to limit the potential pathogen spread."

Given the cleverness of their enemy, Jordan didn't expect they would find anything useful in their roundup. "Is there hope for Gemma?"

Ayaan's shoulders remained stiff as she sat in front of the screens, watching the search and detention happen. "She's feverish."

Nailah patted Jordan's arm. "We don't know the extent of damage her organs might sustain from this, but thanks to your quick analysis, she will live."

Ayaan turned at that. "Jordan figured this out?"

"She came up with the idea that Mala was a biological weapon of sorts, yes."

Ayaan got up and took Jordan's hand. "Thank you. You saved my cousin's life."

"And many others," Nailah added. "We are in your debt, once again."

Jordan accepted their thanks but her mind was on Gemma. This was at least the second time the child was in danger. "When Hadro's wife died and we found the twins, was that a Halabi attack as well?"

"No," Nailah said. "We sent an investigation team to the crash site after your Terran force retreated. The ship data pointed to damage sustained from a debris field. It was an accident."

"This wasn't," Ayaan said, waving a hand at the screens. "It wasn't a direct attack on me either."

Nailah nodded. "He's going to lose political capital over this, certainly." She turned to Jordan. "While his attempts had one lone target, he could claim family revenge for his father's death."

"And my status as an unplanned pregnancy meant I was a less than ideal heir to the Nassien leadership," Ayaan said. "Halabi wasn't alone in preferring I didn't exist."

Nailah's jaw clenched. "Making your full genetic analysis public record eroded most other opposition to you."

"Leaving Halabi," Jordan said. "But now he's hit someone else. And presumably the twins have no real opposition?"

"None," Ayaan said. "Nana will have video shots of Gemma on every news channel within the hour. His associates could turn a blind eye on his attacks against me, but not with Gemma being a casualty of this latest attack."

"And we have Mala's confession as well. An undocumented child of his? We have her DNA to prove he is the father," Nailah said. "He's dug himself a deep hole this time."

Jordan watched the screens. Those in deep holes have nothing left to lose, she thought.

CHAPTER 12

THE DETAINEE PORTION of the ship may not have any official communications network, but the unofficial one had kicked in already by the time Kay went to the dining hall for breakfast the next morning. As a Terran clone in Novan space, she was used to facing down stares, but she hadn't realized that daily chore had disappeared once she'd entered Terran space with Jeffrey. Being blond and blue eyed wasn't the beacon of difference it had been. Yet this morning, faces turned when she stepped into the hall. Some were quick glances, some stares, none particularly friendly.

Two paces into the hall, she was greeted by the same sergeant from the night before. "Word travels fast, Ma'am."

"So I see," Kay said.

The sergeant offered her hand. "Sergeant Pratchett, Ma'am."

Kay shook her hand. "Lieutenant Katherine Draybeck."

They walked together to the breakfast buffet line. "Notoriety has its benefits, Ma'am. We set out some runners last night. Your relatives are at Five-D. Sorry we haven't found out what block yet."

"That's great," Kay said, surprised at Pratchett's efficiency.

"No problem. We created a rotation roster so that one of us is available when you set out."

Kay nodded. "I take it you have the short straw this morning."

Pratchett smiled. "Frankly, Ma'am, it feels good to have an assignment again. Some of us aren't cut out for civvie life."

So Kay had a bodyguard now. Well, it could prove useful once they laid plans on how to take over this crate of a ship. Assuming her bodyguard was amenable to a hostile takeover of the ship.

Part way through breakfast, Desi joined them, and now it was a cozy group of three who headed out for Spoke Five.

"Do we get to travel back to the hub at all?" Kay asked, when they passed the nearest spoke.

"No," Pratchett said. "Separation between *Lazarus* crew and detainees is strictly enforced. Any communication needs to go through the spoke-assigned MPs."

Military police, so that's what Jeffrey got himself assigned as. Kay glanced at the two MPs at Spoke Three. Neither looked particularly alert, but then they were keeping an eye on a mostly civilian population.

"Two military cops per spoke doesn't seem like enough for crowd control," Desi said.

Pratchett glanced back at them. "Each spoke is responsible for their own volunteer police force."

"And you are part of that for Spoke Three?" Kay asked as they progressed down the walkway.

"Civilians only. That's the rule that came up from planet side. They think the military detainees are dangerous." She tapped her temple. "Too many advanced adaptations."

"They think we're all dangerous," Desi said. "That's why we've been accelerating out of the system for days, and why it took so long for our shuttle to catch up."

Kay turned to them. "You found that tidbit out fast."

They shrugged. "Information is survival in a place like this."

Their walk went quickly through the blocks of each successive spoke, twenty blocks each, with ten buildings per block, and then past the guard station and hatchway that separated each spoke section from the other. There were people about in most blocks. Some with a purpose, others just staring out at anything that passed by. This all went by in a dull monotony of white buildings and gray sidewalks. The only interesting features were the different parks in every other block, some with children playing in them already.

Then they passed through the security checkpoint at Spoke Five and it all changed. Gone were the casual civilians and children. Here, there were two civilians with black vests and shock sticks—the local police force. Kay glanced up the stack to see similar monitors on the stack above.

"Spoke Five is restricted," the first police officer said.

Kay stepped forward. "My family is in there."

The officer glanced at her uniform and looked back up at her with wide eyes. "You shouldn't be wandering the stacks, Ma'am. It's not safe for you."

Kay waved at her companions. "I'm well taken care of."

The police let them pass into a section that looked the same as the rest but felt very different. There were fewer people milling about, and those that were watched them pass with a wary eye.

"Not the friendliest neighborhood," Desi said.

"They have reason," Pratchett said. "Been a few altercations since I got here. Like I said, the Draybeck name doesn't sit well with some. I'm surprised they didn't house you here with the rest of your family."

Given the rest of her family didn't know she existed, Kay wasn't surprised at all, but she kept that herself. They crossed block two, and she turned right to head up the steps to the next stack. The buildings between stacks stepped up on either side of the staircase, with a narrow access alley running between them.

Kay glanced to the right. A meaty hand grabbed her and pulled her into the alley on the left. A sizable older woman, gray haired and angry as hell slammed her against the back wall of the Stack C building.

"Who the hell are you?" she growled at Kay.

Desi and Pratchett squeezed into the narrow alley and pried the big woman off Kay. Kay straightened herself out. This whole walking target thing was getting old, fast. "I'm Katherine Draybeck. I'm looking for Helena Draybeck. Do you know her?"

The woman tensed but didn't try to break out of Pratchett's hold. "Yeah, I know Dray. I also knew Katherine. I served with her in the first Novan war. Where she died. You wear her face but the hell you are Katherine Draybeck."

Okay, someone who knew the real Katherine other than Dray was not something Jeffrey prepared her for. Now what the hell was she supposed to do? Kay saw the doubt flicker in her companions' eyes, especially Pratchett. Losing her bodyguard in a back alley with an enraged enemy wasn't top on Kay's to do list for the day.

She set herself on the balls of her feet just in case. "I will explain myself to Dray. If you know her then take me to her."

Pratchett loosened her grip on the woman. "What's your name, Ma'am?"

"Fenton." She took a step back. "I served with Katherine Draybeck, the real Katherine Draybeck. Spent time in a Novan prison with her as well. If she were still alive, she wouldn't look like a cadet straight out of school. She'd be in her fifties."

Pratchett turned back to Kay and then to Fenton. "Best bet is we get to the rest of the Draybecks and see what sense we can make of all this."

Okay, that was fairly neutral. Seems Kay hadn't totally lost her companions. Desi just eyed her with a smirk. Whatever they were thinking, it wasn't a scream of betrayal anyway.

Kay straightened up. "Lead the way to Dray."

Fenton seemed to consider her next move carefully, then shook her head. "Fine. For all the good it will do."

Fenton didn't elaborate as she turned up the stairs, and Kay didn't ask for details. She knew she was on thin ice as it was. Keep her mouth shut and make it to the Draybecks, that was her priority. Of course, that didn't stop the tangle of nerves and adrenaline rushing through her now. Close to a month of work had gone into making this happen and not all of it was to help Jordan. Step by step, she felt her anxiety rise for reasons that had nothing to do with her mission priorities, and it was pissing her off. Yeah, this was family, real, blood kin for the first time in her life. So what?

So what indeed when they walked the length of the first block on stack D and then Fenton opened the door to building five on the second block. Kay looked up at the same facade that covered every building on this ship and rolled her neck until it snapped, releasing some of her tension. She followed Fenton inside.

Apartment seven was locked, not unexpected given the situation. Fenton rapped at the door with her knuckles. They waited. Fenton turned to Kay with a smirk and shrugged, then rapped at the door harder.

"Dray, get up. This is something you'll want to see."

They waited again. If Kay wasn't separated from the door by Fenton and Pratchett, she'd give it a good solid kick in and be done with it. Fenton had her fist up to bang again when they heard the sounds of shuffling inside. The door opened, and there she was, Helena Draybeck.

She was a few centimeters shorter, with short hair tinged with red and a splash of freckles across her face, but Kay couldn't deny the resemblance. This was family.

"Here's a little surprise," Fenton said as she took a step to the side and waved her hand at Kay.

Dray looked at Fenton and then turned her gaze to Kay. One blue eye turned her way and one silver eye. Artificial. Kay's stomach did a flip that threatened to bring her meager breakfast back up for a second visit. Her relative was a freak with visible artificial implants.

Her relative also wasn't standing still any longer. In a blur of motion, Dray was past Fenton and Pratchett and had her hands wrapped around Kay's throat. Nothing like a deficit of air to bring a person to crystal clear focus on priorities. And Kay's priorities shifted in an instant from helping Jordan to surviving this mess.

Dray might be half crazed, but she was smaller, and a couple of months at least in confinement. Kay thrust her arms up between Dray's hands and broke the grip on her neck with ease. She tossed in a sold punch to Dray's midriff for good measure before Pratchett and Fenton got them separated.

And that was that for her first ever family reunion.

Desi stepped forward. "Perhaps we can take this gathering inside. I'm sure there are fascinating tales to tell, but who's to say that the neighbors need to hear it all, eh?"

Desi didn't wait but invited themselves into Dray's apartment. Dray wriggled out of Fenton's grasp and with an angry glare at Kay followed Desi inside. Kay stepped in after Fenton, and Pratchett closed the door behind them.

The apartment might have been bigger than Kay's but it was hard to tell with the sheer mess of it all. Well, mess in half of it. There was a clear demarcation between clean and unclean. Dray dropped herself down in a patch of dirty clothes piled on the unclean half of the sofa. She didn't look back at Kay and that was fine because Kay's stomach threatened to revolt whenever she fell under the gaze of that unnatural eye.

Fenton shoved more junk off a side chair and sat down. "Well, this is Helena Draybeck, just like you asked. Now how's about explaining how and why you stole her mother's face and what you're doing here?"

Kay looked at the faces turned to her, all but one. Dray stared out the window. Whatever had fueled her earlier outburst was gone. What was left looked vaguely familiar, a blank stare, slight twitch in the legs. Kay didn't have time to analyze it though, as everyone else was waiting for her explanation. Fenton's face wasn't one she was going to look at though, so Kay spoke to Desi, who leaned against the open doorframe to one of the two bedrooms in the apartment, the messy bedroom.

"I'm here with Major Jeffrey Franklin. I was sent on behalf of the Nassien Autonomy to extract the Draybecks."

"And you just happened to have Katherine's face because?" Fenton asked.

Kay turned to her. "Because she was my clone mother."

"The fuck she's your mother," Dray said, glancing at her and then turning away again. So something could enliven the wonderful Helena Draybeck. Too bad it was short-lived and fueled by her hatred of Kay.

Kay took a deep breath. "It's the official term the geneticists use for us all."

"All?" Pratchett asked. "There are more of you?"

Kay shrugged. "There were multiple clone generations off that gene line, yes. As far as I know, I'm the only survivor."

"Fucking Novans," Fenton muttered.

"So what's your real name if you aren't really Katherine Draybeck," Desi asked.

Kay looked away. "I have a gene line designation that wouldn't make sense to any of you anyway. I go by Kay."

Fenton stood up. "This is all too convenient. You just happen to be a Draybeck clone and just happen to be on this ship."

"I said I'm with Jeffrey Franklin."

"And I don't know who he is or care," Fenton said.

Kay looked to Dray but she was still staring out the window, her only animation a twitching leg. Kay pointed to her. "She knows. He's family."

Fenton turned to her. "Dray?"

Dray turned. "Brother-in-law."

Fenton waited as if in hope of something more, but Dray turned back to the window again. One step away from useless, and she was supposed to be critical to this plan? Time for some tough love.

Kay stepped forward. Fenton blocked her path, but she held up her hands. "What do you think I can do here with all of you surrounding me? I'm stuck on this crate too, now."

Fenton backed off and Kay crouched in front of Dray until the woman turned that mechanical eye on her. Kay smiled, then gave her a good solid slap across the face.

Fenton was on her in an instant, yanking her back. She stumbled to her feet but the effect on Dray was precious and worth the aggravation of being dragged around by Fenton again.

Dray was on her feet, eyes, even the fake one, glaring. "I will kick your ass from one end of this ship to the other for that."

Kay laughed. "In your condition? Months of confinement. How long did you wait before you started drugging up?"

"You try being hated by everyone around you and treated like a traitor," Dray growled.

"Yeah. Because walking around with an obvious Terran face in a sea of Novan soldiers has been a cake walk. Get over it, princess," Kay said.

Dray glanced at Fenton and sank back to the chair, her face flushed. Tactical error on Kay's part to bring up the obvious signs of being under the influence in front of Fenton. Maybe the woman was some kind of mentor to Dray. Anyway, time to shift tactics.

Kay shrugged out of Fenton's grasp, which had loosened with the realization her precious Dray was taking drugs. "Look, this great plan your brother-in-law dreamed up depends on you. Your wife is depending on you."

Dray looked up. "Jordan?"

"Jordan. She's in Novan space right now fighting for your release. And what are you doing?"

"What is her wife doing in Novan space?" Pratchett said. "That doesn't make sense."

"It does when your own government illegally incarcerates you all as a threat to their pure genes. Jordan has some real political talents. She used her influence with the Nassien Autonomy to fight for the details of the genetic modifications your families were subject to."

"Fucking Novans," Fenton said.

"Yeah, you mentioned that already."

Dray wiped her face on her sleeve. "How is she?"

Kay squatted back down in front of Dray and Fenton let her. Surprise, surprise. "She's fine. The compound she's staying at has a top medical facility on site. She's got the best care available."

Dray frowned. "Is she sick?"

"She's pregnant."

Dray grabbed Kay's sleeve. "It worked? We're having a baby?"

Kay grinned. "Two. She's carrying twins. She and they need you."

Dray stood up. "I need a shower." She looked at Kay. "Wait for me."

Kay nodded. Finally, some progress. The room was silent as Dray disappeared to get herself in order. The conversation with Dray was meant to be private, but didn't end up that way.

Kay stood up and shot a glare at Fenton. "Question now is, what do you plan on doing with the intel you just heard?"

Fenton crossed her arms. "I'm not going anywhere."

Kay took that as tacit agreement to join in.

"Do you really think I wouldn't want to be a part of all this?" Desi asked. "Vastly more fun than I expected so soon in our lovely new prison."

She turned to Pratchett, who must realize she was in a spot if she didn't agree. Question was, could Kay trust whatever Pratchett said now?

"I'm following orders of my superior officer, Ma'am."

"You realize the rank and uniform aren't real," Kay said.

"Real enough in the system that if I punched you right now, I could be court-martialed."

"Military discipline comes in handy," Kay said.

Pratchett shrugged. "Begging the Lieutenant's pardon, but you aren't the top-ranking officer on board. That is where your problems will come with the military detainees here."

"She's right," Fenton said. "I'm a major. That will get us some support, but there will be others here who out-rank me. Your Novans made sure of that when they messed us all up in the first war."

Her Novans when she was in Terran space. Just like they were her Terrans when she was in Novan space. Maybe she could convince Ayaan to take a long vacation in neutral space after this fiasco was over.

Assuming they succeeded and she didn't end up trapped with these people forever.

DRAY STEPPED BACK into the living room an hour later in a fresh uniform and looking if not more awake, at least less apathetic than she had earlier. She turned that mechanical eye to Kay who kept her face blank to mask the revulsion. She'd get used to it, in time.

Everyone around her probably had just as much tech in their bodies as well. She wondered why Dray's wasn't hidden as well, though.

"So what is Jeffrey's plan?" Dray asked.

Kay went over the high level strategy, including the set of Intel personnel Jeffrey was likely in communications with already. She even included the Novan meet up at the end to get the Drayback's off the ship.

"I don't like it," Dray said.

"Excuse me?"

Dray turned to her. "We get everyone off this ship, not just us. At least everyone who wants off."

Fenton smirked at Kay. "And that's exactly what the real Katherine Draybeck would have suggested."

Great, delusional heroes, just what she needed on this mission.

Desi it seemed, knew more about revolution than the rest of them combined. They were entirely in their element with this conspiracy. "You won't get a lot of volunteers in that regard. Oh there will be some like me, rounded up just to be got rid of. But many here have family they left behind, family pure enough to stay Terran. They won't want to risk not being able to get back to that family. Obeying the law is ingrained in our system."

Pratchett agreed. "Being rescued by the Novans that put us all here won't sit well with a lot of people as well, especially the military."

It was the Terrans that put them all on this ship, but Kay didn't bother arguing. She couldn't care less who got off the ship with her, so long as she fulfilled her mission to get the Draybecks off. "We get the ship to neutral territory, then we can debate what happens next."

Fenton and Pratchett went off in search of food, while Desi took off back to their section to feel out possible civilian allies. Kay lingered behind, waiting until she was alone with Dray. Then she stood up.

"Hand over your stash, whatever it is you've been taking."

Dray glowered at her. "You are not my mother."

"No, I'm not. I am an addict though, just like you. Guess that's part of this glorious gene line, too. I know what it takes to stop, and I know it isn't by ignoring it all."

"I'm not an addict."

Kay rolled her eyes. "Fine. Then it shouldn't be an issue to hand over what you have."

Dray crossed her arms.

"Look, this is not some freaking party ship we are on. This is a prison, whatever your Terran government is calling it. Prisons have sources for whatever you want, I know that, too. Just like I know you could give me your stash and go out to refill it within the hour, but think of this. Your wife, your unborn kids, they are depending on you. So is Jeffrey, so am I. In case you hadn't noticed, I'm a prisoner now, just like you. And I didn't give up my freedom just to watch you piss it all away because you're feeling picked on."

Dray shot up. "You have no idea what I'm feeling." She pointed to her mechanical eye. "I got this thanks to you Novans at Chagos."

Kay narrowed her eyes and looked down again at Dray's clean uniform. The symbol wasn't immediately recognizable to her. Why would it be, when it was for a Terran ship. But on closer look, *Rubicon* was clear to read.

She swore and held out her left hand, which was starting to visibly twitch from the anger running through her. "And this I got thanks to you, at Chagos, so now we're even."

Dray's hands rolled into fists and Kay shifted balance to the balls of her feet. She would not take another sucker hit, not for this so-called family, not anymore.

The apartment door opened, causing them both to turn in that direction. A young woman came in, tall, broad-shouldered, solid. She wore a sleeveless tank, dark stains streaked across her forearms, across strong muscles. Her reddish-blond hair was tied in a ponytail, and a faint dash of freckles speckled her nose and cheeks. Another Draybeck.

The young woman approached, her eyes locked on Kay's. Kay sized her up, including the biceps, and realized a hit from this one would more than hurt, it would knock her out cold. Her brain raced to remember the name for this one but it wouldn't come. What did come was the woman's hand, but not as a fist, and not fast. She stood in front of Kay, a few centimeters taller, and raised her hand as if in slow motion to cup Kay's cheek.

"Cara," Dray said. "It's not Mom."

Cara's eyes never left Kay's. "Of course she isn't. I know you're not, but I never got to see my mother outside of old vids." Tears glistened in her eyes.

"Cara," Dray said.

Kay lifted her hand and slowly pulled Cara's away from her cheek. "I'm sorry if my presence is difficult for you."

Cara smiled, a light, airy smile so incongruous to the rest of her it shocked Kay. "Not difficult at all. You're a gift, whether you know it or not, an unimaginable gift." She backed up a step. "Please, sit down. Whatever my sister has said or done, please excuse her, she's not herself."

Dray practically growled her anger but Cara ignored it and took the seat on the sofa next to her, where Dray finally sank back down. Kay lowered herself to her own seat, not really sure how to react to this latest family addition. Was it possible for a Draybeck not to be an angry pain in the ass, like she and Dray were, if she were being honest?

Cara patted Dray's leg with one strong hand. "It's true and you know it. And I don't blame you. I'd be beyond myself if they'd turned off all my implants as well, and I don't have half the tech you do."

Of course, Cara would be loaded up as well, just like everyone here. But it didn't bug Kay to realize that, not when she couldn't see it the way she could with Dray's fake eye.

She turned back to Dray, giving up on all sense of propriety and pointed at it. "So that thing isn't working?"

"That thing as you say, is completely blind. It's integrated to a new experimental implant that's too experimental for them to leave it running when they locked me up." She turned to gaze out the window. "That thing is what caused all of this."

Cara leaned back on the sofa and stretched her legs out. "They would have discovered us all sooner or later anyway. Terran Purity standards are getting tighter every generation. Better they find it with us than with any kids we decide to have."

Dray turned back, her face lit up with something finally that wasn't anger or self-pity. "We're having twins, Cara. Twins."

Cara's smile lit up her face. "Really? Jordan's trip to Gilgar was successful?" She pulled Dray into a bear hug that almost looked painful. "How'd you find out?"

Dray nodded to Kay. "Jordan sent her to us."

"Of course she did. Jordan's not one to sit on her hands, is she?" Cara turned to Kay. "Fenton gave me the highlights. I'm in, of course. Though I have to say, I'll miss this place."

Dray shook her head, but the faint smile didn't leave her lips. "Cara's in love with a ship."

"Wise guy." Cara smacked her leg, and turned to Kay. "It really is a fantastic opportunity though, to see one of the old generation ships in action. I haven't been allowed near the engines of course, but even the systems that keep these quarters in livable condition and self-sustaining are fascinating." She lifted her arm, as if seeing the dirt for the first time. "I was working in the under deck. There's a back flow problem in water reclamation between the stacks."

"Cara lives for engines."

"I'm an astrodrive designer. I did my master's thesis on these ships. What do you expect to happen when I get to actually live on one of them?" Her eyes took on a distant look. "The FTL engines have started up. Looks like we're on to the next pickup point."

Kay looked at her. "You can feel that?" She hadn't felt so much as a tremor.

Cara tapped her head. "Still on inside me. Scientific, not military so no reason to shut me down. I don't have full access of course, but I can monitor certain parts of the ship, based on my prior research grant."

"Yeah, how about you?" Dray asked as her gaze strayed to Kay's temple. "Is that live?"

Kay resisted the urge to reach up and scratch it. "Just a scar, to get me through security."

Dray nodded. "Thorough. The real Katherine would have had a pilot implant."

The real Katherine would have been happy to see her family. Kay wasn't sure the knot of confusion in her belly qualified as happy at the moment, as she stared at the first and only blood relatives she'd ever been allowed to see.

<h1 style="text-align:center">CHAPTER 13</h1>

MORNING SICKNESS HAD passed, but for Jordan, the afternoon naps her body was forcing on her grated against her need to get things done. She woke up from her nap and glanced at the time, not even an hour had gone by. Not sure why she woke early, she rolled her legs off the bed and sat up, rubbing her hand across the slight firmness in her belly.

"Yes, you're worth it," she whispered, "but do you have to take over my entire body?"

Raised voices drifted into her room, and she guessed that's what woke her up. She stretched, splashed cold water on her face from the bathroom, and emerged from her room as presentable as she was going to be. Nailah was in the front room of her residence, along with Zayn and Ayaan. More surprising was Manji's presence, along with her primary body guard.

Zayn was standing between them, fury written all over his young body. "I'll declare vendetta!"

Nailah sighed. "No, you won't. You're too young, and the attack didn't affect you at all. Now would you sit please?"

Jordan whispered to Ayaan, "What have I missed?"

"Gemma suffered organ failure this morning. The doctors have stabilized her, but the chances she won't have permanent damage from the pathogen are slim now."

Ayaan might have been sitting, but Jordan realized she was as angry as Zayn, just more restrained. Except for that tapping hand against her thigh. Jordan wondered if she even knew she did it.

"Zayn, my mother is correct. You aren't eligible for vendetta," Ayaan said. "But I am."

Nailah threw up her hands. "Not again. We've had this discussion before."

"And you convinced me not to file the last time. Look what it's gotten us?"

Mother and daughter stared at each other. Jordan attempted to break the tension with the obvious question on her mind. "What is vendetta, besides the obvious?"

"The obvious," Nailah said.

Ayaan glared at her mother. "More than the obvious. Vendetta is a legal filing of one party against another, based on direct personal harm. It gives me the legal right to openly go after him."

"And gives him the same right to go after you," Nailah said.

Ayaan shrugged. "He's already doing that. Besides, the filing gives me the ability to go after all his assets as well."

"Mother," Nailah said, turning to Manji. "Are you going to add to this conversation or not?"

"The child is correct." Manji smiled that cold smile. "She was raised to wield political power, Nailah. Now that she's about to finally do that, you wish to stop her?"

"It could get her killed!"

"And doing nothing could get us all killed. Halabi has overstepped," Manji said. "I wonder if he's even realized just how far. Based on the attack alone, his political associates are distancing themselves from him. With a legal filing of vendetta and a court order to freeze his assets, he will be considerably weakened."

"Weakened and cornered with nothing left to lose," Jordan said. "My apologies, ser, but it seems to me he will get increasingly desperate based on these measures."

Manji nodded. "Desperate men make mistakes. It is up to Ayaan to ensure those mistakes go in our favor." She stood up. "The legal team will write up the documents for your signature by the morning. Prepare your security team. As our honored guest has said, this will make Halabi act openly and rashly. Be ready for that."

It was a few more days before Jordan could visit with Gemma, and she'd been warned what to expect, as the girl was being held in a coma to help aid the healing process. What Jordan didn't expect was both the vast security measures now in place around Gemma, and the opulence in the hospital room for an unconscious patient. After two security checkpoints and a final bio-scan, she was let into a hospital room that looked more like a luxury hotel suite. A broad window with lace curtains looked out onto the hotel garden, sunlight filtering through the green canopy. The light paneled walls wrapped around the isolated hospital bed holding Gemma, with two green bamboo plants acting as pillars on each side of the headboard. Whatever equipment existed had to be remote, as the only visible electronics was a wall vid opposite the bed that played a vid of beach surf.

A long cushioned bench with throw pillows took up the space under the window, where the young clone, Katie sat rather stiffly.

Jordan approached and sat next to her on the bench. "Has there been any change?"

Katie flicked her a brief glance, then pressed a button on the remote console next to her. The vid surf display switched to a crammed display of medical readouts. "She was taken off the respirator yesterday. Kidney function remains limited." She flicked another screen up. "Brain function shows some degeneration, but they won't know the full effects until after she's taken out of the coma."

Jordan wanted to ask why Katie was here, but she knew the answer likely lived only in Manji's head for now. "How is Zayn?"

Katie flipped the screen again, and after a brief pause, Zayn showed up on the display, in what looked like pajamas, though it was mid-afternoon. "Hey. Any change?"

"None," Katie said. "Jordan asked for you."

Jordan didn't dispute Katie's incorrect assumption that she wanted to talk to Zayn. "How are you doing?"

Zayn yawned. "Bored. I've been moved to a secure location until the Halabi vendetta issue is resolved. It stinks and I hate being here."

So the pajamas suggested he was in a different time zone, or even a different planet. It was a crazy way for kids to live, with this level of threat.

"Jordan," he said. "I need a favor."

"If I am able," she said.

"Ayaan is putting a bullseye on herself because of all this. With your Tarquin contacts, can you get her out of system, if the worst happens?"

Jordan nodded. "If it comes to that, yes I can, and Gemma, too." Fast access out of New China was a plan she already had in place with the Tarquin Embassy. Getting two others onboard wouldn't be the problem. Three, she corrected, looking back at Katie when she ended the vid call. The difficulty would be getting high-profile Nassiens to agree to any last-ditch escape plan.

She looked back at Gemma's small frame and prayed none of them would need a last-ditch escape plan.

Legal affairs in every human culture bore the same stamp of extended debate, rigorous wording, and extraneous protections aimed more at saving the lawyers than the plaintiffs, but two days after Jordan's visit to Gemma, Ayaan had her legal filing of vendetta against Halabi. Freezing his assets would take considerably longer, but Jordan was sure he knew it was coming. The question became, what would he do while he still had the financial and physical means to do something?

AFTER A TWO hour trip up to a secure docking station in orbit above New China and a short walk to another docking bay, Jordan finally settled in the seat across from Ayaan, who looked more tired and distracted than even Jordan felt. The combination of active vendetta proceedings, heightened security, and no direct contact with her lover on the *Lazarus* must be taking its toll on Ayaan.

Jordan shifted the seat harness to a less awkward position across her belly. Weeks in Novan space had given her more weight, less patience, and a penchant for Dovarien spice noodles that she blamed on the twins inside her. The pilot on the FTL courier was an older woman in an ill-fitting green Nassien guard uniform. She was absorbed in her pre-flight check with a precision that had to come from a military past. Jordan watched her process with a lingering sense of nostalgia. The ship seemed simple enough—fast passenger ship, FTL ready, and, as Jordan was learning to expect, heavily armed given who owned the ship and who the passenger was. Being close enough to peer over the pilot's shoulder, Jordan saw the armament controls in a central console between the pilot and empty copilot seat. The missile launchers were obvious before she boarded and she recognized the controls for them in the console. She didn't know if the ship had any more hidden secrets, but assumed they wouldn't need any of it, given the rest of the armada that would be following them to Volga. Nailah wasn't taking any chances and had assigned two Nassien guard ships to follow them on their trip.

Joris stepped through the hatch a few minutes later, sealed it shut, and took the co-pilot's seat. The pilot finished the preflight check and flipped on the launch imminent signal, shifting their small cabin to an orange glow.

Jordan turned to Ayaan. "Thanks, for all this," she said with a wave of her hand. "It can't have been easy to coordinate this visit to Volga."

Ayaan gave her a distracted smile. "Nothing is easy right now, but it will resolve itself shortly. Meanwhile, the Russian Federated Union is the last major player with a stake in Project Troy. If we can get their agreement, we'll have the gene record release approval in place."

Jordan nodded, keeping to herself the thought that it might have been simpler if she had travelled to Volga on her own. Ayaan was insistent about accompanying her, so that turned a simple trip into a multi-day planning and coordination mess. Still, Jordan was glad to have Ayaan's considerable influence, even if it delayed their departure.

"You believe you can negotiate a temporary home for the detainees with Gilgar?" Ayaan asked.

Jordan smiled. "I believe my mother can, yes. She's heading there already. Gilgar has always been neutral, so it would be an ideal temporary home, until we can settle the detainees legal status." It wouldn't be a perfect solution, but the political ramifications of having Terrans taken in as refugees by another government should add pressure to resolve their status within the Terran space. And anything was better than having them all floating in a generation ship in some political limbo. Much though Ayaan might not agree, it was a more acceptable solution to the detainees and their families than being declared Novan citizens.

Ayaan tapped her fingers against the seat rest, staring blankly ahead.

"Any news on the *Lazarus*?" Jordan asked, taking a guess at what might be distracting Ayaan.

Ayaan didn't even look down at her data pad. "I can't reach Kay's tracker from this ship. My mother will keep us informed of any changes."

"Have they jumped yet?" For the past two weeks, the *Lazarus* had jumped exactly every three days, presumably picking up detainees.

Ayaan frowned and turned to her. "Not yet."

Day five and no jump. Had they finished their sweep of detainees? Or had Kay and Dray managed to take control? The worst part of waiting was as always, the waiting. That's what she told herself. Maybe the unusual delay in the *Lazarus* jump schedule was distracting Ayaan, but Jordan didn't think so.

"I didn't get to see Gemma again before we left," Jordan said, hoping to engage Ayaan in a better conversation. "She's doing well?"

Ayaan nodded. "Very well. Sorry you were blocked access to her since they lifted the coma. She's had to endure two surgeries and considerable cognitive evaluations."

"And the results?"

"Inconclusive. She's had considerable speech difficulties, which is one reason she's kept isolated. Physical recovery will take time, but she should have reasonable mobility and quality of life, eventually."

Eventually was a hard timeframe for a young teen to come to grips with.

With a low rumble, the ship pulled free from its docking bay. Jordan looked out her portal as the ship rotated and she got a good parting view of the orbital station. It was considerably smaller than the public access station she came in system from. Where that one had space for close to a hundred civilian and cargo transports, this smaller station looked limited to less than ten docks, two of which held military shuttles, if Jordan was correct in her guess.

As the ship accelerated out system, Jordan saw one of their two security ships off their port side. She guessed the other was shadowing them as well, somewhere out of her view. Something else caught her eye. She leaned against the portal to block as much internal light as she could.

"Is that another ship with us?"

She turned back to Ayaan, who leaned across to look out the same portal.

"Not that I can see, but it's a busy system." She leaned back in her seat and closed her eyes.

So much for that conversation, Jordan thought. It would take three hours to get up to FTL jump speed, so Jordan settled back into her own chair and let her body's needs take over.

CHAPTER 14

TWO WEEKS ON the *Lazarus* taught Kay two important lessons—Cara was a doll and anyone would be lucky to have her as a sister, and Dray was a jackass. Okay, maybe jackass was too strong a term, but Kay had no delusions they'd ever be bosom buddies. Cara was another matter though and made the risky trip worth it.

They all sat in a cafe that Desi had taken over as proprietor. The rest of the stack avoided it once it became obvious that the Draybecks were involved, and that pariah status served them well.

Dray put down her fourth cup of coffee. "I don't like it."

Kay sighed. "There's not much you do like."

Dray shot her the same glare she always used then turned back to Cara. "The maintenance tunnels you found gain us access to the hub, but how do we know the tunnels are still functional."

Cara smiled. "We go find out." She raised a hand to forestall Dray's exception. "I can oxygenate them as part of a regular maintenance check. We have the safety equipment if something goes bad. Breathers and exposure suits from stack maintenance."

"Not good enough for full space exposure," Dray said. "If the guards find out what we're doing, we can all be vented to space."

"Not quite vented," Cara added. "There's no direct access to space from these tunnels. But they do have fire control. If that gets triggered, things get uncomfortable."

"Then they can't learn what we are up to," Kay said.

Dray nodded. "We split the team. I go through the tunnels, Cara leads the diversion force that goes right to the spoke access."

Kay folded her arms and counted to three before Fenton broke in with the obvious.

"Kay leads the tunnel force," Fenton said. "She's ground force battle experienced. Cara's a genius, but hasn't so much as fired a pea-shooter since she got out of flower skirts."

"I never wore flower skirts," Cara corrected.

"Anyway," Fenton said. "Dray is the best diversion we can have. This entire stack is on special alert because she lives here. It'll be no surprise if she goes after the spoke. And she's too politically important for them to just shoot her on sight."

"Thanks for that," Dray said. "So I'm the fake fight and Kay gets all the fun."

"Kay gets to lead the backup plan," Kay said. "Franklin is responsible for the spoke gate you attack. If his team is in place, you are the ones who will break through to the core first."

What Dray lacked in trust for Kay, she made up for in tactical planning. The final plan had three separate attack fronts, with Cara leading a third effort under-deck with Fenton to cause enough problems in other decks and stacks to draw away as many guards as possible.

Kay's force was limited by the number of breathers and exposure suits available to them. She had Pratchett, two other soldiers, and a few civilians recruited by Desi. Then again, if they succeeded, it would be by stealth, not force of arms. She glanced down at the handful of stun sticks they'd stolen from local civilian police. Definitely not by force of arms.

It was another three hours before they were fully coordinated with Jeffry and managed a test run on one of the access tunnels to verify it could be oxygenated. At the night shift, within a maintenance corridor two decks away from Dray and her team, Kay coordinated her small group.

"Suits on, breathers hooked to your belts. With luck, we won't need them."

Kay pulled the drab brown exposure suit up over her Terran uniform. Once she settled the hood over her head, she heard Desi laughing at her. "I can find one of these for you, too, you know."

They held up a hand. "My role is far less vital, dear. I'll be rousing the rabble once Cara starts getting systems to shut down on the other stacks. It's a job few would want."

Kay grinned. "And few would love it as much as you."

Desi bowed. "You know me too well in so short a time."

She held his arm with her gloved hand. "Stay safe."

Desi pulled her into a hug. "Stay alive."

They took off, leaving Dray with Pratchett and the other members of her tunnel team. Kay adjusted the ear piece that would provide communication with the other teams, once they broke radio silence. Once they broke through to the hub. She eyed each member of her team in turn. Soldiers she trusted, as much as she could a bunch of Terrans, but it was the civilians that had her on edge, two wiry older women who were retired military, like Fenton, and three brothers who had the brawn to make up for their lack of real weaponry. Physically, they were perfect for the mission, but psychologically? She didn't have a lot of experience with civilians, and the ones she met on New China hadn't given her a high opinion of civvies, in general.

Thoughts of New China and Ayaan threatened to distract her. Kay picked up a couple of the stun sticks to pass out, but Pratchett pulled Kay to the side first. "As far as this team is concerned, you are an officer, Ma'am."

"Your point, Pratchett?"

"My point, Ma'am, is officers delegate."

Kay glanced at the two sticks in her hand, as if she were examining them, then put them both down.

"Staff Sergeant Pratchett," she said. "Hand out the stun sticks, your judgment."

Kay waved off Pratchett's offer of a stun stick. Kay had two of the largest kitchen knives hidden in her suit, something she trusted more than the civilian stun stick. She glanced at the chrono built into the cuff of her suit.

"One minute, ten seconds."

Pratchett gave each soldier a stick, one to each of the civilian women, and one for the brothers to share. She kept none for herself. Kay raised an eyebrow. "Nothing for yourself?"

Pratchett nodded. "I'm as unarmed as you are."

Kay smiled. Pratchett would have been a friend, if she wasn't Terran. If Kay wasn't Novan, at least in name. Hell with it all.

"Let's go."

Brother One of the three pried open the stack access hatch and crawled in first. Somewhere, a bored hub admin would get a blinking notification of the breach. But Cara and Fenton would be doing their best to mask that notification in a swarm of other alarms going off in multiple other stacks. No reason to think anyone would pick this minor alarm to pay real attention to. No reason, except luck was never one of Kay's gifts.

She pushed back her doubts and approached the open hatch to go next, but with Pratchett watching with a raised eyebrow, she stepped to the side. Officers weren't the first in the line of fire, either. Officers sucked.

Pratchett went first with Brother One, then a soldier and the two women. Kay moved into the middle of the troop with the other two brothers, and the last soldier took up the rear post to make sure the civilians stayed moving. This was a side tunnel, close enough to benefit from the stack's atmosphere, temperature, and gravity.

The exposure suits had built in lighting which illuminated the cables, pipes, and general grime that surrounded them. Cara could have pointed out what each item provided, but in another ten minutes, Cara would be busy messing with the cables and pipes from another stack, and Fenton repeating the effort in a third stack and deck to maximize the disruption.

Brother One paused at a T junction, and Pratchett came up next to him.

"Breather on," she said and pulled her own in place.

Kay and the rest put their breathers on. This was the long tunnel, parallel to the spoke that would, in theory, gain them access to the hub. In theory, Cara's oxygenating effort would still be in effect.

Kay hated theories.

Brother One opened the access panel to this hatch, tore off the cover, and exposed the batch of wires underneath. The jumble made little sense to Kay from behind a few onlooking shoulders, but this guy was chosen by Cara for his technical skills. A nod from Pratchett and he separated two wires, cut one of them, and used it to form some kind of jump with another connection. With a hiss, the hatch unsealed itself and swung outward, forcing Pratchett to step backward and lean into the soldier behind her.

"My lead, now," Pratchett said, and Kay bounced back on her heels.

Being mid-point was going to get on her nerves, fast. Cold air slid out the open hatch, key point being, actual air. She crawled inside on her turn and scanned the monitor built into the sleeve of her exposure suit. Temperature would be chilly, but not dangerous while in their suits, and it had an obvious and safe air flow.

She pulled off her mask. "It's breathable."

Gravity in this tunnel felt a little less, but movement was more cramped, forcing them single file behind Pratchett's lead. The rear guard soldier shut the hatch behind them as their column progressed into the spoke tunnel, which at least didn't have the grime that the prior access tunnel had. Less atmosphere interaction would do that, Kay supposed.

The shout from the front of the column didn't really surprise her, and she had a kitchen knife in each hand, taking in the reactions of the two women in front of her. One was stunned and slumping to the deck. Kay heard the sound of a stun stick firing behind her and glanced back to see one of the brother's down and the other pushing into her to get away from the rear guard soldier and his live stun stick.

She had to trust Pratchett to take care of the front of the line. She elbowed the still-standing brother. "Get down!"

One boot on his squatting form and she was over him and facing a Terran soldier, an enemy she knew only too well. If the narrow tunnel wasn't helping her, it was even worse for him as he scrambled over the stunned body of the other brother. His was a hand weapon meant to incapacitate a belligerent civilian. Hers was lethal and projectile.

He glanced at the body beneath him to get sturdy footing, and Kay flung the first knife at his face. Kitchen knives weren't aerodynamic, but for once, luck was on her side and it sliced into his cheek. His shock was all she needed to lunge forward and bury the second knife in his chest. She shoved his dying body off the stunned brother. "Pratchett!"

There was no way to easily move through their column, but Pratchett knew how to handle unplanned situations. "Two down, stunned. One deserved it, Terran soldier."

So much for trusting the military on their team. "One stunned, one dead," Kay reported back.

Her thoughts about what to do for the innocent stunned ones were drowned out by the radio broadcast in her ear bud blasting to life with Cara's voice.

"Emergency Jump. Hold Fast! Hold Fast!"

"Hold fast!" Kay repeated. Hold fast to what?

Brother One came up with the answer. Damn she needed to remember his name. "On the deck, back to a wall. Tuck your knees in and head down!"

Kay complied as it was the best they had. No one thought to put hold fast straps in an access tunnel for obvious reasons. Because who in their right mind would schedule a jump with people in the tunnels? Like ducks in a row, they lined up as best they could. The near brother shoved his unconscious sibling between him and Kay. It wasn't going to help.

"Shove his head in your crotch," she said. He glared at her, then nodded as he must have realized his unconscious brother's greatest risk would be snapping his neck in the sudden acceleration. Pratchett followed suit with the unconscious woman.

Kay ducked her head and wrapped her arms around her knees as the telltale FTL jump nausea struck. Unlike during secured jumps, nausea was the least of her problems. She slammed sideways into the woman next to her, and then it was a rapid succession of pain and collisions that seemed to last ages but was more in the order of seconds.

Kay spit out blood from her split lip when the jump transition steadied. She was in a pile, sandwiched between two other bodies. Pain laced through one knee, and she felt blood trickling on her cheek, but couldn't tell if it was hers or the person above her. When that person didn't move fast enough, Kay gave a good shove. The now thoroughly dead body of their rear guard attacker slid off her. She did the same off the body beneath her, who was definitely alive if the elbow in her gut was any indication.

She pushed the dead soldier further away. "Report!"

To her relief, Pratchett answered from further down the tunnel. "Two injured, one critical. I'm still mobile."

Kay put more weight on her injured left knee and grit her teeth against the pain. "Mobile here as well." She aimed her cuff light toward Pratchett and the two brothers squatting next to the still form of the stunned brother. "How is he?"

"Hard to say," Brother One said. "He's breathing, no obvious external bleeding."

Kay nodded, then switched on her com link. After the emergency jump mess and Cara's broadcast, radio silence wasn't worth maintaining. "What the hell happened?"

"Kay! Are you okay?"

Split lip, bashed knee, and more than half her team down. Did that qualify as okay? "I've had better days. We were ambushed by two of our team. Terran soldiers. Pratchett and I are mobile, and two others, but we have injured that need help. What's your sister's status?"

"Dray's through the hub, but locked out of bridge control. That emergency jump was beyond risky. No telling how many people on the decks didn't get into a safety harness on time. Hold on, I'm getting a message in from Dray."

Kay tried a few short steps in the limited space she had and was surprised that she was in fact, mostly mobile. It wasn't an outright lie for once. Pratchett was already a step ahead of her and had used the belts from both Terran soldiers to restrain the stunned but still alive one to a pipe running along the floor of the tunnel. It wouldn't hold him for long, but it was something.

Cara's voice came back online. "Kay, take whoever you can and get through to the hub. Dray's got a plan but she wants you. Is Marcus mobile?"

"Marcus?" Kay said. Brother One looked at her with a nod. Finally, a name. "Yeah, he's mobile. One of his brother's isn't, along with one other civilian. I'll need to send some back your way."

"Good. You'll need Marcus to open the hatch at the other end of the tunnel. I'll contact Desi to send some help for your injured people."

Kay ended the com call and looked back at Pratchett. "You, me, and Marcus will continue. Dray and her team are through the hub and working on access to the bridge. The rest of you will go back to the stack. Desi is sending help to move the stunned and injured. Thanks for what you've risked to get us this far. Remember, we're not in full command of the ship yet."

So much for her motivational speaking skills. Even Pratchett couldn't hide her smirk as the three of them crawled over the remaining survivors and walked, or in Kay's case, limped the rest of the way through the spoke tunnel.

Once at the end, Marcus flipped off the cover to the tunnel exit hatch and with similar skill, had it opened in short order.

"Where'd you learn that handy skill?" Kay asked.

"I taught electrician class at the local prison. Picked up a few extra-curricular skills from my students," he said with a grin.

"Handy," she said as he pulled the hatch open and she stepped through. To hell with being a fake military officer. Marcus wouldn't know the difference, and Pratchett knew the truth.

Two gray-clad guards stood at attention and saluted her as she stepped through the hatch. Damn, so much for dropping the pretext. "Sit rep."

The taller of the two, a deeply tanned woman handed her a ship-safe pistol. "Lieutenant Commander Draybeck ordered us to escort you to her. We control all the spoke access and have locked fifteen of the twenty ship's crew in the rec room under guard. The non Intel guards have handed in their weapons already and will be relocated into the stacks."

Not bad. Jeffrey had some skill after all.

It was a dead-quiet march from the hub to the bridge access. Unlike the grand expanse of the stacks and decks, this area of the ship felt more like a ship. Narrow passageways, drab gray, and the faint smell of grit and machinery that wasn't masked by moisture and soil smells in the stacks. Finally, something that felt like home.

They climbed a ladder to bridge access with Pratchett in the lead. Kay was the last to pull herself up and join their mutinous group. Jeffrey was the only face she recognized in the small cluster of guards.

"Where's Dray?" she asked.

He nodded, indicating something behind her. "In there."

She turned to see an open hatchway half way down the passageway. She stepped through with Jeffrey at her heels. Dray was there, bouncing on her toes with more enthusiasm than Kay thought called for, given they were still on the wrong side of the bridge access hatch. Kay couldn't place what the original purpose of the room might have been, but it was set up now with a drop-down table wrapped in white, with a collection of tools she didn't want to know the purpose of.

She turned back to Jeffrey as he shut the hatch behind her. She flicked a thumb at Dray. "Time to turn the lights back on in there?"

Jeffrey nodded. "With a little help, yes."

She turned to Jeffrey, thinking he was the one with the knowhow on flipping Dray's switch, or however it would work, but was surprised to see him and Dray looking back at her. This did not feel right.

"We needed a way to get the access codes past security," Jeffrey said.

No, this didn't feel right at all. "You fixed me up like a damn drug mule in my sleep," she growled.

He smirked. "Not that dramatic." He tapped his temple. "And you were awake for the whole procedure."

She reached up to the healed scar, the so-called dummy pilot implant. "What the hell's in my head?"

"Just a data chip," he said. "Nothing active to you, but something the security scans would assume was part of your pilot implant."

"The one I don't really have."

"The one you don't have, yes. Now if you'll hop on the table, I can extract the chip and use it to, as you say, turn the lights back on."

She glanced at Dray and saw the expectant look on her sort-of sister's face. "Drug mule," she mumbled as she sat on the nearest table.

Jeffrey pulled back her hair and gave a quick spray of surgical freeze. For someone not medically trained, he had a steady hand. She felt little besides the warm trickle of blood down her cheek before he had it all sealed off again. He gave her a cloth to wipe clean with and dropped whatever was stuck in her head this whole time into a tray. It didn't look like much.

"Your turn," she said to Dray as she hopped off the table.

Dray smiled. Not a smirk, but an almost guilty-looking smile. "Sorry, my half of this experiment is less bloody."

Jeffrey cleaned off the data chip from Kay's head and placed it into a small electronic device she didn't recognize.

"I had to have that stuck in my head, but you can walk right through the front hatch with the scanner that will flip Dray's switch?"

Jeffrey held up the device. "Not quite. This might be new to you, but it's standard medical equipment on any Terran ship. It's for implant debugging, deactivation, or in this case, reactivation. That part, given the nature of Dray's special implant, required access codes and a firmware upgrade to this."

He pulled a thin cord out of the device, then pulled down Dray's back collar. Kay couldn't see anything there but skin, yet she could see the cord snap into place.

"Magnetic?" she asked.

Jeffrey nodded. "They gave Dray a hard stop on all her implants when they took her into custody. It requires direct contact to reboot."

Half human, half a piece of hardware. Kay kept her shiver to a minimum, but Dray smirked at her anyway. "Jordan has the same reaction whenever she sees implant work."

"Smart woman."

"Okay. In theory, this won't hurt a bit." Jeffrey flipped something on his device.

Dray shut her eyes and slumped forward. Kay reached out to catch her, but Dray recovered and stood straight again. She opened her eyes, and this time, instead of seeing one blue and one dead, Kay saw the slight expansion and contraction of an electronic pupil colored a matching blue to the other eye, and the vastly larger expansion of a shit-eating grin across Dray's face.

"Follow my finger," Kay said, playing eye doctor.

Dray's grin widened. "I can scan your finger down to the molecular level, upload it back to the ship mainframe, and verify your identity." She blinked. "Yep, Katherine Draybeck, right in the ship passenger manifest. You really are genetically identical to my mother."

"Terran Unaltered," Kay said without explanation and dropped her finger. "Well, guess it's time to get this ship turned around."

CHAPTER 15

THE SHUTTLE PILOT'S voice interrupted Jordan's nap to announce FTL jump was in five minutes. Jordan hadn't gone through the FTL transition since first arriving in New China space, but thanks to the Novan doctors, she had a pill to prevent the nausea and any potential vomiting. She took the medication out of a pocket and slipped it under her tongue to dissolve. The doctor had warned it might make her sleepy, but sleepy for the FTL journey was better than losing her lunch. She felt the transition, but it was more like a distant sensation than anything upsetting. She drifted off after that for a nap.

Jordan felt a hand shaking her awake. She opened her eyes to see Ayaan with a head-set on and a VR display slipped down over her eyes. "We drop out of FTL now. You need to be ready."

"Ready?" Jordan asked. "FTL should have taken seven hours." There's no way an anti-nausea pill would knock her out that long.

Both the pilot and Joris were engaged in FTL drop prep, which seemed excessive for such a relatively short jump. Something was happening, something she was deliberately kept out of the loop about.

"Coming out of FTL in three, two, one," the pilot said.

Jordan felt the FTL transition drag at her senses, and she shut her eyes against it. Seconds later, the ship took a sudden swerve that threatened to upend her stomach regardless of the drug she took. She opened her eyes as the ship flipped on its central axis. Streaks of close-range laser fire shot past her portal. They were under attack. The what was obvious, as was the who. No one had caused any trouble except Halabi. The how and why were questions for another time.

"How can I help?" Jordan asked.

Joris was firing their missiles, and from under her feet, she felt the build-up and then jarring release of what had to be ship-mounted cannons. The pilot was engaged in maneuvers, and Ayaan, Ayaan was obviously commanding their multiple escorts. This wasn't a surprise attack. The ship's capabilities, the pilot with advanced military training, and Ayaan's ability to coordinate all three ships spoke of considerable planning. Jordan gripped her seat arms, knowing there was nothing she could do. This was all planned around her, an issue she'd take up with her supposed hosts later. If they all survived this.

The ship took a jarring hit on the port side, and Jordan peered out of her portal to see what was after them. Between the pilot's maneuvers and the minimal view, she could only tell more than one ship was involved. Whether there was more than one attacker in the mix was hard to say, but given three Nassien ships and the number of hits this one was taking, it had to be more than one opposing ship or a very large one. On the plus side, they were heading for a planet. Whether it was Volga or some other place was anyone's guess, but if they could get help from there, they had a chance.

Jordan didn't know what registered to her first, the solid hit on the starboard side, or the burn of the flash fire that it triggered in the cockpit. She bit her lip against the pain along her right hand and knee. The cabin pressure shifted, causing her ears to pop seconds before flame retardant sprayed through the cabin. The retardant dissipated quickly thanks to the air filters, but the smell of burnt flesh wasn't going anywhere, neither was the intense pain of her own burns.

The pilot was obviously dead. Joris looked unconscious, with significant burns on his upper torso from what Jordan could see. Ayaan, furthest from the hit and fire, looked disoriented.

Jordan gritted her teeth against the burns but knew she was lucky to escape that hit with only minor injuries. She started to unbuckle her harness. "Help me move Joris."

Ayaan stared at her over her VR display.

"Help me, dammit! The pilot's dead, Joris is maybe alive, but if we don't take over, this ship is a simple, straight-moving target, and frankly, I'm not up for dying today."

Ayaan blinked, then pulled out of her harness. "We won't take another direct hit. Halabi wants me alive."

"Great," Jordan said, unhooking Joris' harness. "How about we don't make it too easy for him, then?"

Between the two of them, they shifted Joris into Jordan's seat. He had a pulse, that's all that mattered. She left Ayaan to strap him into the seat while she slid into the copilot seat. She brushed the remnants of retardant off her console and catalogued the controls in an instant.

She also took in the two ships behind her and doubted they were Nassien. Jordan flipped the ship and dove out of the current plane of battle. She didn't hear any shouts so assumed Ayaan was strapped back in.

Another flash starboard took out one of Halabi's ships in a massive explosion.

"What kind of firepower do you have on these ships?" Jordan asked.

"Not us. Military pinnacle-class, compliments of my mother," Ayaan said.

The second Halabi ship let loose its arsenal at Jordan's ship. She tried to avoid a direct hit, but with no one to trigger the defensive countermeasures, their ship took another hit aft that crippled their maneuverability.

"We're going to be trapped by the gravity well." Jordan fought to maintain the ship with little luck. "Is that Volga?"

"No, but this ship can't survive landfall. We need to get to the escape pods."

Jordan locked the controls into a low orbit, for all it would do them with the ship so crippled. She released her harness and joined Ayaan by Joris's seat. "Can we get him to a pod?"

Ayaan closed her eyes. "No pulse. He's gone."

Patience wasn't top on Jordan's list right now, and she pulled Ayaan aft. "Mourn later, survive today."

Ayaan hit the hatch controls to the escape pods. The ship had two pods, each of which would hold four people. The ship took another hit, and Jordan screamed as something hit her on the same right side. She dropped to her knees to keep from passing out from a wave of intense pain. She placed a shaking hand on the point of pain, and felt some piece of cabin debris sticking out, slick with her own blood.

"Don't pull it out," Ayaan said. "The angle is too close."

Jordan knew what it was too close to without asking. Her womb. Her breath came in short gasps as Ayaan helped her strap into one of the vertical harnesses and pull on the oxygen-enabled helmet. Jordan shifted herself so the shard in her side would not be in contact with either harness or cushion and nodded.

Ayaan, already strapped in, triggered the pod release. Jordan was slammed into the pod's protective cushioning, sending another wave of pain through her injured body, but thankfully nothing jolted the shard. A vid screen showed the rapidly shrinking sight of their crippled ship that had already started to burn on orbital re-entry. Logically, Jordan knew their pod was a similar fireball to anyone on the planet who saw them, the difference being these pods were designed for both planet-fall and extended space survival.

"The pod has some emergency aid capabilities. Stay still." Ayaan played with the pod controls. Jordan's mid-section was coated in an instant with a quick-hardening immobilizer.

"That will prevent further harm, for now. I can give you a pain killer, but that might make you unconscious as well."

"No pain killers." Jordan could only see Ayaan's profile in the protective cushion next to her, but sympathy wasn't her strongest emotion right now. "How much of this did you know in advance?"

"Enough to prepare."

"Not well enough," Jordan growled. "In case you hadn't noticed."

"I noticed," Ayaan said. "We aren't out of yet, if you haven't noticed. If Halabi is still alive, and I'm betting he is. He's tracking us."

"So is your mother," Jordan said, but left it at that. It would be a race to see who got to them first.

Jordan watched the vid display as they raced below the cloud cover on what turned out to be a settled planet after all. The first image showed a deep blue-gray body of water, possibly an ocean, given it dominated the display. The pod shifted, and she turned to Ayaan.

"You're steering us?"

Ayaan nodded. "The pod itself can find safe landing, but we're not alone out here."

The display shifted, and Jordan saw two planetary craft heading for them. When the first shots fired, her unasked question was answered—foe, not friends were on their tail.

"Any weaponry on this pod?" Jordan asked.

"Are your hands free?"

"Just the left one," Jordan said. Ayaan played again with her controls, and Jordan's helmet came alive with a tactical heads-up display showing the two enemy planes and their incoming ordinance.

Ayaan rotated the pod away from the missiles. "You'll find your left-hand console now has missile and short-range gun control. We only have three air-to-air missiles."

In other words, use them wisely, Jordan thought. She closed her eyes as Ayaan banked again. "How far to the landing point?"

"Five minutes."

Jordan rotated her first two missiles and locked both onto the first target. It was a gamble, but if she took it out completely, the other plane would likely move out of range, at least to recalculate the pod's capabilities.

"Locked on target," she said. "Prepare evasive maneuver on my mark."

Jordan sounded the count and fired. Ayaan dove the pod down and away as Jordan watched her HUD. First and second explosions went off. Not enough of that plane was left to track on the pod's tactical display. The other plane looked to have taken some damage as well.

"We got lucky," she said, shutting her eyes against a new wave of pain as her breath came in shorter gasps. With or without pain meds, she didn't think she'd stay conscious much longer.

She opened her eyes. The remaining plane was still tracking them, but at a distance that made both their weapons systems useless.

"Safe until landing," she said.

Ayaan eased the POD lower. Blue transformed into brown, then green as the tops of a thick tree canopy came into view. Jordan didn't even realize she'd drifted into unconsciousness until the slap of humid air hit her exposed flesh. She opened her eyes to see Ayaan standing in front of her with a loaded gun. Jordan reached for her harness release, then remembered the immobilizer.

"Stay in the pod. It will protect you from any small-range weapons," Ayaan said.

Jordan shut her eyes a moment, then opened them to check her HUD. "The pod's guns are intact. If there's an opening . . ."

"Use them." Ayaan sealed the pod shut, and Jordan switched back to watching the external world on a split between the vid display and her tactical HUD.

Sadly, the dots forming in front of her eyes weren't coming from either display. "Keep it together, Bowers."

She had access to the emergency medical options, and chose what she hoped was the lesser of two evils, just enough pain meds to take the edge off, but not enough hopefully to push her into unconsciousness. A needle jabbed her lower left thigh, and seconds later, she felt a minor level of relief, enough to restore her breathing at least.

She keyed audio into her helmet. "Plane landed. I'm tracking six hostiles."

"I see them," Ayaan said. "They are forming a wide arc. Don't let them come at me from behind."

Jordan shifted the pod guns. "Got you covered." She couldn't be sure of the enemy's weapon range, but they weren't firing yet, so when three enemy targets lit up on her HUD, she marked them and let the gun's AI take over. Two were down immediately, the third evaded long enough to get off a few rounds, but wasted them on the pod instead of searching for Ayaan.

"Three down," Jordan said. "Locking on four."

"Hold your fire," Ayaan said.

Jordan took her eye off her HUD to glance at the vid display. Once again, Nassien technology failed them. Jordan looked back at her HUD to see a gray dot to denote the presumed neutral person on the field of battle. That neutral person had a name, and a knife on Ayaan's throat.

"Mala," Jordan growled.

Her HUD showed only one other enemy target so Ayaan must have taken out five and six herself. Jordan's target four came into view, an older, balding man, limping heavily. Good.

"Halabi," Ayaan said.

Less good. "He's still locked into the pod's target," Jordan said. If she fired, Mala could cut Ayaan down in an instant. Again, less good.

Halabi took a wide circle away from the pod and stood a few paces in front of Ayaan with a pistol pointed at her. "Tell your friend to get out of the pod."

"She's useless to you and injured. She's immobilized."

"She killed three of my guards." He waved the gun." Get her out."

Jordan watched Ayaan approach, with Mala and the knife at her side. "Will my HUD still control the pod when I'm out?"

Ayaan gave a barely perceptible shake of her head. So much for that option. A moment later, the pod hatch lifted free, and she saw Ayaan in front of her with the ever-present Mala at her side.

"Mala," Jordan said. "I thought you'd be dead from the pathogen."

Mala smirked and raised her free had. "Subcutaneous blood packets, and I'd already been immunized against it. Too bad it didn't take out the two brats."

"Get her out of the pod," Halabi shouted.

"Sorry," Ayaan said as she triggered the pod's first aid release. The immobilizer weakened, then pooled off in a liquid goo.

Jordan gasped in renewed agony as blood flowed around the shard in her side once again. Black dots formed in her vision, but she caught Ayaan's eyes shifting to the tactical console. Jordan released her one remaining shot.

Halabi fell in a clump. Mala wasted a precious second to scream her rage. That was enough for Ayaan, who shifted away from the girl's delayed knife thrust, taking a slice across her thigh instead of anything vital. She threw herself on top of Mala, where gravity and size took over.

When Ayaan knelt up, Mala was on the ground with the knife between her ribs. Hands slick with her own blood, Mala couldn't remove it as life slowly faded from her eyes.

Jordan's HUD lit up. "More incoming."

"Friendly, this time," Ayaan said, with a weary smile.

Jordan couldn't have returned the smile if she wanted to. The black dots in her vision morphed gently into complete, blissful unconsciousness.

CHAPTER 16

PRATCHETT STOOD TO Kay's left in the passageway outside the sealed bridge access hatch. "So what sort of miracle are we waiting for here?"

Kay shrugged. "You're asking the wrong fake Terran. What do you know about implants and what they can pull off?"

"Depends on the implant. They can range from highly specialized to generalized but superficial. What's your . . . What do you consider Draybeck to be to you?"

Good question. "Let's stick to relative of obscure designation."

Pratchett nodded. "What kind of implant does she have?"

"Something fancy," Kay said as Dray and Jeffrey joined them in the passageway.

Dray had that shit-eating grin Kay already recognized as her extra happy face. What she had to be extra happy about was anyone's guess, given that they were all still on the wrong side of ship control and staring at an impenetrable bulkhead and hatch that looked to have been recently hardened against unauthorized access.

"Got a G-3 explosive in that special head of yours?" Kay asked as Dray stood next to her.

"Better. Override command codes." Dray turned to the group assembled around them, most in the gray guard uniforms like Jeffrey. "Bridge crew is on second shift, two corporals, a fresh from the academy first lieutenant, and the junior pilot."

Jeffrey let out a soft sigh but didn't interrupt as Dray went on. "Cara's in control at the engines, so no bridge commands will take affect anymore. The people behind this hatch are hanging high and dry."

"And safe," Kay said. "What's going to keep them from firing on us when the hatch opens?"

Jeffrey stepped up. "Common sense, I hope. That last FTL jump was unplanned, and from our review of the ship's logs, it wasn't authorized from the bridge. The ship captain is being escorted up from his quarters, but he's being less than cooperative. My guess is he had an emergency jump programmed into the system. No way of knowing what impact that might have had on this junior pilot if he was linked into the ship at the time."

A lot of ifs and a lot of guessing. For once, Kay had no desire to be first in line. She stepped back and let Jeffrey's armed buddies take positions on either side of the hatch. The rest of them used that much hoped for common sense to flatten against the bulkheads and out of firing range.

Jeffrey flipped on the com link beside the hatch. "This is Major Jeffrey Franklin, Terran Intel. I am about to open this hatch. It would be best if we all kept a calm head and refrained from firing on each other. We control the ship and the stacks. Under Intel authority, I am taking command of this ship. Please stand down."

He nodded to Dray, who stepped up and keyed in the command override code that was floating around in her special head now. Or however the implant worked. Maybe that fake eye had a built in HUD. That could be convenient.

The hatch hissed open. No projectile fired out. So far so good. The guards, who had at least some body armor, stepped in first, then one shouted, "Clear."

Jeffrey straightened his uniform and stepped in. Kay, Dray, and Pratchett followed. Kay looked around. Wasn't every day that a grunt like her even saw a bridge, Novan or Terran. She took in a ton of screens flashing who knows what, an important looking chair that held a less than important looking scared lieutenant, and a seat that looked more like a torture device, with cables and controls surrounding a body, slumped and unconscious.

"The pilot?" she asked Pratchett and got a worried nod in return.

Dray stepped up and lifted the pilot's head. He was another young man, olive complexion with black hair and a scar on his left temple that matched the fake one Kay had—his pilot implant.

Dray looked around and her focus landed on Pratchett. "Can you take him down to medical? He looks in bad shape."

"He tried to stop the jump," the first lieutenant said, his voice higher than expected, before he cleared his throat and tried again. "You shouldn't have forced an FTL jump. Who knows how many injured we have now."

Kid had a backbone after all, Kay thought.

"We didn't trigger it," Jeffrey said. "But your captain should be here any minute. Maybe he can explain how we ended up in FTL."

With the help of the two corporals, Pratchett got the unconscious junior pilot onto a gurney and maneuvered it off the bridge.

Kay watched them leave. "Tell me we have another pilot on this ship."

Dray's grin widened. "Oh yeah, we do. She's on her way here already."

Jeffrey frowned again. "She's not going to be happy."

Kay heard voices from the hatch and turned to see Fenton step in, followed by a tall woman with hair dyed red and the telltale pilot's scar on her temple. Her expression shifted from wary to shocked to pissed off in little more than a second.

"Damn it to hell, Draybeck! Couldn't you stay in your little luxury prison until this fiasco was over?"

Dray grinned back. "Good to see you too, Mallory."

Jeffrey coughed to get their attention. "Senior Pilot Grace Mallory."

Mallory turned to him, then turned to Kay and looked her up and down. "This your baby sister, Karen?"

"Cara," Kay said, "and no. Related, but way too complicated to explain. I take it you two know each other."

"Grand reunion," Mallory said. "One I could have lived my whole life without."

"Mallory was on that ship where Jordan met your girlfriend's uncle," Dray said.

Mallory frowned at Kay, then turned back to Dray. "What asinine mess have you gotten me into this time, Draybeck."

"First off," Dray said. "There are three Draybecks on this ship right now. So you might want to just use Dray. This is my half-sister, Kay."

Half-sister? Well, it made a certain sense, since half of Dray's genes matched Kay's.

"Lovely," Mallory said. "Now how about explaining why you fried my off-shift replacement. I saw him being carted away. Do you have any idea what the impact is to a pilot when a jump is forced on them?" She didn't wait for an answer but turned to Kay. "You know."

"Sorry, fake." Kay tapped her temple and shook her head. "Seriously, it's a long story."

"All Draybeck stories are." Mallory sighed and slipped into the nearest chair.

"First off," Jeffrey said, "we didn't force the jump. But maybe he can explain." He pointed to the hatch, where an older man, gray hair in a short buzz cut, stepped in.

The man stood at attention and practically shouted, "Captain Jaques Lambert. Your presence on this bridge is a violation of Terran Naval law."

Great. A by the book jackass.

Jeffrey saluted him. "Major Franklin, Terran Intel."

Lambert glared at him. "You won't hold that honor much longer."

"Yes, we can debate our relative futures later. Did you authorize this jump, and if so, where is it leading to?"

Lambert turned his gaze to Mallory. "I order you not to assist this mutiny."

Mallory stood and saluted her commanding officer. "Respectfully, sir, our junior pilot is incapacitated. If we are to leave FTL safely, I need to know our destination and expected exit time." She looked between Jeffrey and Lambert. "Could one of you please let your remaining pilot know the facts here?"

Lambert's jaw clenched. "The destination is classified."

Mallory pinched the bridge of her nose. "Can you tell me the duration?"

"Classified."

Kay watched the sweat start to bead on the Captain's brow, and threw out a guess. "He doesn't know."

The look he gave her said her guess was spot on. His bravado slipped for a moment, then he set his spine ramrod straight again. "My orders were clear. In the event of an uprising that looked to be successful, I would trigger the last jump this ship will ever take."

"No Terran commanding officer would give the order to murder thousands of detainees. The political backlash alone would guarantee swift retribution," Jeffrey said, staring at the captain. "You're a Purist."

Lambert smirked. "And you lot are all traitors." He glared at Dray. "And mongrels."

Mallory sank back into her chair. "A suicide mission." She glared up at Lambert. "That's why this crew is all so junior. And I was just picked as the lucky one to join you in your death wish."

Kay turned to her. "How do you know it's suicide?"

Mallory glanced her way. "An FTL jump with no destination. It's a classic pilot training exercise to make sure the communications between pilot and navigation are always double and triple verified. No FTL destination input at the jump start means there's no end to this journey." She shot a glare at her captain. "It means we run until the FTL engines fail. Then we die."

Kay crossed her arms and closed her eyes. Some days, it just didn't pay to get out of her bunk.

"Wait a minute," Dray said as her smirk started to fade. "There isn't some kind of failsafe to protect against that?"

"There are multiple. FTL navigation requires a source and endpoint. That's the first level of safety." Mallory turned to the captain. "But you just randomized the endpoint, didn't you?"

He didn't reply.

"Modern ships include a sophisticated navigation A.I. that validates all endpoints. In a modern ship, he couldn't have done that. But this is an archaic crate retrofitted with the barest minimum to pick you lot up and hold you without looking like a prison."

"So what does this have for navigation?" Kay asked.

"Just a set of destinations to pick up detainees." Mallory swiveled her chair. "Navigation—list preprogrammed routes on console three."

The console screen to her left came to life with a list of gibberish. At least gibberish to Kay. "Any chance we are just on a trip to one of those locations?"

"Not a chance, mongrel," Lambert said.

Kay rolled her eyes. "Seriously, if I were a mongrel, my life would have been a shit ton easier. Sadly, I'm one of the few pure Terrans here." She nodded to Jeffrey. "How's about we get Captain Useless out of here? Unless you want me to interrogate him a bit with my fists. I'm up for that."

"It wouldn't work, anyway. Purists are beyond logic." Jeffrey ordered his guard to escort Captain Lambert back to his quarters and keep him there under guard.

"What are our options here?" Dray asked.

"Wait until FTL fails," Mallory said. "That could take up to a month, and then likely die. Or do an emergency FTL shutdown, and die sooner."

"Well," Fenton said, "not to be crazy optimistic, but death isn't guaranteed."

Mallory shrugged. "Not guaranteed. But coming out of FTL in the vicinity of any sizable matter results in an explosion that would be glorious to witness, assuming you weren't part of it, of course."

Kay's ear piece came to life, and she turned aside the same time as Dray and Jeffrey.

"What is it?" Mallory asked.

"It's Cara. She's locked herself in the engine room. Seems the captain's not the only Purist on staff." Kay looked to the junior lieutenant. "Assuming you're not another one of those clowns, can tell how many are attempting to break into the engine room?"

The lieutenant waited for Mallory's nod of consent before huddling over his terminal and speaking a series of commands. It took a moment before the navigation list on Mallory's console was replaced with a video shot showing a passageway with five crew members holding stun sticks and one officer with a gun.

Kay looked to Dray. "Can you keep that hatch locked?"

Dray looked to the distance. Yeah, that special eye had to have a HUD built in. Could be convenient.

"No. It's ancient technology. Most of this ship is."

Kay nodded and turned to Jeffrey. "I need another gun, Pratchett, and at least one of your Intel soldiers."

"What's your plan?" he asked, handing over his gun and waving another soldier to join her.

"Secure the engine room," she said, taking the extra gun and her stun stick.

"That's as deep as your plan goes?" Dray asked. "That's my sister in there."

"And my half-sister." Kay put a hand on Dray's shoulder. "I'm a grunt. This is what I do. Storm the target area and secure it for the fancy-ass people like you."

She turned back to the Intel soldier. He was broad shouldered, with curling brown hair. Most importantly, he had an armored vest. "Got a name?"

"Yariv Sharon, Corporal."

"Can you get us to the closest cross passage to that one?" she said, pointing at the console.

"Yes, Ma'am."

"Then let's go." She tapped her ear comm. "Pratchett, meet me at the central shaft, level three."

She stepped out of the bridge hatchway and followed the corporal down the passageway double-timing it to the central shaft that joined all levels at the central hub of the toroidal ship. Pratchett was waiting for them when they got there.

"Trouble?" Pratchett asked, accepting Kay's stun stick.

"Never a dull moment on this ship. We need to secure the engine room. We have five hostiles outside the engine room hatchway, most with stun sticks. At least one visible side arm."

"Our approach?" Pratchett asked.

"If they have any sense, they are watching access from this lift. So we come at them from above and below. They don't have enough people with guns to watch all entry points." She pointed to the corporal. "Sharon, meet Pratchett."

The corporal nodded.

"What's your experience with that gun, Corporal?" Kay asked.

He glanced down at his side-arm. "Haven't fired it outside of the range, Ma'am."

She waved her hand and he swapped the gun for Pratchett's stun stick. She looked over her own the gun—standard Terran side-arm near as she could tell. She checked the cartridge—ten ship safe bullets. She clutched the gun it both hands to hide the tremor from the others.

"Pratchett and I come from above and below. Corporal, you take the elevator to level zero. Be on your knees and have your hands up when it opens. Leave the stun stick tucked out of view. Ask for help or whatever comes to mind. Your goal is to grab their attention so they don't see us coming from the ladders."

With surprise on their side, and maybe enough luck that her tremors won't screw up her shots, this will all work out.

Or, it'll go to hell in a hand basket real fast. Either way, it was time to move. "Corporal, you and I take the shaft elevator down to level minus one. Pratchett takes the ladder down. When we are in place, then you Corporal come back up to level zero in the elevator. Once we hear you, we'll act. If it goes sideways, you're armor should protect you. Get back in the elevator and report back to Dray."

He nodded and they got in the elevator together. Kay focused on releasing the tension in her shoulders. She needed calm for this. Coming from below, she would have the first shots before the enemy could fully react. The corporal's life might depend on that.

The elevator stopped at Level minus one, and Kay got out. "If they aren't idiots, they'll have heard us go past. Remember, be on your knees with your hands up when the elevator doors open."

He nodded and held the doors open while Kay walked to the access ladder. She did the one stupid thing you never did with a side arm, and shoved it in a pocket as she stepped up the first rung of the ladder. She was three quarters of the way up when she heard the elevator doors shut below. Three more steps up and she was just below deck level. She pulled out the gun and took two calming breaths. Pop up, one shot for the guy with a gun. No sane person faced a gun with a stun stick. The rest should surrender.

Voices nearby.

"They're coming!"

"Not your problem," someone else growled. "Blow the hatch, and we'll shut down FTL before they get here."

A blown hatch, a gun. Five against Cara. The odds were bad, and Kay recognized the sound of panic in those voices. She couldn't wait for the corporal's diversion.

She crouched on the second to top rung, one last breath, and popped up the ladder well to sprawl on the deck facing the hatch, arms outstretched with gun in two steadying hands. One man with a hand on explosives. First two shots and he dropped. Second target acquired and she took out the officer with the gun just as she heard the elevator ping and open. She was pulling herself up off the deck when she heard the return shot and felt a searing pain in her hip and dropped back down. Shit, more than one gun.

Pratchett's head popped down from the opposite ceiling ladder and fired, dropping the second gun owner.

Kay dragged herself to the bulkhead and scanned the remaining enemy targets, one woman and another man. Both dropped their stun sticks and raised their hands.

The corporal came out of the elevator to Kay's side, and Pratchett flipped out of her hanging position.

"Fancy," Kay said. "Teach you that in Terran NCO training?"

"Gymnastics for seven years, if you can believe it." Pratchett tossed hand ties to the corporal who secured the two remaining enemy combatants. "How bad are you?"

Kay looked down at the blood slowly staining her Terran uniform. "I'll live." She keyed her ear comm. "Dray, we're secure here."

Seconds later, the hatch opened, and Cara stepped out with an emergency med kit.

"Watching me on the vid?" Kay asked.

Cara squatted at her side. "You are rapidly overtaking Dray as the most interesting sibling I have." She tore open the hole in Kay's trousers and wiped away the blood. Cara's hands were shaking, and Kay pushed them gently to the side and took over.

"Clean in and out, near as I can tell," she said, taking a med sealer from Cara. "Still hurts like a bitch."

Cara sat back against the bulkhead with her knees drawn up. "The nerves of steel gene that you and Dray have must have passed me by."

Kay pulled herself off the deck and tested some weight on the leg. Shit that hurt. She waved Cara up as well. "You make up for it in the smarts and common sense she and I didn't get."

Cara smiled and leaned down so Kay could use her for support. "If these two can guard the engine, Dray wants us on the bridge."

CHAPTER 17

JORDAN HEARD THE electronic beeps that were ever-present in any medical room. It took a moment for her mind to catch up to why she was hearing those beeps. When it did, she tried to raise her right hand, but found it immobilized. She reached over with her left hand to where the shard had been stuck in her side. She felt a bandage, but something wasn't right.

She pressed her stomach and her eyes shot open. The small hardness of her belly wasn't there anymore. She looked around, and saw Gemma in a recliner next to her bed. "I lost them."

Gemma shook her head, then quick-typed into a handheld and a synthesized voice spoke. SAFELY MOVED TO INCUBATOR. DOCTOR CAN EXPLAIN MORE.

Jordan let out the breath she was holding. Novan incubators were so popular even the war hadn't put a dent in their imports to Terran space. She looked closer at Gemma, noting the slight droop to the left side of her lips.

Gemma typed again. STROKE. OVER WORST OF IT NOW.

Jordan nodded. "I'm glad to see you, but how are you here on Volga?"

NOT VOLGA. NEW CHINA. FOR THREE DAYS.

Jordan shut her eyes. Three days.

NEED YOUR HELP.

Jordan opened her eyes again. "Whatever you need."

TERRAN IMPLANTS. FIX STROKE DAMAGE.

Jordan nodded. She knew there were limits to Novan biomedical innovations. "They can restore some of what you've lost. But are you ready for that?"

The door to Jordan's room opened before Gemma could answer. Ayaan stepped in and signaled Gemma to leave them. Gemma stepped out, but before the door closed, Jordan heard the electronic voice.

READY.

Ayaan paid no attention as she sat in the chair Gemma just vacated. "We've lost track of them."

Maybe it was the pain killers, or just regaining consciousness, but Jordan couldn't follow the conversation shift. "Lost what?"

"The *Lazarus*. It disappeared six hours ago. Terran news is already spinning this as a freak FTL failure."

Jordan put her hand to her belly, feeling for the remnant of Dray inside her, but they weren't there. This was too much, just too much.

Ayaan placed her hand over Jordan's. "It's a false report. Our analysis shows no FTL speed up before the jump. It just happened."

Jordan opened her eyes, ignoring the tear trailing down the side of her face to the pillow below. "How is that not an FTL failure?"

"FTL engines don't just start themselves. It takes commands and a path. Someone initiated it." Ayaan leaned closer. "I think they succeeded. Jeffrey and Kay. Maybe they initiated the jump to get out of Terran space."

"Maybe." Jordan said a silent prayer that was the reason for this disappearance. "How are the twins?"

Ayaan frowned.

"What?" Jordan said. "Gemma said they were safe"

Ayaan raised her eyebrows. "Yes, yes they are. Sorry. I, I'm sorry I put you in that danger. I had no right."

The botched Halabi attack. Of course. "No, you didn't have that right." She wasn't letting Ayaan off the hook. "You nearly took me and two innocent unborn with you. That's one of the reasons vendetta never became legal in Terran space. It's archaic."

Ayaan lowered her gaze. "I won't try to convince you of the necessity and the lives I've saved by wiping out an aggressive enemy to my family." She looked to Jordan again. "When Gemma and Zayn became targets as well, I acted to protect my family."

"We are nearly family as well. If you marry Kay."

Ayaan stood up and tried to pace the short space around Jordan's bed. Seems Jordan hit on a sore spot with that one.

"Do you intend to marry her?"

Ayaan sat back down. Her thigh tapping began in earnest. "There are complications. Even if I could get my grandmother to agree, Kay is not considered a Novan citizen."

"That no longer remains an obstacle." Manji stepped into the room to the tap tap of her cane, followed by her bodyguard. "Your political efforts have borne fruit, child. The Novan International Refugee Committee has agreed to extend refugee status to all participants of the gene infiltration programs and their descendants. Novan citizenship is an eventual option to any who apply thereafter."

Ayaan turned to her grandmother. "You would agree to a marriage between me and Kay?"

Manji raised an eyebrow. "You would wait on my approval?"

Ayaan's hand stopped tapping her side as her expression seemed almost surprised. "No. No I would not."

"And long since time you accepted that fact about yourself." Manji waved her cane. "That doesn't excuse you from making the ruler of the Nassien Autonomy stand in her old age."

Ayaan hopped out of the chair, and Jordan hid a smile. The battles there were hardly over, but she recognized the signs of a truce for now.

JORDAN WAS RELEASED from the hospital a day later. She'd spent all available time in the incubator cubicle, talking and recording her voice for playback. Thanks to the time she spent in her own recovery, the hospital had four days' worth of recordings of her heartbeat, respiration, and other vitals to customize the incubator to her personal rhythm. She only wished she had Dray's voice recordings as well for the twins to mature with.

Much to Manji's amusement, Jordan had to walk with a cane for the next few weeks as well, until her damaged muscles recovered. The wily old woman even offered her a model similar to her own, but Jordan declined. She didn't need a hidden laser cutter close at hand. She hoped.

She met Gemma and Ayaan in the Nassien compound that afternoon. Gemma gave her a half smile and started typing away with two hands now. SENT PROBES TO SITE OF FTL JUMP. WORKING ON A THEORY ON FTL TRACE RIPPLES.

She typed again, and the Nassien A.I. Took over. "Gemma's theory has proven intriguing," it said. "The fundamental principle is that faster than light travel for any given vessel produces a unique space/time warp, a ripple if you will, that with the appropriate deep scan measurements, can be traced from origin to destination."

"We don't have a destination," Jordan said.

"No," the A.I said. "But we have a trajectory that we can follow with an appropriately adapted vessel. Gemma had been running experiments on a subset of my cores as her thesis on tracking and providing legal prove of origin for pirated vessels based on this unique ripple signature. Adapting this to the *Lazarus* case is elementary."

ELEMENTARY EXCEPT FOR ANALYZING THE PROBABILITIES OF DIRECTION AND POSSIBLE DRIFT. THE A.I. CAN BORE YOU WITH DETAILS, BUT THE LONGER WE WAIT, THE LOWER OUR CHANCES OF FINDING THEM.

Jordan turned to Ayaan. "So we go hunting?"

"With the fastest ship we can. We're already a day behind."

"I can have a Tarquin fast courier ready in two hours." Jordan turned to Gemma and recognized that combination of fear and hope in her eyes. "Gemma needs to come as well, in case we need adjustments to this FTL chaser she's developed."

Ayaan nodded. "We'll be ready with the largest portable A.I. extension as well, to compute the drift."

Jordan rushed back to her assigned rooms. With Ayaan's help, she had an encrypted call to her mother within minutes. Luckily, their secure communication could still find her mother wherever she was located.

"Jordan, I'm so sorry. You've heard about the disappearance of the *Lazarus*?"

"Yes, Mother, and we have a possible solution to finding them. I'll be leaving here shortly."

"Be careful, Jordan. The ADF is also searching for the *Lazarus*. At least two fast cruisers have been diverted to its last known location. Whatever happened to that ship, don't rule out sabotage."

"Point taken, Mother."

"One other thing you should know. The remaining Draybecks are with me, and we've left Terran space. A warrant was released twelve hours ago for our arrests in connection with the *Lazarus* disappearance." Jordan tried to apologize but her mother waved it off. "It was only a matter of time really. I've contacted the Arbatova family, and they are willing to sponsor all of us for Novan port of entry. I'm not sure if I'll take them up on it or not."

Jordan recognized her mother's ambivalence as the Arbatova connection reminded her too much of Jordan's father's death. "We can resolve all that later. Thank you for taking the Draybecks with you."

Jordan terminated the call and sent the Tarquin ambassador the coded message she'd planned before this mission. It was supposed to get her and Jeffrey out of New China in an emergency. Now it would get her, Ayaan, and Gemma out and on the trail of the *Lazarus* faster than any other vessel. She just hoped it would be fast enough.

CHAPTER 18

"SO EFFECTIVELY, A properly equipped vessel could use its own FTL trace to track where it's been traveling and use it to estimate possible termination points," Cara said.

Mallory stared at her. "Obviously this is where all the brains in the family went. Still, has anyone taken this theory of yours and put it to use?"

"Oh, it's not my theory," Cara said. "It was published a year ago and picked up by the university I got my doctorate from."

Kay leaned against a chair. They'd spent more hours than she cared to remember on this bridge and frankly, she was getting sick of it. Any theory was better than just blasting along at FTL speed into oblivion.

"The theory itself is fairly straightforward," Cara said. "But the math is, well, beyond anything we have onboard here."

And so much for that one.

"How far can we get then, with the ship computer?" Dray asked, who sat rather too comfortably in the captain's chair.

"Not far," Cara said. "But what we can do is analyze the ripples we are currently creating, and use that signature variation over time to estimate the proximity of large mass entities we are passing."

Kay looked at Dray and recognized the same blank expression she was likely sporting herself.

Luckily, their pilot seemed to grasp the details.

Mallory leaned forward with more enthusiasm than Kay had seen in the last twenty-four hours of their acquaintance. "So if we can detect a pattern, we can shut down the FTL drive at the lowest probability of collision with a large mass entity."

"Our lowest calculable probability," Cara said.

Mallory leaned back. "Yes, lowest we can calculate based on the weak compute power of this flying crate." She ran her hands through her long hair and then sighed.

"Do you agree with Cara?" Dray asked her.

"Best we've got," Mallory said. "It changes our chances from guaranteed dead to mostly dead, but maybe not."

"How long do we measure before we act?" Kay asked.

All eyes turned to Cara. "Give me a day's worth of data, then we analyze the patterns."

Kay had the feeling this would be the longest day of her life. Possibly the last. Still, she'd sat through many last possible days before. She knew how to pass that time.

Five hours and two six packs of beer later, Kay looked up as Dray wandered into the small crew mess hall where she and Pratchett were working their way through the alcoholic supplies.

Dray sat in the empty seat next to her, cracked open a beer, and took a good long drink. Failing to mask a belch behind her fist, she turned to Kay. "I never said thanks, so thanks."

"For?"

"For possibly getting yourself killed. More than once, to come get us. We wouldn't have gotten this far without you."

Kay shrugged. "You wouldn't be in this mess if it wasn't for me. Or well, the people who own me."

"Nobody owns you but you," Dray said.

"Trying to be poetic?" Kay asked with a smile.

"Trying to be a sister. Or, whatever we are."

"Half-sister makes sense to me. Maybe by the time we get out of this mess, your Jordan will have gotten your records released along with mine. So you'll know what the Nassien military fiddled in your genes to make you special."

Dray leaned back and closed her eyes. "For as long as I can remember, I've been fighting against the rumors that my mother was a traitor. Guess I was the misinformed one all along."

Kay leaned forward and grabbed Dray's sleeve. "She was never a traitor. She was a P.O.W, a lab rat, and from what Fenton tells me, a war hero multiple times."

"That prison escape was a farce. They let them all go."

"Her final battle wasn't," Kay said. "From what Ayaan could dig out of my gene-line records, the first Terran Unaltered generation was cloned right after your mother died. Seems what she did to control those other ships not only saved the mission, it sparked a deep investigation into what she was capable of. The Novans wanted that capability."

Dray looked at her. "And do they have it?"

"Whatever it is, I guess so."

"WHAT HAVE YOU got for us," Dray said the next day, for once not in the captain's chair which was occupied by Mallory at the moment.

Fun little power play going on there. Dray was leaning over a console beside Cara. Both Draybecks looked well beyond tired, but even Kay knew what sleep you got before a mission hardly counted as rest. More like passing the time in a less than conscious state for a couple of hours at a stretch. If you could grab it. From the looks of it, Cara hadn't managed even that much. Kay recognized the look of someone who'd taken more stims than her body could handle.

Cara pointed at the numbers on her console. "Over the past twenty-four hours, we've passed fifty-seven large-mass clusters. The trace isn't as clear as I'd hoped, but that could be due to the relative distance from the objects and our trajectory."

"So what does it mean?" Kay said, not willing to even pretend she was following all this.

Cara looked up at her. "Well, in our favor, space is full of basically nothing, light-years of nothing significant to a ship this size. Scattered around that nothing are the stars and planetary systems. I think we passed fifteen solar systems and one possible binary star pair that may or may not have had any large mass entities in orbit." She turned back to her console and typed some commands. The display changed to a star chart.

"You know where we are?" Dray asked.

"No, this is just to help explain my point," Cara said. She pointed a shaky hand at the display. "This is a star chart of the Terran controlled space. Each of the color dots are star systems where we have a presence—some planetary, others mining resources, and some just scientific at this point. The gray dots are systems we claim but haven't any real presence there. If I brought up a Novan map, you'd see something very similar. My point is there is a lot of empty space between the dots. That's where we drop out of FTL."

"So if we're in clear space now, we exit now?" Dray asked.

"No," Mallory said. "Now we wait until we pass the next large-mass entity. Cara wrote a program that took the Terran star chart as input and estimated a pattern to what the FTL ripples might be for a ship of our size passing through on hundreds of possible trajectories. Seriously, Dray, are you sure you're related to her?"

"Nice," Dray said. "So what's that tell us?"

Cara pulled up another set of numbers that meant nothing to Kay or Dray. Maybe Mallory got it. Or maybe Mallory just pretended so she could get under Dray's skin.

"I ran ten thousand trajectories. The patterns aren't predictable," Cara said, "but they do show gaps, as we'd expect between the star systems. I measured the lowest gap, the one that would be the shortest distance between two systems. I think we halve that, and use it as the delay from when we pass our next large-mass entity and when we shut down FTL."

The math was beyond Kay, but the logic made sense. "Pratchett and Jeffrey are in the stacks, attempting to keep the peace. How much time will we have once we pass the next star system before we exit FTL?"

"Five minutes," Cara said.

"That is not a lot of time to prepare the stacks," Kay said. "I'll let them know to get into FTL lockdown now."

"It's worse than that," Cara said. "I can only run the analysis from the bridge computer, but I need to be in the engine room to shut down FTL. I can't get there in the available time window."

Dray looked at Mallory. "Can you run the analysis?"

"No. While I understand what she's describing, I can't see the pattern when it happens. And I'll need the full five minutes to lock myself into the pilot system for when we do drop FTL. I'll need to map and track any near-location objects and maneuver to slow down and avoid any hazards. Large-mass entities will vaporize us, but even small mass entities can damage the ship or worse."

Dray got that distant look that said she was accessing her implant. That would be a real weakness in a battle scenario, but then fancy-ass implants weren't put in the heads of frontline grunts anyway.

"I can do it," Dray said.

Mallory snorted. "Don't get delusional. You don't have the math to track the pattern up here, and you certainly don't know how to shut down an FTL engine. I barely know the details of that, and only in theory."

Dray's eyes snapped back to local focus. "No, I can link to the engine room computer from here. They're not networked together, but I have access to both through my implant." She got that distant look again, and then console two came to life about the same time as she planted a grin on her face. "Can you work with that, Cara?"

Cara shifted to the chair in front of console two and started typing. "This is great! I have full access to the engine room computer now."

"Congratulations, Dray, you've just become a human network cable," Mallory said.

That didn't dampen Dray's grin, but Cara's next words did. She still needed physical access to unlock the override.

"That I can do," Kay said. "Assuming it's just physical work."

Cara looked at her. "It's a bit more complicated than that, but yes, I can talk you through it. This will work!"

THAT INITIAL EUPHORIA for having a plan settled down into the usual boredom of mission wait. They passed one large-mass entity before Kay was in place in the engine room, so they had time for one dry run of what she had to do. Seemed easy enough. So now she sat. And waited.

The problem was, planets and stars didn't come by in fixed patterns. Sometimes it was ten minutes, sometimes it was thirty-five. She looked at the chrono. It was going on twenty minutes since last large-mass detected.

The engine room wasn't what she expected. She expected big machines, lots of noise. What she saw was just another set of blank screen consoles and a couple of well-padded chairs with safety harnesses. The rest of the ship kept its archaic style from the original Generation ships, but the bridge and engine room showed where all the modernization was put in to make this a portable museum ship capable of traveling FTL for tourist stops.

What was important in this room for Kay was the locked keypad to the right of her console. She had the manual key on a chain over her neck. And the keypad entry would come from the bridge via Dray.

She stood up and paced. Five steps, pivot, five steps. Damn. This waiting was worse than mission wait. At least with a real mission, she knew what to expect. Jump out. Shoot. Don't get killed. For this, it was wait, fiddle some bits, hope they didn't turn themselves into a vapor cloud.

Speakers blared to life with Dray's voice. "Emergency FTL shutdown imminent! Hold Fast! Hold Fast!"

Kay dropped back into her chair and tapped her ear com. "Dammit, Dray, couldn't you have told me first? Jumped out of my skin with you shouting through the speaker!"

"Sorry, wanted to give the stacks first warning. You have the keypad open?"

Kay looped the chain over her neck and inserted the flat key into the slot. The reader scanned the key and clicked. She lifted the keypad cover. "I'm in. What's the code?"

"Repeat after me as you type. Delta seven seven."

"Delta seven seven."

"Nine seven Foxtrot."

"Nine seven Foxtrot."

"Bravo zero zero. End of code."

"Bravo zero zero." Kay held her breath. The console in front of her displayed FTL OVERRIDE at the same time that Dray echoed those words in her earpiece.

"Strapping in," Kay said. She couldn't feel any change in the engines, but Cara told her she wouldn't until the transition out of FTL. She locked the four-point safety harness in place. "Dray?"

"Yeah?"

"It was worth it."

There was a pause before Dray answered. "Yeah, it was."

Kay's anticipation didn't last beyond those words. The stomach churning transition started, and she closed her eyes, focusing on not losing all those beers she put down earlier. The harness tightened around her as she felt the pull of booze revisited in the back of her throat.

And then it was done. Out of FTL, no vomiting. Kay opened her eyes. They survived. She lifted a hand to unlock the harness just as a warning alarm went off from the ship speaker. COLLISION IMMINENT. COLLISION IMMINENT.

"Dray? What's going on up there?"

"Comet trail! We're taking damage. Hold fast!"

CHAPTER 19

JORDAN DID NOT come out of sedation easily, but she insisted on being awake once they picked up the FTL trace of the *Lazarus*. She was up, but her brain felt like she was both drunk and massively hungover, all tied up with a bad case of the flu. Looking at Ayaan's face hovering nearby told her Ayaan wasn't handling the Baeron drive effects well either.

"How long have we been out?" she asked as she grabbed a steaming mug of tea to go with the stims she'd just swallowed.

"Day and a half," Ayaan said, slumped in one of the two chairs available in the tiny mess hall.

Jordan took the other seat. "Gemma?"

"Doing better than the two of us."

"The resilience of the young," Jordan said. "We're tracking the *Lazarus*?"

"Yes, Gemma's probes are doing the job."

It had taken all of Jordan's negotiating skills to convince the Tarquins to allow Gemma to attach her probes to the ship's hull and run physical cables through the hull to protect the measurements from external interference while in FTL. That had delayed their departure by half a day. Now it was just a game of chase, faster than light.

"What about Katie?" Jordan asked.

Ayaan shook her head. "Had to sedate her again. I'm not sure why my grandmother insisted she come along."

"You're not?"

Ayaan smirked. "Okay, yes, I know why. Now that we know the gene trait targeted by Kay's gene line program, it's obvious. My grandmother wants Katie trained as a bodyguard for Gemma. She expects my guards to train her on this mission, but no luck there if she can't stay conscious long enough."

Jordan passed those two guards as she'd entered the mess hall. She didn't think either of them could focus on much more than just staying vertical and glaring ominously.

"I don't agree with my grandmother anyway, and Kay certainly won't. Katie has a right to make her own decisions."

"Agreed."

"With the release of the Project Troy details, it will be fairly straightforward to have them both offered full citizenship. Then their decisions and future are in their own hands. No more external manipulations."

Jordan patted Ayaan's arm. "What about you? Where do you go from here?"

"Assuming we're successful?"

"Always."

Ayaan leaned back and stretched. "The first step is ensuring the safe relocation of the *Lazarus* detainees. We've yet to get a neutral party to agree on where to take them in."

"Don't give up on the Gilgarans. I'm close to convincing them of the urgency and need for neutrality until ultimate citizenship is determined. Once we find the ship, we can find a home."

IT WAS ANOTHER groggy, sick, day and a half before Jordan was woken up suddenly by the Tarquin pilot's voice broadcast over the ship com.

"We're dropping out of FTL. Prepare for transition in five."

Five minutes? Had Gemma's experiment worked that quickly that they've found *Lazarus*? Jordan didn't have time to ask questions. She pulled the safety straps over her legs and torso, and pulled the padded safety bar up on her bunk.

Baeron drive transitions were the worst. It felt like someone pushed a fist through the back of her head, yanked out her spine and then shoved it back inside again. Her vision faded in and out and she managed to bite her lip so hard it bled by the time the transition ended and the All Clear signal sounded.

Jordan unstrapped herself, and dabbed at her bleeding lip as she switched on her bunk com. "What's happening?"

"We lost the FTL trace," the pilot said.

"Did the ripples change?" Jordan pulled herself up and put on her uniform jacket.

"No. It just stopped. Your youngster is analyzing the data now."

Jordan rolled off her bunk and met Ayaan in the passageway as they both rushed to the control room. Her head finally felt clear, but her pulse raced. Gemma sat at a console, flipping through streams of data as they entered.

"What could cause a stop in the trace? Could the pattern have shifted?"

"NO," Gemma typed. She scrolled back on her stream of data and pointed at a batch. "HERE IS WHERE IT STOPPED. LOOK AT THE NUMBERS AND COMPARE TO OUR TRANSITION OUT OF FTL." She paused as she switched to a different set of data. "THIS IS US. YOU CAN SEE THE SAME ABRUPT TRANSITION."

"Which means?" Ayaan asked.

"THEY DROPPED OUT OF FTL. WE KNEW THEY WOULD AT SOME POINT. WE SHOULD BE ABLE TO PICK UP KAY'S BEACON SIGNAL SOON AND CAN TRACK BACK TO THEM FROM HERE."

Close, so very close. It meant one more Baeron drive FTL transition, but if it brought them to Dray and Kay, it would be worth it.

CHAPTER 20

TWENTY MINUTES LATER, after ensuring the engine room was properly guarded, Kay stepped through the bridge hatch into pandemonium. Mallory was slumped on the floor next to her pilot chair. Still conscious, which was far better than the junior pilot who was still unconscious from their transition into FTL. Dray leaned over the console with the first lieutenant, scanning a whole lot of red.

"How bad is it?" Kay asked.

Dray looked up. "Could have been a lot worse. We've got fires burning on three stacks and a loss of hull integrity that sealed off these compartments." She pointed to some of the red on the screen. "Fenton's reporting injuries on some decks closest to the outer torus. Most are minor, but a couple have already been put in emergency med evac shells."

"Not bad," Kay said.

Dray stood up straight. "The real problem is the damage to our communications. We have no long-range communications, but the ship itself is sending a broadcast beacon automatically, probably compliments of the Purists in case we survived the FTL drop. We can't figure out how to shut it off."

"Yeah, about that. Your little chip wasn't the only thing I've been a mule for." Kay tapped her shoulder. "Novan beacon stitched under the skin before we left New China. Wonder who finds us first?"

Mallory sat up straighter. "How about we figure out where we are to start with, before we start the bidding war on who gets to blow us up first?"

Dray helped her off the floor. Mallory glared at her pilot chair and chose a console seat instead. "Navigation—chart our location."

Navigation responded after a few seconds delay. "Current location is 22 parsecs from Gil-120 planetary system." It updated console two with a detailed map of the surrounding location.

Mallory leaned over as they crowded in front of the screen. "Gilgaran space. Must be our lucky day. First we don't get blown to bits, now we land in at least neutral territory." She scrolled through the available information. "Well, mostly neutral. If our data is valid, this system is claimed by Gilgar, but has never actually been occupied."

"We should get someone's attention anyway," Kay said. "So still a guessing game on who's first, Terran, Novan, or Gilgaran."

"Tarquin," Dray said, with that distant look.

"How do you get Tarquin in that mix?" Kay asked.

"Because they're here, now." Dray spoke into her console and the damage report was replaced with a distant flashing beacon. "At least this ship identifies it as Tarquin. It arrived in system two minutes ago."

Kay leaned over her. "How far away?"

Dray studied the output. "Close enough we aren't outrunning it, for sure. In theory, they're neutral as well. We can start a short-range communication link with them. At this distance, the time lag on response is only a matter of minutes."

"Incoming message," the first lieutenant said. "I'll put it on bridge speaker only."

Seconds later, a voice came in. "This is Jordan Bowers of Terran Intel. Please state your condition, *Lazarus*."

Dray jumped out of her seat and lifted Kay in a bear hug. The woman was shorter but solid muscle. "Yes!"

In-system ships travelled at a crawl, even fancy Tarquin ones. It was another four hours before the Tarquin courier maneuvered into a docking position. Four hours of listening to what was broken on the *Lazarus* and what was fixable in short order. Four hours where Kay wasn't paying the least bit of attention, and for the most part, neither was Dray. They were both outside the docking bay thirty minutes early. It looked the same as when Kay had arrived, but waiting from the inside this time.

After thirty long minutes of approach, docking clamps extended, dock seals secured, the dock lights finally turned green. Dray keyed open their end of the dock access and the hatch hissed its release and opened. The first off the dock was Jordan, looking rough. Not that Dray noticed. She ran to her wife and buried herself in Jordan's embrace.

Next off, the ever-present Nassien guards. Two, heavily armed and marching toward Dray and Jordan.

"Reunion time might be better elsewhere," Kay said.

Dray finally paid attention. "Ah, you have company?"

"She does," Kay said. "I work with these two, and they take their duties seriously."

Next off the dock was a sight for sore eyes. Kay stepped forward. "Dray, may I introduce Ayaan Nassien-Nomani, heir-apparent to the Nassien Autonomy."

Dray looked at Kay and mouthed the words *your girlfriend*?

Kay grinned and stepped up to Ayaan. She expected the usual formal nod since Ayaan wasn't one for public displays. She was wrong. Very wrong. Ayaan threw her arms around Kay and pulled her close.

"Next time, we go together or not at all," Ayaan said. And then Kay lost herself in a deep kiss.

The walk back to the bridge took considerably longer since Ayaan's body guards insisted on securing every passage way and intersection before the group could proceed. Kay took it in stride. Dray couldn't seem to figure out what to frown at, her wife with the obvious injuries and sporting a cane, or the guards with more armaments between the two of them than the entire ship had all together.

When they came to the bridge, Kay stepped to the front of the guards. "I'll secure this first, please. These people are already on edge."

They handed her a stun gun, and she automatically stepped back into the role of Ayaan's personal guard. She nodded to Dray, who spoke over the bridge com. "Be advised that we have an armed escort with us, as you've likely been following on the bridge cameras. This is a Novan diplomatic mission."

The bridge hatch opened from the inside, and Kay stepped in first, scanning the room. Mallory sat in the Captain chair. The lieutenant stood by console one.

Kay lowered her stun gun. "Ayaan Nassien-Nomani." She repeated the full title as the bodyguards and then Ayaan stepped through the hatch, followed by Dray and Jordan.

Mallory stayed in her seat but introduced herself and the lieutenant.

Ayaan cleared her throat. "Given my current status within the Nassien Autonomy . . ."

"And the multiple assassination attempts," Kay said.

Ayaan nodded to her. "And that, I'm required to travel with an armed escort. Please do not assume this is a Novan takeover. We are here to ensure the safety of the members of this Terran vessel, and with the authority of the Novan Government, I'm authorized to extend refugee status to all on board, and eventual Novan citizenship to any who wish to emmigrate to a Novan planet."

Mallory looked past Dray to Jordan. "So this crazy rescue was your idea?"

Jordan smiled. "I can't take all the credit. I had a lot of help. Including one very tired teenager you might remember from the last time we were all together and waiting for a rescue. She's asleep now, but eager to meet you and Dray when she recovers."

"How did you find us so fast?" Kay asked.

"Gemma. She worked out the math to trace you through FTL."

That kid was a genius.

Mallory just shook her head. "Well, I'm glad to see the sane one in your marriage is finally here. Jordan, you look like you've seen some rough times yourself."

Dray glared at Ayaan. "Yeah, I'd like to hear some details on that one."

"Forthcoming of course," Ayaan said. "That said, I believe the easiest option would be for Kay and I to return to the Tarquin ship while we work out the logistics of where we go from here."

The Tarquin ship that was not owned and flooded with Terrans who had no reason to want the presence of the Novan family that created this genetic hodgepodge decades ago. The reality of her own status sunk into Kay once again. She was either Terran to the Novan worlds, or Novan to the Terrans on this ship, and no actual citizenship in either worlds.

The difference now though, was she had family.

THE PLAN WAS to spend the next few hours resting, her and Ayaan on the docked Tarquin ship, and Jordan on the *Lazarus*. It gave time for catching up and explanations and generally to lessen the tension from the arrival of a ruling Nassien.

And the catching up was a real eye opener.

"He's finally dead," Kay said.

"Dead. Though I don't know if or when Jordan will forgive me for including her in the final vendetta set up."

Kay shrugged. "It all worked out. And there's another clone?"

"Yes, just the one. Teenager and experimental. Calls herself Katie."

Someone who looked just like her, but younger. That might take some getting used to. Key stretched out on the single bunk they were sharing, though it had more room than a Novan or Terran bunk, given the relative size of your average Tarquin. She'd just shut her eyes when com beeped for access and Ayaan's head guard popped in.

"Terran vessel has just arrived in system," he said.

Kay rolled off the bunk and stood, followed by Ayaan in what was now a cramped compartment.

"Vessel type and distance," Ayaan said.

"Battle cruiser. The Tarquin pilot estimates twelve hours before this ship is within its target range."

Ayaan led the way out. "Contact the *Lazarus* and let them know we are coming onboard."

"Ser," he said. "That is not advisable. Our best course of action is to undock and leave the system."

"Not an option," Ayaan said as she marched them down the passageway.

They were back on the bridge of the *Lazarus* twenty minutes later. Jordan looked a bit better for the minimal rest, Dray looked worse. Someone got the news of who happened to have control of their unborn twins and wasn't taking it well.

"If you leave," Mallory said to Ayaan, "maybe that battle cruiser won't come in with gun ports open."

"If I leave, there is nothing to keep them from destroying this ship and all on board. As I recall, they tried that already."

Mallory shrugged. "Purists. They are a small contingent. I can't believe they would have control over an entire battle cruiser. But if they find out The Grand High Mucky-muck's granddaughter is on board, maybe they take a few pot shots at us anyway."

Ayaan shook her head. "You underestimate my value to the Terran propaganda machine. Alive, I am on your newscasts for months. Dead, I'm just another excuse for the Novans to prolong a war that should have ended in stalemate years ago."

"Amen to that." Mallory turned to Dray. "This is your shit show. What now?"

"If I may," Jordan said. "Ayaan is correct. Her presence here is a good delay tactic. We are in neutral space so there are repercussions to any act of aggression. Gilgarans take their neutrality very seriously. They can't be far behind if the Terrans are here."

From her words to some random-ass Deity's ears. The lieutenant broke into the conversation. "Another vessel just entered the system."

"Ship type?" Mallory asked.

"Origin Novan."

All eyes turned to Ayaan, who frowned. "There was no plan for a vessel to follow us here."

"Like your grandmother would just let you go," Kay said, wiggling her fingers.

Ayaan hovered over the lieutenant. "Open a communications link to the Novan vessel."

The lieutenant had more backbone that Kay thought. And interestingly, it was Mallory's nod that got him in action, not Dray's. Seems the lines were drawn pretty close now.

With the link open, Ayaan identified herself and manually keyed in a passcode that would have to now be changed since it was recorded on a Terran vessel.

The link responded. "You finally resolve one long-term death threat and what do you do? Go chasing down another one."

Ayaan smiled. "Hello, Mother. Can you please refrain from opening up another war front that may bring the Gilgarans out of their traditional neutrality and on the Terran's side?"

"No promises. But I didn't come alone."

The lieutenant confirmed. "Third, no fourth vessel in system. Signal confirms—Gilgaran destroyers."

Ayaan stepped back. "I suggest we all go back to sleep. It will be some hours before all parties can decide where and how to negotiate our collective status."

"And who negotiates for us?" Mallory asked.

"You seem rather comfortable in that captain's chair, senior Pilot. I vote for you." Ayaan didn't wait for an answer, but marched them back through the passageways and onto the Tarquin ship.

"Now what?" Kay said.

"Honestly," Ayaan said, taking off her uniform jacket. "It's mostly out of our hands. We've set up negotiations between Terrans and Novans, with the Gilgarans acting as a neutral facilitator. The rest will take time, but you achieved the goal of securing the safety of the Terrans on this ship."

"Me and my family." Not like she did it alone.

Ayaan smiled. "And how do you like that family now that you've gotten to know them?"

Kay sighed. "About as much a pain in the ass as your family, but without all the armed guards."

Ayaan laughed. "Families never are simple, are they? But what do you want to happen next?"

Kay sat on the edge of their bunk. "I don't really fit in either place, not Terran, not Novan."

"But you do fit in with two families now. One Terran, one Novan." Ayaan yawned. "We have time to figure things out. How about sleep?"

And true to form, she lay down for a nap. Who was Kay to go against such thought-out plans? She curled up around Ayaan and was fast asleep in minutes.

EPILOGUE

KAY PULLED THE hood tighter on her borrowed parka, trying in vain to keep the icy snow from stinging her cheeks. She held up her binoculars and scanned the frozen tundra that extended in an unbroken plain of white for kilometers around their refugee encampment.

"Any sign of them?" Dray asked.

"Not yet." Kay lowered her binoculars. "Ayaan's going to tear them both a new one for this."

Dray shrugged. "Gemma needed this. In eight hours, she goes under the knife as one of the first high-rank Novans to accept a Terran implant. If that's not an excuse to haul out and take a road trip with her best friend, what is?"

"Won't stop Ayaan's temper tantrum later, even if Katie's already learning the whole bodyguard routine."

"Oh please, you call that extended leg slapping a temper tantrum? Your fiancé keeps herself so tightly under control it's a wonder she isn't the one who finally snapped and drove off into a snowy sunset."

Kay eyed the engagement ring on her finger, still dazed at how she became both a Terran Draybeck and a Novan citizen all in the past eight months. She looked off to the horizon. "At this latitude, the sun's not setting for another four hours."

Dray yawned, sending a cloud of mist into the cold air. "It's past midnight and my toes are freezing in these boots. Can't we just assume they are coming back, and we can all go to bed?"

"Ayaan's already under the microscope as the Novan liaison in this refugee facility, working day and night to release everyone's genetic data and see to their citizenship status. The least I can do is make sure one stray kid gets back safe." A kid that was family to her, like Dray. She wondered if Basri would approve of her new sense of purpose, running security on this compound, and bridging that gap between Terran and Novan for the refugees.

"There," Dray said, pointing to her left. "They're coming back."

Kay raised the binoculars again and slowly scanned the across the snowscape. "I don't see them."

Dray tapped her temple by her electronic eye. "You need one of these my friend. Twice the range of those binoculars. The twins will be waking me up in another couple of hours. I promised Jordan I'd take the morning shift so she can sleep in. Can we go in now?"

"Fine." Kay lowered the binoculars. "Wake me when the twins get up. I'll help you."

Dray patted her on the back. "Bucking for favorite aunt status already?"

"It's not much competition since Cara stayed on the *Lazarus* while it shuttles more refugees here." She turned and walked back into the bunker door and down the flight of stairs that led to the underground facility the Gilgarans set up to house the refugees while their status was finalized. Waiting for the details of all modified Terrans and their descendants, they would be here on this Gilgaran ice planet for at least a year.

Kay pulled off the hood of her parka and shook the snow off so that it hit Dray in the face. Not such a bad way to spend the next year. Might even find a nice iceberg to hold her wedding on.

This is where an author would normally include her biography. In place of that, Sandra included the following four tidbits about herself. Three are flat-out lies, one is a true:

- She was arrested as a teenager, but her police officer uncle got her off with a warning.

- She is terrified of balloons. Terrified.

- Spiders on the other hand, are a-okay after she ate one on a dare in the sixth grade.

- She paddles her kayak in the sheep pasture when it floods.